an
as
ne.
m,

as
ly
er
se.
be

Visit David Belbin's homepage at
http://www.geocities.com/SoHo/Lofts/5155

P●INT CRiME

THE BEAT

Fallen Angel

David Belbin

■SCHOLASTIC.

Scholastic Children's Books
Commonwealth House, 1–19 New Oxford Street,
London WC1A 1NU, UK
a division of Scholastic Ltd
London ~ New York ~ Toronto ~ Sydney ~ Auckland
Mexico City ~ New Delhi ~ Hong Kong

First published in the UK by Scholastic Ltd, 2000

Copyright © David Belbin, 2000

ISBN 0 439 01305 4

Typeset by TW Typesetting, Midsomer Norton, Somerset
Printed by Cox & Wyman Ltd, Reading, Berks.

10 9 8 7 6 5 4 3 2 1

In memory of
Don Scott
1951–1999

The city in these pages is real. The events described in them are not. All of the characters, together with the police station where some of them work, are imaginary. I'd like to thank everybody who helped me with this series. Friends, police officers, publishing people, many others – you know who you are. I'd also like to thank all the readers who have written to me about "The Beat". I hope you enjoy the ending.

David Belbin

PROLOGUE

Jan kept waking up. This was the worst thing about doing shifts, the way it messed with your sleep patterns. She'd just been on holiday and had become used to rising late. Today, though, she had to be on at six. Jan would get up at five and take Henry over the road to Carol, her childminder. Carol was an angel. She didn't mind fitting in around Jan's unsocial hours.

Jan should be able to sleep. The house was quiet. Kevin was on all night at the hospital. Henry had gone straight off at eight. Jan had dozed off at ten, then was woken by the pubs putting out. Now there was only the occasional animal noise to disturb her, but she was wide awake. Thoughts began to crowd her mind.

Her marriage was in trouble, that was becoming obvious. Even on holiday, she and Kevin hardly talked. They'd only made love once. When Jan tried to discuss things, Kevin quickly changed the subject.

Something was badly wrong. Working the hours they did, it was easy to drift apart. Kevin had given up trying to persuade Jan to leave the police force, have another baby. That was a bad sign. Jan wasn't sure whether she still loved her husband, but they were a family. They would make do, as families did. Anyway, who else would have her, past thirty, with a two-year-old in tow?

Next, Jan worried about Carol. The childminder might be an angel, but her husband was no saint. Bob was nearly twice Carol's age. Carol had known him since she was a schoolgirl, delivering papers to his house. She'd married him at sixteen, had a baby at seventeen. Now she was eighteen and Bob had started knocking her about. Carol hid it well, but Jan was a police sergeant. She knew how to read the signs. Yet whenever Jan tried to raise the subject, Carol closed her down. She'd mentioned her worries to Kevin, who said it was a bad idea to get involved in other people's marriages. He was probably right.

Jan thought she heard someone outside the house. Who could that be, after midnight? Just her imagination. She began to think about Clare Coppola, her partner, who was due back at work soon. Clare had been through the mill recently.

She'd lost her boyfriend, who'd been shot dead. Shortly afterwards Clare was off work for weeks, injured. On top of all that, a childhood friend of hers had been brutally murdered. How would Clare cope with being back on the beat?

More noise. Jan sat up straight. There was definitely somebody moving about downstairs. Jan got out of bed and went to the wardrobe, where she kept her gear. She took out her truncheon and ventured out of the bedroom. How cheeky can you get? The burglar had even turned a light on! Jan walked downstairs. It sounded like a drunk, blundering about. My god! There was blood on the door handle, blood on the carpet. He must have cut himself breaking in.

Jan was only inches from the phone. She was about to dial three nines when she heard water running. Another possibility occurred to her. She raised her truncheon, then tip-toed to the down-stairs toilet, which had a sink by it. The door was closed. Jan took a deep breath, opened it.

"Kevin! What the hell happened to you?"

"Sorry, love," he mumbled, showing two broken teeth. His nose was bleeding and his shirt was badly torn. "Didn't mean to wake you. Go back to bed."

"Who did this to you?"

"A patient went psycho on me."

"Then why didn't they clean you up at the hospital?" Jan asked.

"What is this?" he sputtered, "an interrogation? Just go back to bed."

"Don't speak to me like that!" Jan said, sharply. He wasn't wearing hospital clothes, she noticed. He'd been lying about being at work tonight. She realized, then and there, that her marriage was over.

Two cheaply dressed men, one in his late teens, the other in his early thirties, arrived at a bar in Amsterdam. They entered separately, but sat down together. It was midday. Despite the hour, they were surrounded by twenty-somethings smoking dope and drinking beer like it was going out of fashion. These two, however, didn't smoke. They ordered coffee, then sat down at a table in the darkest corner of the room.

"It's no good," the younger told the older. "We'll never get proof."

"Not direct proof of racist activity," the older, who was called Simon, replied. "But there are other ways of bringing him down. Do you remember how they finally put away Al Capone?"

"The gangster?" the young man said, looking round anxiously as the coffee was brought over. "No, I don't remember how they got him. Was it the Valentine's Day Massacre? I saw a film about that."

Simon shook his head. "Income tax evasion. The authorities didn't have to prove where Capone got the money from, only that he hadn't paid tax on it."

"You think that Jagger's evaded income tax?"

"I think he's taken money," Simon replied. "And I know a woman who works for the Front National in France who can help us prove it."

"Why would she help, if she's in the FN?"

Simon grinned. "She joined the FN for the same reason that you joined Combat 18. She's a mole, like you were."

"I see." The younger man, whose name was Jed Sutcliffe, had infiltrated a fascist group called Combat 18 earlier in the year. His mission had been partially successful. The small fry – racist bully boys – had been caught. But the big fish – Nottingham solicitor Ian Jagger – had swum effortlessly away.

"What do we do with the proof when we get it?" Jed wanted to know.

"Confront Jagger. Make him admit it, on tape."

"You think he'll meet us?"

"He's getting married," Simon explained, "to a woman called Charlene Harris."

"I don't remember her."

"She joined his firm after you left the city. Word is he's crackers about her. And – get this – *she's black*."

Jed didn't know what to say to this. If Jagger was marrying a black woman, what kind of racist did that make him?

Simon went on. "If we time it right, threaten to show Harris what we've got, Jagger's bound to panic, try to pay us off."

"Jagger's not the panicky type," Jed asserted. "Also, he must know that I didn't get involved in all this for money."

"Trust me," Simon said. "You don't know how people like Jagger think. In their eyes, *everybody's* in it for the money. We get Jagger to admit where his money comes from, *on tape*. Then, when he offers us cash, we walk – straight to the broadsheet newspapers."

Simon used to work for the *Financial Times*. He knew what he was talking about. He was well aware of exactly how much proof the serious press needed before it printed a story. Jed trusted him, relied on him. Yet he still felt uneasy.

"The way I see it," Jed said, thinking aloud, "Jagger's got half the Nottingham police force in his pocket. That's why they didn't follow up his fascist connections back in March. Jagger's friends could get us arrested before we get near the *Guardian* or the *Telegraph*."

Simon nodded. "Fair point. But you had a lot to do with the police. You must have come across somebody in the Nottingham force who you trust."

Jed thought for a moment. "There was a young Inspector, uniformed guy. What was his name? Grace, I think…"

Simon gave Jed an odd look. "You've not seen the British papers, have you?"

"Hardly."

Jed had been holed up in Munich for months, writing an account of how he'd infiltrated Combat 18.

"Inspector Paul Grace was murdered a few weeks ago."

Jed swore beneath his breath. "How? Why?"

"Shot outside his home. Grace was the key witness against the motorway team, a bunch of big-time burglars. When he died, the police had to release the lot, though I think they picked some of them up again later."

"Poor sod," Jed commented.

"Is there anybody else you trust?" Simon asked.

"There's a beat copper called Ben Shipman. I don't really want to draw him into all this again, but he's…" Jed tried to think of the right word "…sound."

"OK, Ben Shipman it is. But don't contact him yet. I've got to get the papers first. Getting in touch with this girl is a very delicate matter. How's the book coming on?"

"Finished." Jed slid a computer disk across the table.

"Good. I'll start on it straight away."

Simon was going to edit Jed's book, improving the style, checking for mistakes, cutting any details which might break the British libel laws. This was what Jed and Simon were meant to be discussing, not some blackmail plot. If things went according to plan, Jed and Simon would make a little honest money out of the book. Jed was fed up with living hand to mouth, surviving on handouts from anti-racist groups. But the money wasn't the important thing. What counted was nailing Jagger.

"Won't what I've written destroy Jagger?" Jed asked Simon. "I don't see…"

"I'm looking forward to reading the book," Simon interrupted. "But, the way I see it, if you want it published in Britain, you need more proof. If you want to sell a lot of copies, you need plenty of publicity. And if my plan works, you'll get both. So what do you say?"

"I'll think about it," Jed promised.

"Don't take too long," Simon warned.

NOVEMBER

1

At eight on a Monday evening, two women – one white, one black – sat in the Limelight Bar. They'd been drinking for two hours. Both were attractive and in their early twenties. Several men had tried to chat them up, without success. Now it was quiet. Most of the after work crowd had drifted home. But the women were in no hurry. Clare Coppola had no one waiting for her. Charlene Harris's fiancé was working late. Slightly drunk now, they agreed that it would be sensible to order food. They moved to a table in the restaurant area, and, once they were more private, Charlene picked up on something which Clare had said earlier.

"So you and Neil did it at last," she commented, jokily.

Clare smiled with slight embarrassment. The

information about her one night stand with Neil had just slipped out. Normally, the only person she would have discussed it with was her best friend, Ruth. Ruth, however, was away.

"It just happened. A one off. Neither of us planned it."

"You are on the pill," Charlene stated, a lawyer establishing the facts.

"Actually, no. I was, when I started sleeping with Paul, but when you're working shifts, taking it gets complicated and I started putting on weight so..."

"You should take the morning-after pill," Charlene urged.

"It's two mornings after."

"It works for up to seventy-two hours."

"I've heard that, but..." Since her boyfriend was murdered, nearly two months before, Clare hadn't had a period. But she wasn't pregnant. She'd taken a test. Her whole system seemed to have shut down, that was all. Stress could do that to you. She told Charlene some of this.

"I'd still take the morning after pill. Better safe than sorry."

"Yeah, maybe I will," Clare said.

Charlene went to the loo and Clare found herself in a fantasy about being pregnant. Half of her wanted to have Paul's baby. At least, that way, there would be something of him left behind. Clare had never been in any doubt about wanting children.

But not as a single parent. On TV, in magazines, having a baby had become the latest fashion accessory. It might be all right if you were a rich pop star or could afford a full time nanny. That wasn't real life. Real life was a girl like Julie Wilder, bringing up a kid on her own at seventeen, poor and pissed off all the time, waiting for a Prince Charming to save her.

Julie had been lucky. Charlene's ex, Ben Shipman, had played the part of Prince Charming. Rumour had it that he'd even moved in with her.

"It won't last," Charlene had said, when Clare told her this. "I know Ben. What he really wants is a strong woman to boss him around at home and push him hard in his career. He's slumming."

Had Ben been slumming when he went out with Ruth? Clare wondered, but wasn't tactless enough to ask. There was, however, one thing she had to know.

"Ben has this thing about Ian being a racist," she said. "Have you ever asked him about that?"

Ian Jagger, distinguished solicitor, was both Charlene's fiancé and her boss.

"Of course I have," Charlene said. "Ian said there was nothing in it."

"You think jealousy made Ben invent the story?" Clare asked.

"No," Charlene told her. "The opposite. Ben didn't want me in Nottingham so he made up the story about Ian having far-right connections to scare me off."

"If you say so," Clare murmured, though she thought that the situation was murkier than that. It was only eight months since there had been a race riot in the city centre. Ben wasn't the only person who thought that Jagger had had a hand in instigating it. Some people suspected Jagger of hiring Charlene Harris, not because she was a talented lawyer, but because she was black. Hiring her showed that Jagger wasn't a racist. But he'd hardly marry her for the same reason, now would he?

"If Ian was a racist," Charlene asked, as if reading Clare's thoughts, "would he be marrying me? His first wife was black, too. Did you know that?"

"No," Clare said, surprised. "When did they divorce?"

"They didn't. She died in a car crash, seven years ago."

"Did they have kids?"

"No. Pamela was only thirty. They were about to start a family, Ian says."

Their meals arrived. The two women ate in silence, contemplating the dead.

"Do you plan to have children?" Clare asked after a decent interval.

"Ian's keen. He's not getting any younger. I want to get more established in my job first."

It was funny, Clare thought, her and Charlene getting close like this. It was good. There was one topic that they avoided, the ongoing investigation into the murder of Mark Murray. Firstly, the situation was too sensitive. Secondly, neither woman was involved in the case any more. Clare, after a brief attachment to CID, was going back on the beat the next day. Charlene, as she explained between mouthfuls of pork, was up to her neck in custody cases.

"A lot of which are far nastier than criminal cases, though crime's what I was hired for."

"Crime can get pretty monotonous," Clare said.

Before parting, they arranged to take in a film the following weekend. Then Clare headed to Slab Square for a bus. Charlene had only a short walk to her flat in The Park.

Clare turned and called out, "Will you be safe?", for the wide streets were poorly lit.

"You bet," Charlene assured her. "See you on Sunday."

Jo McCord finished her homework and went downstairs to watch the telly. Unlike most of her friends, she didn't have a set in her room. She knew that, if she did, she'd never stop watching it. There was nothing on anyway. Mum and Dad were watching yet another new cop drama. Jo didn't want to watch something where people got killed. Her idol, an actor called Mark Murray, had just been murdered. The day before it happened, Jo had got to meet him. This was the first time that someone she'd met had died. Thinking about it kept her awake at night.

"Have you walked Trigger yet?" she asked Dad.

"Nah. After this."

"I'll do it," she said.

"I don't think so, dear," Mum butted in. "Not at this time of year."

It was all right for Jo to walk the dog in the light summer months, but her parents weren't comfortable with her going out in the dark. Not that they lived in a particularly dangerous area, but you were always reading stories in the papers. And then there were all those cop shows.

"I'll carry my personal safety alarm," she promised. "And a torch. Come on, nobody's going to attack me when I'm with Trigger, are they?"

Mum and Dad looked at each other. Jo could read those looks. Mum was wavering. Dad didn't want to deal with the situation, he wanted to unwind and watch the show. Jo played her final card.

"I've been cooped up in the house doing homework for *hours*. I won't be long, honest…"

"All right," Dad said. "But stick to streets that are properly lit. There are some funny people about."

"I will," Jo promised.

In the hall, she put on her fleece. All that fuss, just to take the dog for a walk. Trigger, seeing her pick up his lead, began to whelp excitedly. The torch just fitted in her front pouch. Jo didn't know where her rape alarm was. She'd probably lent it to someone months ago and forgotten to ask for it back. But there was no need for Mum and Dad to know that.

Outside, the weather was mild for November. Trigger strained the lead. He wanted to go where he wanted to go – probably the playground two streets away, which would be locked up now. But Jo meant to keep to well lit streets, like she'd promised. She paused at the gate to calm Trigger down. Across the street, there was a shuffling sound. The house opposite had been empty for months now. Its owner, Mrs Dole, had Alzheimer's and had gone into a nursing home. The son had only just got round to putting the house up for sale. Mrs Dole's stuff was still there and there'd been a burglary a couple of weeks ago. So Jo listened, just in case, but there was no further sound. She and Trigger set off on their walk.

As she crossed Wellington Circus, Charlene tried to make up her mind which flat to go to to – her own, or her fiancé's. They were only five minutes apart, but hers was nearer and it was turning cold. Also, Charlene didn't like Ian to see her when she was drunk, not even a little drunk, which she was now. Ian liked a drink, but always remained in complete control.

Once inside, Charlene turned on the heating, poured a last glass of wine and rolled herself a small joint, mixing mild tobacco and strong weed in equal proportions. This was another thing which Ian disapproved of, but turned a blind eye to. Dope relaxed Charlene better than alcohol, and didn't give her a hangover.

Charlene put some Miles Davis on the hi-fi, *Live Evil*, and drooped on to the sofa. She'd enjoyed the evening. She hoped her friendship with Clare would develop. In the eight months she'd been in Nottingham, Charlene had found it hard to make friends. The other lawyers in the firm were friendly at first, but kept their distance once they knew that she was going out with the boss.

There was a network of black professionals that Charlene could have hooked up with. Yet, at university, Charlene and Ben had always resisted defining themselves by their colour and Charlene continued to resist. Ian Jagger had introduced her to a far more influential élite, one which happened to be a hundred per cent white. But they weren't people she could fully relax around, never mind share a spliff with. Yet, if Ian could fit in, why couldn't she? Ian wasn't born into an élite. The opposite, in fact. His father had worked at Raleigh Bicycles, but died of a heart attack when Ian was twelve. His mother had been a cleaner. Cancer took her when Ian was at university. Even Ben, son of a bus driver, had been far better off. Charlene's roots were affluent middle class by comparison.

Charlene often found herself thinking about Ben. How had he taken the news of her engagement? She wanted him to hurt. It hurt her, hearing about how he was shacked up with a seventeen-year-old in the Maynard Estate. How he had fallen! If Ben had taken Charlene's advice and become a lawyer, instead of a police officer, he would be far better off. Not only that but, Charlene was sure, he would be the one she was marrying, planning a family with. Sometimes it seemed to her that she was marrying Ian in order to spite Ben.

She loved her fiancé, but in a slightly abstract way. For all Ian's gentility, his kindness, his handsome, distinguished looks, theirs was not a red hot romance. Ian was more experienced than her. That was inevitable. He was also cleverer than she was, though he never rubbed her nose in it. They weren't equals, as she and Ben had been. In bed, things were fine … more than fine. And Ian had made it clear that he didn't expect Charlene to be faithful to him if she chose not to. *You're only young once* he joked, then implied that he would choose to be faithful to her, whatever she did. This was the way they did things in the élite that he belonged to.

She thought about the racism issue which Clare had brought up. That was one thing, Charlene decided, she ought to sort out before their marriage.

Ian had never fully explained what had happened. It was just before she came to Nottingham, last March. There had been a bloody battle in the centre of the city. The riot took place practically outside the Central Police Station. The racists had been set up, were heavily outnumbered. What was the infiltrator's name? Jed something.

Charlene's head swam. She decided against a bath, setting the alarm in time for a shower in the morning. She undressed. Momentarily, as she cleaned her teeth, the dope and alcohol seemed to fuse the different parts of her brain together, giving her the illusion of crystal clear thought. Charlene's head and heart combined to tell her that she was marrying Ian Jagger for all the wrong reasons. Then she got into bed and instantaneously fell asleep.

The phone was ringing when Clare got in. Her landlady, Sam, would be at her boyfriend Steve's. Ruth was still away. Gary, the other lodger, would be at *his* boyfriend's. Clare was stuck in an empty house. She let the machine take the call.

"Clare, if you're there, pick up!"

It was Ruth. They hadn't spoken in several days. Clare picked it up.

"Hello stranger! When are you coming back?"

"That's what I'm calling about, Clare. I'm not."

"Not what?" Clare asked, high spirited, still drunk.

"Not coming back," Ruth said in a small voice.

"Pardon?" Clare said, thinking this was the lead-in to some kind of joke.

"I'm staying here, in Halifax."

Clare paused before asking the next question.

"You're transferring?"

"No, I'm quitting. I was never cut out to be a plonk, Clare. I'm going back to my old job, radio operator. There's a vacancy and… I'm sorry to desert you. I know that you've been having a shit time, but…" Her words trailed off.

"There's nothing to be sorry about," Clare said. "You were there for me. But I don't understand. I thought you liked Nottingham."

"I do," Ruth said, "but I like Halifax, too. It's home. To be honest, Clare, I left to get away from my dad. Now that he's dead…"

Her father had died earlier in the month. They hadn't got along, though Ruth had never really explained why.

"Mum and I had a long talk today. I think it's for the best. Will you give Sam my notice on the room?"

"Yeah, sure, but…"

"And promise to come and see me."

"I will. Oh, Ruth…" Clare was crying. On the other side of the Pennines, Ruth was crying too. They talked for a while longer, both too emotional to be very coherent. Finally, they pledged eternal friendship and ended the conversation. Clare felt drained. How was she going to get by without Ruth?

2

Jo heard the footsteps behind her, but didn't turn around. She stopped. The footsteps stopped too. They had been there since just after she left the house. Jo was uncomfortable. People walked at different speeds. They either overtook you or you out-paced them. They didn't keep pace with you for a street and a half, as this person had. When Trigger stopped to do his business, Jo reached into her pouch for the torch, just in case. Then she looked around.

It was a young bloke. Hard to tell how old in the dark. His hair was short and he wore a brown, mid-length coat, quite stylish. As he came closer she saw that he was smiling.

"Nice dog," he said, in a warm voice. "What breed is it?"

"Irish wolf hound," she told him.

"And what do you call it?"

There was nothing creepy about him. He was only trying to chat her up. Jo didn't mind that. It often happened when she was walking the dog.

"Trigger," she said. "One of my dad's jokes. To do with westerns – *The Lone Ranger* or something like that."

The guy smiled again. He had a nice smile, kind of shy but intelligent. Trigger finished taking a crap and pulled at the lead.

"Mind if I walk alongside you?" he said. "It's lonely, going for a walk on your own."

Jo liked being on her own, and she wasn't exactly short of company. But she had never been any good at saying "no" to people.

"Sure," she said. "My name's Jo."

"Kieran."

He held out his hand. Jo shook it. His grip was surprisingly strong. Then, hesitantly at first, they began to talk. Kieran worked in computers, he said. Jo admitted that she was still at school.

"A levels or GCSEs?" he asked.

"I'm younger than I look," she told him, not wanting to admit that she was in Year Nine, had only just turned fourteen.

"I'm older than I look," Kieran said.

Under a streetlight, she saw his face better. He had high cheek bones and dark eyebrows, which gave his face character. He was handsome, she decided. Not Mark Murray-handsome. In a western, Kieran would play the leading man's side-kick, the one who got killed, or the honest but vulnerable sheriff.

"Have you been to university?" she asked.

"I'm not *that* old."

"Wouldn't bother me if you were," she said, then wondered why she'd said that. Was she being flirtatious? Were they flirting? Jo didn't really know how to deal with a bloke this old. Yet he seemed more awkward than her.

"Do you mean to go to university?" he asked.

"If I get the grades, I guess."

"That's good."

They were at the edge of a main road. Jo had come further than she meant.

"I turn back here," she told Kieran.

"Oh. Right."

"Enjoy the rest of your walk," she said, with a smile, and began to turn. Would he shake her hand once more? No. He stood there, like a big dummy, another bloke she would never see again, Jo thought. Trigger began to drag her, anxious all of a sudden to get home. Then she heard the sound of running feet.

"Jo?"

She stopped. Trigger growled.

Kieran looked uncertain. "I was wondering… I'd

24

offer to take you for a drink if it weren't for the dog, but … would you like to go out with me sometime?"

Jo hesitated. This was a stranger, a guy she'd met on the street. What would her parents say? Stuff them. What would her friends say? They'd be jealous, probably. Kieran was at least nineteen, she reckoned, maybe a bit older.

Jo was into older men, but she wasn't looking for a boyfriend. She was in mourning for Mark Murray, who they buried in two days' time.

"Maybe," she said. "Give me a ring if you like. We're in the book. McCord." She spelt it for him. "Montague Street."

Now he knew where she lived. Maybe he would phone. Maybe he would think better of it. Jo had no idea where he lived. Round here somewhere, presumably. What would he think when he saw her in the daylight, realized that she was under-age? Jo was never short of offers, but they always came from the wrong people. She wouldn't get her hopes up.

The football season was not going well. Over a third gone and Forest were in the bottom three of the Premier League. They hadn't won a league game since September. Their best young player, Dean Sutherland, had been sold to Motherwell for a song. The owners wanted to sell the whole club, so weren't putting any money in. But there were no takers. The manager kept threatening to resign, especially after a veteran striker was sold without his being consulted. Twice a week there were rumours in the papers that the team were about to unload their most valuable asset, the Italian international Umberto Capricio.

The valuable asset nuzzled Gary on the sofa. Umberto turned off Sky Sports, which had just finished showing their Monday night Premier League game. The team below Forest had scored a handsome, unexpected victory. Now Forest were second from bottom. Umberto got up, poured himself some more cranberry juice and asked Gary whether he wanted any. Gary shook his head.

"If things don't get better by Christmas," Umberto said, as he sat down again, "I may have to move on."

Gary wasn't sure he was serious. "People will say you're a rat deserting a sinking ship," he commented.

"Let them say what they want," Umberto told him. "You know the truth. I was promised that they would be strengthening the squad. Instead, they've sold off the best players. The team spirit is terrible and getting worse every day. It's like being with a bunch of bad-tempered children."

"Where would you go?" Gary asked, his voice so soft that he wasn't sure if Umberto heard him. He felt forsaken.

Gary had never been in love before. He'd thought that he was in love with Lauren Knight, from the year below him at school. He'd been round to her house a few times in the summer holidays when she was fifteen, but nothing really happened. Then, one day, he'd gone round on the off chance. Lauren was out, but her big brother Wayne was in. He'd asked Gary if he fancied a drink. Within an hour, they'd been in bed together. Although Wayne looked a little like Lauren, Gary had never thought of himself as being in love with him.

There'd been plenty of sex since then – one night stands, mostly – but Gary believed that love was something that happened to other blokes. And then he'd met Umberto. Within weeks, they were saying the words to each other. Maybe Umberto used those three words with every man he dated, Gary didn't ask. But it was the first time that he'd used them, and Umberto knew that.

Now his lover sat on the edge of Gary's armchair and began stroking his hair.

"Come to bed."

"You didn't answer my question," Gary whispered.

"I won't do anything without consulting you, *tesore*. Come to bed."

Hand in hand, the two men went upstairs.

Kieran tried to enter the house quietly but his mother's voice cut through the night air like a frantic bird call. "Is that you, son? Come up here."

"In a minute."

The stair lift was on the upstairs landing, which

meant that Mum was already in bed. She'd be watching telly, the way she always did until she fell asleep. Knowing that she was safely upstairs, Kieran got his tiny digital video camera out of his coat. He'd bought the machine for a song from a man in a pub. He connected the machine to the mains adaptor, then rewound it.

Mum interrogated him about his walk: where he'd been, who he'd seen. Mum was virtually house-bound, which was why Kieran stayed at home. She had no idea that her son spent half the time he was out in an empty house on Montague Street.

"There's a bit of colour in your face," Mum pointed out. She missed little.

"It's cold out, that's all."

Something happened on the late film which distracted her. Kieran took her bed pan to empty, leaving the room with a mumbled good night. Downstairs, the electric bar fire had begun to heat the room and the tape had finished rewinding. Kieran wasn't expecting much from tonight's crop. For once, real life had been much more exciting than the stolen moments on tape. Even so, he set up his transferring leads and got out his secret highlights tape, which was concealed in a case marked *Rear Window*, though *front window* would be more appropriate.

The window he filmed from was directly opposite Jo's bedroom. It also gave a good view of the

McCords' living room. This had nets along the lower half of the sash windows, but they made no difference to Kieran. Looking down, he could see nearly everything. There was Jo, on the TV screen, still in her school uniform, on the sofa. She was sipping coffee and watching *Neighbours*, thoughtlessly scratching her left leg. He'd got in quite close on her face. She watched the show with great seriousness, as though it was Shakespeare or something, rarely smiling. He liked that.

When it was over, she went upstairs to get changed. Jo was a modest girl. She never changed near the window. Often her body was concealed by the wardrobe door. Even so, earlier in the year, he'd got several minutes of her in bra and knickers and one tantalisingly brief side-shot of her naked. This evening she had closed the curtains before taking off anything at all. After that, he had had a long wait.

While he was waiting Kieran had become hungry. When he was sure that the McCords were in the back of the house, eating their dinner, he'd gone to the chippy. He hoped he hadn't missed anything. After dinner, there was a light on in Jo's room for ages but, with the curtain closed, there was nothing to see. Kieran did think about going home. When Jo's light went off, he'd decided to give it ten minutes before packing in. Often, she'd go downstairs and watch telly, but not tonight. The curtains were closed in the living room, too.

He was going through the back door when he heard the dog bark on the street. Instead of going down the back alley, Kieran tip-toed to the front of the house. There she was, taking Trigger for a walk. Jo hadn't walked the dog, to his certain knowledge, for a week and a half. It had to be a sign. His time had come.

So he'd followed her. Like a fool, he'd got too close. She'd noticed him. Otherwise, why had she stopped? Kieran didn't know what to do. If she saw his face, had him down as some kind of nutter, that would be it. He would never have a chance of going out with her. So he'd thrown his fate to the winds, gone straight up and introduced himself...

Their meeting had been everything he'd hoped for, and more. Up close, Jo was both younger and more beautiful than the flickering image on his TV screen: virginal, even. Her voice in conversation was sweeter than when she talked to her mates. It was warm, sensuous. How long could he leave it before he called her? How long before he told her how he felt?

The stalker sat in the car, watching her house from the dark end of the street. He could see her front door, her bedroom window. She was unlikely to spot him, parked beneath a broken street lamp. This was futile, he knew, but he had to see what he was up against, had to know if she came home alone.

Tonight she did. Someone so beautiful should not be walking unaccompanied on the city streets. Where had she been? To a film, maybe, or a concert, though it was a little early for either event to have finished. Ten. Down the road, at Canning Circus Station, the shifts would be over. A light came on in her bedroom. For an instant, he saw her at the window, closing the curtain. She never went to bed this early, did she? The light went off.

Maybe it was time to call it a night. Go back to his lonely house, open a can, watch TV. Since it happened, he'd been finding it hard to sleep. Being here was a mistake, sure. Yet knowing that she was up there, alone, was comforting. He wasn't going to rush things, but, if she was alone, there was still a chance...

Suddenly, she was at the door, a jacket draped over her arm. She was walking towards him. No, not towards him, but towards the dark alley which led down on to Ilkeston Road. It wasn't an alley that a woman on her own ought to use. There had been muggings, and worse, in it. He ducked his head so that she wouldn't see him.

Only she wasn't going to the alley. Melanie banged on his passenger side window. Neil wound it down, embarrassed.

"What the hell do you think you're doing?"

He had no answer.

"Work," he said, finally. It was conceivable that

CID could be staking out somewhere other than Melanie's flat. A suspected drug dealer, for instance, lived in this cul-de-sac.

"Right," she said. "You won't mind if I call the police, will you? Tell them that some weirdo who I used to go out with is hanging around outside my house, watching my bedroom window. What do you think you are, Neil? Invisible?"

"I'm worried about you," Neil said, hopelessly.

"Why? I've got a new boyfriend. I'm happy, except when you turn up. I tried to let you down easily, Neil. Now it's over. Here, take this."

For the first time in the conversation, he turned round and looked at her, though the sight of Melanie was hard to bear. Strands of her long brown hair blew loose in the night breeze. How had Neil ever managed to pull a woman like her? That grey sweater. How many times had he lifted it over her shoulders and, and...

"Take it, Neil. I don't want it."

She thrust the leather jacket through the open window. He had bought it for her twentieth birthday, the Saturday before. He had hidden it in her flat. Only Melanie had dumped him before he could give it to her.

"I don't want it either. You'll look good in it."

"I don't care what I look like, it's from you and I can't wear it. Take it, Neil. Get a refund. And please leave. That way we can both have good memories. It was nice for a few months, Neil, but now it's over. Leave, please."

Neil turned on the engine and drove off without looking back. He drove, the leather jacket on the seat by his side, passenger window open, cold air blowing in. He circled the city slowly, looking at everything but taking in nothing. It began to rain, but he left the window open. He drove until the car made the clanking sound which indicated that it was almost out of petrol. Realizing that he had next to no money on him, Neil parked on a side street near the new business park on the south side of town. He sat there for a while, watching the rain. When it stopped, he walked home, slowly, with his head down, Melanie's unworn leather jacket draped around his shoulders, a pathetic figure of a man.

3

"And today we welcome back one of our probationers, Clare Coppola. Jan will partner you today, Clare," Inspector Winter told the shift at five to two on Tuesday afternoon. Clare didn't like the way that the recently arrived Inspector referred to her as a probationer. This was a reminder that, although, she had been on the shift for a year, Clare still had four and a half months to go before she was a fully qualified copper. At least Winter hadn't put Clare on foot. Her damaged ankle wasn't a hundred per cent yet.

"When's Ruth coming back?" John Farraday, Ruth's partner, asked.

Clare kept quiet.

"Your guess is as good as mine," Winter said. "Until then, we're still one under par."

Minutes later, Jan and Clare were alone in the Parade room. Jan looked haggard. There were lines beneath her eyes and her skin was sallow. The sarge was only thirty-one or -two. Today she looked ten years older.

"It's hot in here," Clare said, taking off her jacket.

Jan did the same, then gave Clare an appraising look. She pushed the door to.

"Clare, please don't think me insensitive, but … you're not … are you?"

She was looking at Clare's stomach. Clare was embarrassed.

"No, I'm not… I just need to enrol in a gym, go on a diet," she said, then quickly moved the conversation away from herself. "How about you? Isn't it time that you started on a little brother or sister for Henry?"

"I'd have to find him a father first," the sarge replied, in a bitter voice.

Clare did a double take. Jan's husband, Kevin, was a hospital registrar. Shift work made their marriage doubly difficult, but Clare hadn't realized that they were in trouble.

"What's happened?" Clare asked.

"We're getting a divorce," Jan told her, then added, *sotto voce*, "I don't want it spreading round the station."

"Of course not," Clare said. "Is there … someone else?"

"For him," Jan said, "Yes. Took me months to work it out."

"Another doctor?" Clare asked, in a gentle voice. Jan shook her head.

"A nurse?"

"Worse than that," Jan told her. "Our child-minder, Carol."

"Carol Ward, as was?"

"That's her."

"It only seems like five minutes since she was our paper girl!"

"I thought we were friends," Jan said. "They've been at it behind my back since last Christmas, can you imagine that?"

Clare closed the door and made them both a coffee. "When did you realize?"

Then it all came out.

"On holiday. We hadn't … done it … for months, but even when we were both relaxed, Kevin wasn't really interested. He denied that he was seeing someone, but I didn't believe him. I started sneaking home in the day, never found anything untoward. You know what the really humiliating thing was? It wasn't me who caught them, it was Carol's husband. Kevin came home one night when he was meant to be working. He had a black eye, two teeth missing and blood all over his shirt. I threw him out. That was three weeks ago. Now he sees Henry every other weekend."

"No chance of a reconciliation?" Clare asked.

Jan's eyes burned with resentment. "He's moved in with her. I don't want him back anyway. Things haven't been right since … since…" she hesitated. "Things haven't been right."

"You haven't told anyone else at work?"

"The boss knows," Jan said. "Who else am I going to talk to? You're my partner, but your boyfriend got murdered, you've been ill, then attached to CID. I used to see Neil socially now and then, but we've hardly spoken since he's been seeing Melanie…"

"He's not any more," Clare told her.

She filled Jan in on what had happened, leaving out the part where she and Neil slept together, since it seemed to reflect badly on both of them. Suddenly she remembered the morning-after pill. Too late to do anything about that now. By the end of the shift, her seventy-two hours would be up. Unless she told Jan and went to a clinic this minute … but that would be awkward.

"Poor Neil," Jan said. "I thought it was too good to last. Want to know the conclusion I've come to? Coppers should only go out with other coppers. Failing that, they should find someone stupid enough to spend all their time looking after them, like Ben's Julie. Melanie was good for Neil, but she had her own life."

Reluctantly, Clare agreed. "How are you coping, looking after Henry on your own?"

"It seems like I've always been looking after Henry on my own," Jan told her as the phone rang. "I hardly miss Kevin at all. The hardest part was finding a new childminder." She picked up the phone, listened for a minute, then continued talking. "Somebody's burnt out a car on the edge of that posh new business park. Security there want it towed away pronto because *it gives the wrong image. Aah, diddums…* Do a check on the number would you?"

She read the registration number out.

"That number sounds awfully familiar," Clare said, as she typed it into the computer. Once the car's details appeared, she understood why. A Carrington address appeared on the screen, followed by the owner's name. Neil Foster.

Jo spent most of Tuesday daydreaming about Kieran. Stupid, when she would probably never see him again, but it was better than dwelling on Mark Murray's murder. The funeral was tomorrow. Yesterday's *Evening Post* had stressed that only friends and relatives would be admitted. Fans were asked to stay away. Jo had met Mark once, had even got a kiss out of him, but could hardly count herself as a friend of his. She would mourn alone.

She got home from school at a quarter to four. Mum was still at work. Jo's younger sister, Grace, always stopped off at a friend's. Jo had an hour to

herself. She fancied a nice, long soak without anyone hassling her because they wanted to use the
bathroom. But before she could feel the tank to
check that there was enough water, the phone rang.

Jo hurried to it in order to beat the answering
machine, which always came on after five rings. Her
heart began to beat fast. The phone was on a table
in the living room. She grabbed the receiver and
said the number.

"Is that Jo?"

It was him. *Play it cool*, she told herself.

"Yes. Hi. Who's this?"

"Kieran, from last night. I wasn't sure if you'd be
home yet."

"I just got in."

"How was your day?"

"Oh, pretty good, the usual, you know."

He didn't know anything about her usual day, but
he was starting a conversation, and that was good.
When boys from school rang her, they were often
too tongue-tied to ask for a date, which she nearly
always refused anyway. Jo kicked off her shoes, got
herself into a comfy position on the sofa and asked
him about his day.

"So, so. Work was pretty boring. The most
exciting thing that happened was somebody left a
burnt out car right outside our office. The boss has
been trying to get the police to tow it away all day,
but it's still there."

"Will you be in trouble if you're caught talking to me?" Jo asked.

"No chance, I'm on a break and I'm using my mobile. They monitor all the calls going out through the switchboard – you know what computer companies are like these days, always watching you."

Jo didn't know anything about computer companies, but it was flattering that Kieran thought she did. He asked her what she was up to that night and she mentioned homework, a book she was reading, maybe having a bath.

"Not taking the dog for a walk?"

"No, Dad usually does that. He says it's the only exercise he gets."

"Are you on the internet?"

"Not at home. We have it at school."

"Pity. We could e-mail each other. Maybe you could come round to my house sometime. I'd like to show you my computer."

"Maybe," Jo said. "Where do you live, anyway?"

Kieran told her the street, though not what number. Jo had a vague idea where it was, a mile or so away in a humdrum part of town. His home was in the opposite direction to that in which he'd been walking the night before. Kieran must like long walks. The conversation faltered a little.

"Do you think," Kieran asked, more hesitantly, "that we could go out together sometime. For a drink, maybe? Or a film?"

"A film would be good," Jo said.

Jo had nothing against drink. She could make herself up to look eighteen, but it was a risk. Also, her parents would never let her see Kieran if they knew he was taking her to a pub.

"What night?" Kieran asked. "Tonight?"

"No," Jo said, with a laugh. "You'll have to wait till…"

She hesitated, because it would be better if the next day were not a school day. However, it was only Tuesday and Friday seemed an eternity away. "I might be able to make tomorrow," Jo said. "Give me your home number and I'll call you later, how's that?"

"I'll give you my mobile number," Kieran said. "I have it with me wherever I am."

"OK," Jo said, though mobiles cost more to call and Dad wouldn't like it.

"I can't wait for tomorrow night," Kieran said.

He was coming on really strong. Jo nearly said *me neither*, but instead murmured, "See you then" before hanging up.

She started the bath running and, excited, went into her room, where she undressed, scattering her school clothes on the floor. Then something odd happened. Jo glanced across the road, conscious that she was nearly naked. No lights on. Nobody in the street, either. Yet opposite, in the upstairs front window of what was supposed to be an empty house, she could swear that she saw something move. Jo froze for a moment and stared. Nothing. Her imagination was playing tricks on her. Even so, she grabbed her dressing gown and put it on before closing the curtains. She finished undressing in the bathroom.

Ben should have been starting afternoons today, but had to be in court instead. He and his partner, Gary, had apprehended a flasher who'd been hanging around a playground in the Meadows. They'd been waiting to be called since two. If they weren't on soon, the trial would be adjourned to the next day and both men would have to give up a free morning.

"Isn't that your ex?" Gary said, pointing to the back of a tall, well dressed woman. Charlene was shaking hands with a barrister.

"That's her," Ben said. He hadn't seen Charlene in weeks, not since he'd had to visit her office to interview the convicted paedophile she'd been representing.

As the barrister left, Charlene turned around and saw him. He smiled. She smiled back and walked over. Awkwardly, Gary excused himself.

"I'll be in the lav if they call us."

Not like him to hurry off like that, Ben thought, as Charlene sat down next to him on the cushioned bench.

"Successful day?" he asked.

"Very. Hardworking father of three just got custody off the crackhead mum, who spends all the child benefit on drugs. Restricted visits. Everything we wanted, in fact. You?"

"Still waiting to be called. A flasher. No big deal."

"Started studying for your sergeant's exams yet?"

Ben had only finished his probationary period earlier this year, but Charlene knew how ambitious he was.

"I'm putting in ten hours or so a week," he told her.

"Not good enough. It ought to be twenty. Your teenage girlfriend's taking up too much of your time, is she?"

"You heard about her, did you?" Ben said, a little embarrassed.

"The city isn't that big," Charlene told him. "I suppose you heard about me?"

"What?"

She looked mildly surprised. "It was in the evening paper."

"I don't always read it. Tell me your news."

Charlene took a deep breath, then used her most matter of fact voice. "I'm getting married."

"You're *what?*" Ben thought that she was kidding, but the look on her face was serious. "I didn't even know that you were seeing someone."

"For quite a while now. I didn't think it was serious at first but…"

She showed him the ring which was laden with diamonds, set in antique silver.

"Looks pretty serious to me," Ben said, nearly swallowing his tongue. He struggled for words. "Do I know the guy?"

"You've met him," Charlene said. "You don't *know* him."

"Who?" he asked, in a small voice.

"Ian."

"I don't know any Ians."

"You know this one," Charlene said, gently. "My boss. Ian Jagger."

Again, despite the serious tone of her voice, Ben thought she was kidding. She wasn't.

Ben had never really understood the meaning of the phrase *seeing red* before this moment, yet now a red mist seemed to form before his eyes. Ben struggled to breathe. Somehow, he sputtered out six words. "Don't-you-know-what-he-is?"

"You got him all wrong," Charlene said.

Ben suddenly remembered a brief conversation he'd had with Jagger the previous week. *No hard feelings*, the solicitor had said. Ben had wondered what the hell Jagger was talking about. Now he knew.

"He's old enough to be your father," Ben argued.

"Yeah, but the wrong colour," Charlene joked, "so I don't think there'll be any confusion. Chill out, Ben. We're in love with each other."

When she said that, the red mist really descended. Ben was dimly aware of Charlene going, of Gary returning, shaking his shoulder.

"They're calling you, Ben. Come on. They're waiting for you in court."

Clare finally got hold of Neil at half past four. He was at home, but had been ignoring the phone. The Mark Murray murder case had used up all of CID's overtime budget, so Neil had taken a day off to make up for time worked at the weekend. Clare had also worked the weekend, but, no longer being with CID, couldn't take time off in lieu. In March though, when her probation period was completed, she could apply to join CID. All the work she'd done for them would make it hard for DI Greasby to turn her down. Only Clare wasn't sure whether she would still want the job by March.

Neil sounded sick, or hung over, which was how Clare had felt earlier in the day. "What's it about?" he asked Clare.

"Your car. You haven't reported it stolen, have you?"

"That's because it isn't. I ran out of petrol, so I had to dump it. What's happened? Has it been towed, wheel–clamped?"

"Worse," Clare warned him. "Wait there. Jan and I'll come to pick you up."

They got to Carrington ten minutes later. Neil

didn't want to let them inside but Clare and Jan got a quick look at his living room while he was putting on a coat. There were crumpled beer cans on the table. The normally tidy room had two plates on the floor, together with an empty bottle of wine and one half full of whisky. The place smelt of stale booze and pizza. Poor Neil.

"The three of us ought to hold meetings," Clare told Jan. "The Broken Hearts Club."

"Better than drinking alone," the sarge agreed.

Neil reappeared and the club set off across the city.

To get into the business park, you had to get through a security barrier, which was raised for them.

"Funny area to leave a car," Jan commented.

"I ran out of petrol." Neil.

"Couldn't you get one of the boys in blue to bring you over a can?" Clare.

"I didn't feel like talking to anybody," Neil replied, in a tone which implied that he didn't feel like conversing now, either.

"What kind of insurance have you got?" Jan asked.

"Third party."

"With fire and theft?"

"I think so," Neil said. "Why?"

"Take a look."

Neil's car was blocking the slip road on the other side of the far exit barrier. Its windows had been smashed in, but that was a minor matter. The bodywork was singed black. The tyres were melted on to the wheels. The bonnet was open. Beneath it, the engine was a molten mess.

"That's my car?" Neil said, incredulous. "But I left it further down the road. It wasn't blocking anything."

"We figure that somebody decided to do a joy-ride," Clare told him. "They thought they'd have a little fun, smash through the barrier. Only there wasn't enough petrol to get up any speed so they pulled over and torched it instead."

"There was enough petrol and oil for a decent fire," Jan pointed out. "We thought you'd want to see it in situ before it's towed away."

"Thanks," Neil.

"We'll use our discretion to let you off the parking fine." Clare.

"Very generous. What about the towing fee?"

"You'll have to sort that out when they come," Jan said. "Why don't we go inside this building, check if there were any witnesses?"

The office had an entry system. Clare showed her warrant card and had them buzzed in. In the reception booth was a smart looking young guy in a white shirt and tie.

"Have you come to sort out that car at last?" he asked.

"Yes," Jan told him. "This is the owner."

"Oh. Sorry, mate."

Neil took up the questioning, even though he wasn't in uniform or on duty. Force of habit, Clare supposed.

"Was it here when you got to work in the morning?"

"I wasn't here this morning," the receptionist said. "It was the other guy."

"You're only part time?" Clare asked.

"Not really, but people who rent offices here tend to work long hours. So the office is open from seven until eleven. I do three to eleven. The other guy does seven to three. He told me that the car was there when he came on this morning."

"We'd better get his name and address," Jan said, "just in case."

"I don't know his address," the receptionist said. "You'd have to ask the landlord. But his name's Kieran Manders. I can give you his mobile number if you like…"

Jan took it. Outside, the tow truck was arriving.

"Had any trouble like this before?" the sarge asked.

"None at all. This is a highly secure area. No break-ins. Nothing."

"All right. Thanks for your time."

Outside, Neil watched his car being lifted on to the truck. It was the first car he'd owned and he'd hung on to it for far too long, Clare thought. He should be able to afford something better.

Behind the building were two big, ancient brick buildings which, for some reason, had so far avoided demolition. A fire had taken the roof off the bigger one, yet there was still a textiles firm using the third floor. It was fully lit. The other, newer-looking building was derelict. Behind it was the tall tower of the city incinerator, belching out smoke. Clare found it odd, standing here in the city's hi-tech future, staring at its industrial past.

"Penny for them," Jan said.

"I was thinking about that diet," Clare lied. "Got any suggestions?"

"Eat less, exercise more," Jan told her. "And don't become a slave to the tyranny of body shape. It's hard for a woman with your build to stay slim. I hope I didn't insult you this morning."

"No, no," Clare assured her.

"Any chance of a lift home?" Neil asked them.

"Go on," Jan said. "That is, if there's a brew in it. This is a quiet day. We've got nothing better to do."

4

At school the following day, Jo could hardly restrain herself from telling someone. Natalie was the obvious person, but she was skiving off. Jo was friendly with Gemma Day but Gemma was in a funny mood. She was wearing her sister's black blouse, which was too big for her as well as being against the school dress code.

"Nice blouse," Jo told her anyway.

"I thought you'd be wearing black," Gemma said.

"Eh…?"

"Nobody invited you to the funeral, then?"

Jo was mortified. It was Mark Murray's funeral today and she had forgotten all about it! Only eight days ago, she and Gemma had waited outside the Theatre Royal, waiting to get a glimpse of the star.

Jo had burst into tears, then Gemma had as well, and the two girls had comforted each other throughout the lunch hour. Jo was glad that she had told nobody about her date.

This included Mum and Dad. What was it people said about the oldest child? They were the ones who had to unlock the doors which their younger brothers and sisters find open. It had taken Jo all year to get her curfew moved to eleven. Last week she had caught hell for coming home twenty minutes late. So Jo had to play it carefully tonight. She rang Natalie to ask if she'd cover for her.

"I'm meeting him by the lions in town at seven-thirty and we're going to choose a film. But I've told Mum and Dad I'm watching a video with you."

"It's my night round at Curt's," Nat told her, referring to her boyfriend. "So if they call you here, you're screwed."

"Will your mum be in?"

"No, she's got a bar job."

"Then if they say they called, I'll say we were playing music loud and didn't hear the phone. It'll be all right."

"What's he like then, this Kieran?"

"Tall, dark, sweet sort of face, nice voice."

"How old?"

"Old enough. I didn't ask him."

"He at school?"

"No, he's got a job, computers. Real money."

"Lucky cow," Natalie sneered jokily. "When do I get to meet him?"

"Never! You might try and take him off me."

"Curt would kill me," Natalie said, as though this was a good thing.

"Gotta go," Jo told her. "I want a bath before everybody gets home."

Tonight she closed the curtains before undressing. She peeped through the gap in the middle to see if there was any movement opposite. Nothing. Probably her imagination. Jo was always daydreaming, fantasizing about what might be. Blokes, especially. Kieran was no fantasy. He did, however, seem a little shy. Shy could mean trouble. When Jo was in Year Eight, Martin Todd, a Year Ten boy who she really liked, had asked her out, then never shown up. At school the next day, Jo marched right up to him and asked where he'd been the night before.

"I thought we were just messing about," he said, red-faced.

That was six months ago. Since that day, Martin had never once looked her in the eye. Martin was still a boy, even though he was the same age as Curt Wilder. Kieran was a man. And Jo had his mobile number. She'd already called him on it once. If he didn't show up, she would call him again.

On the regional news, at six-thirty, they showed a few seconds of Mark Murray's funeral. Some of the mourners were from the soap opera that Mark used to star in. Jo recognized PC Coppola, who had interviewed her a few days before. She was in her own clothes. Had she known Mark, or was she a fan too? It was hard to think of police officers having a life outside their jobs. The police woman seemed to be crying. Jo shed a few tears herself. Then she went upstairs to get changed. She wore the red bra which she had treated herself to when shopping with Natalie, the one that Mum didn't know about. You could see its outline through her nearly translucent top. Nat reckoned that the top made her look at least seventeen. Jo put on a tight black wool skirt with a baggy jumper over the top so Mum wouldn't be able to tell that she'd dressed up. She hurried downstairs.

"That skirt's for best," Mum said as Jo put on her coat.

"But it's really warm," Jo explained, "and it's cold out."

"So wear jeans," Mum said, but didn't make her change.

"And don't be back after eleven, or you're dead," Dad yelled from the living room.

"I'll do my best, but it's two buses back from Nat's."

"Then leave in good time," Mum warned. "We worry."

On the bus, Jo improved her make-up, adding

blusher and eye-shadow to make herself look older. It was hard to do right, what with the bus moving about and people looking, but she made a pretty good job of it. Would she tell Kieran how old she really was? Not if it would scare him off. But she wouldn't lie, either. That was no basis for beginning a relationship.

The dark alley at the end of Wellington Square gave Neil plenty of cover. He had his warrant card with him in case anybody complained. That wouldn't protect him from Melanie, though. If she put in a complaint about him, he would be in serious trouble. So he'd better make sure that she didn't see him. Last night, she'd come in at six. Her mate Lorraine had come round at nine, left at half-eleven.

Tonight, Neil had tried to stay away, but couldn't. He'd been hanging about since six, breaking off only to avoid people using the alley. Melanie hadn't come home. She was always home by seven. Where was she?

Neil's behaviour was irrational, he knew that. Borderline illegal, maybe. But he was in love, and love made you do crazy things. He knew what he ought to do. Clare had been to a funeral today. She would be low. He could go round, take her out for a drink, watch a video with her, whatever a friend would do.

But being with Clare was suddenly complicated.

Neil had gone out with her for the best part of a year, yet they'd never gone all the way. This was because she was a good Catholic girl, or so he'd thought. They were going to wait until they were married. Only, when he worked up the courage to propose, she'd dumped him.

This weekend just gone, six months after Clare turned down his proposal, she'd seduced him. At least, that was how he remembered it. Six of one and half a dozen of the other, probably. They'd had the best part of a bottle of vodka between them before going to bed. If Neil went round tonight, Clare might think that that he was after a repeat performance. He wasn't. But Neil was only human. If sex was on offer, he'd find it hard to turn down. And if they did it again, there would be implications. Neil didn't want to be implicated. Not with Clare.

So he stayed in the alley, fifty yards from Melanie's flat, waiting.

Kieran was already there when Jo got off the bus, waiting by the big stone lion on the left of the council house. He wore a suit with a T-shirt. Very cool, Jo thought. "You look fantastic!" he told her.

"Thanks. You look pretty good yourself."

He could have kissed her then and she would have let him, but he didn't even try to hold her hand.

"I've got a paper with the films in. Want to go for a drink and choose?"

"Sure."

"There's a place up here which is all right."

They walked up Chapel Bar, where the old cinemas were, and went to a bar called *Sinatra's*. The walls were covered in signed, framed photographs of celebrities – movie stars and musicians, most of them. Jo looked at them after ordering a Malibu.

"Do you think all the autographs are real?" she asked. "They can't be, can they?"

"I don't know," Kieran said. "We could ask when the waiter comes back."

"If they're fake, he'd lie."

"You cynic!" Kieran said. "How can somebody so young be so cynical?"

She blushed, thinking he'd guessed her age, but then he started telling her about his wonderful job in computers.

"I'll show you where I work sometime," Kieran promised. "It's a neat place."

Before they knew it, the time was eight-fifteen and they hadn't begun to talk about which film to go to.

"Most of them haven't started yet," Kieran said, looking at the paper. "We could go across the road and make a quick decision. Or we could stay here and talk. Which would you rather?"

"Stay here," Jo said, shyly.

"Great," Kieran told her, and ordered another drink.

"Why are you in such a foul mood?" Julie asked Ben.

He'd just got in from work. They were standing in the kitchen where Julie was making some supper. Normally, they both liked it when Ben was on the afternoon shift. They got to spend long mornings in bed and Tammy was fast asleep by the time that Ben got home.

"I'm not in a foul mood," Ben told her, then realized that he needed to give a reason, preferably one which did not involve an ex-girlfriend getting married.

"You are."

"How much longer's Natalie going to be here?" he asked, irritably.

"Ten minutes. Then Curt'll walk her to the bus stop so that she can get the last 91. So you can eat your supper in peace."

A *Star Trek* video was still playing in the other room.

"Anyway," Julie said, putting some baked beans on, "Natalie wasn't here yesterday, and you were in a foul mood then, too."

"I'm fed up with baked beans," Ben said, trying to change the subject.

"OK, I'll eat them. What do you want instead? There's some frozen peas."

"Fine," Ben told her, then joined the two kids in the living room. Sitting in front of the telly was better than being interrogated. They were watching an old episode of *Deep Space Nine*. It was intercut with scenes from the first series of *Star Trek*, made back in the sixties. In some scenes, the new characters seemed to be in the same shot as the ones from the sixties. Clever. Ben wished he'd seen it from the beginning. He needed something to take his mind off things.

He and Charlene used to watch *Deep Space Nine* together when they were students. Back in the sixties, in the original *Star Trek*, Lieutenant Uhura was the first black woman to kiss a white man on television. Charlene had told him that.

Ben couldn't concentrate on the end of the show, though. He kept picturing Charlene with Jagger. Charlene wanted a white wedding. They'd discussed it. Now she wanted a white man, too. What pissed Ben off was that everybody knew before he did. It had been in the paper last week, yet nobody had thought to mention it to him. Did they assume that he knew? Was he supposed not to care?

It wasn't that Charlene was getting married. She was only six months out of a five-year relationship. It was too soon, but, over the same period, Ben had got through one girlfriend and started living with another, so it would be hypocritical to complain about that. What drove him crazy was who she was marrying. Ian Jagger couldn't deny having racist connections. His closest friend was Roger Wellington, the former Home Secretary, who was well to the right of Attila the Hun. Jagger was well connected. He belonged to the Round Table, the Freemasons too, probably … anyway, he had an MBE, or an OBE, one of those. He knew half the senior police officers in the city. He was virtually untouchable.

"See you, Ben," Natalie called, but Ben didn't respond.

Julie came in with his supper: two sausages on toast with pale peas on the side. It wasn't much of a meal, but she was eating beans on toast herself. It was what she was used to. If Ben brought pizza or fish and chips home, Julie thought they were living in the lap of luxury.

"Want a can of beer?" she asked.

He shook his head. Somehow, he had to get Jagger. He had to prove to Charlene that she was making a huge mistake. Was this about jealousy, or hubris? Neither. At least, not entirely. He and Charlene went back a long way. He ought to stop her from making a big mistake.

There were only two ways that Ben could think of to get at Jagger. The first was to find Jed Sutcliffe. The lad would be eighteen now. As far as

Ben knew, he had been in hiding since March. Somebody would know where to find him. The other was to dig into the death of Jagger's first wife, Pamela. Ben knew little about how she died, but recalled that Neil had looked into it after the Scott Travis murder, when Jagger was, briefly, a suspect. Neil said the circumstances of her death were never completely explained.

"Ben, you're not eating. What's wrong?"

"Not hungry. I need to make a call. It's work, so I'll do it upstairs."

He rang Neil from her bedroom, but there was no answer. Maybe he'd already gone to bed. Ben left a message asking Neil if they could meet for a drink when his shift finished tomorrow. Then he went back downstairs to Julie, who looked at him strangely, but said nothing, because Curt was back.

5

Kieran was always early for work. It had taken him ages to get a decent job, and he wasn't going to risk losing it. The job paid pretty well and, always an early riser, he liked the hours. He liked the people he worked for, too. They always said "Hello" when he buzzed them in. Most of them were young, well dressed. Just after he started working here, Mr Slater, a scientist who worked in bio-something-or-other, struck up a friendship with him. He even took Kieran to Paul Smith to buy a suit in the sale, the suit he'd worn last night. Slater let Kieran use his discount card, so it cost less than half price. The scientist was gay, but didn't try it on. Kieran made it very clear that he had a girlfriend.

Kieran hadn't actually had a girlfriend, then,

hadn't even spotted Jo at that point. But one day, early in September, he'd gone for a walk around town after work, and there she was. Jo was with another girl who looked younger. They were both in school uniform. He'd followed them along Lower Parliament Street, across the road and into the Victoria Centre. The two girls had a look in HMV and River Island, then went into Jessop's, where they took the escalator to the third floor. He'd stood two stairs behind Jo on the escalator, close enough that he could actually smell her: so fresh, so pure.

On the first floor, the girls went to the lingerie department, so Kieran had to hang back. He'd pretended to look at jewellery and watches, hoping all the time that he wouldn't miss them. He didn't shop at Jessops, didn't know that there was a back entrance which led straight on to the bridge over Lower Parliament Street. After ten minutes, he panicked, and hurried to where he'd seen them last.

"I'm looking for my sister," he said, and described Jo: tall, honey blonde, in school uniform, with a dark-haired friend who was smaller.

"You've just missed her," the sales assistant said, pointing at the back entrance. "But you should be able to catch her up."

And he'd ran, slowing down only when he was over the bridge, past the discount bed shop and almost on the stairs which led down to an anonymous street full of stalls selling batteries and baked potatoes. The girls were at the bottom. Kieran slowed down and followed them to the Market Square. The dark girl got on a bus heading towards Sherwood. Jo waited for a bus which would take her to Wilford. When one came in, Kieran joined the queue. He had a bus pass, so didn't need to know the price of her ticket. On the bus, he sat well away from Jo. He watched as she hid her purchase in her school bag. He'd guessed what it was. Did she have a boyfriend who she wanted to turn on? He prayed not.

Following her home was the hardest thing. Somebody else was getting off at Jo's stop, so he didn't have to stand next to her. Once off the bus though, Jo dawdled. It was hard for Kieran not to overtake her. He had to pretend to tie his shoe, to consult something in his wallet, then stopped a couple of times as though he might be at the right address, but wasn't sure. Jo only lived three streets from the bus stop, but it seemed much further.

Kieran couldn't believe his luck when he saw that the house opposite hers was for sale. That night, he'd returned with a screwdriver and a telescope, and broken in. Getting in and out of the house was a doddle. There was no alarm. He'd found a key to the back door and had it copied. The break-in was noticed a few days later and a window repaired, but there'd been no extra security, presumably because there was nothing worth taking. All Kieran had to do was walk along a narrow ginnel. It served three houses and came out two doors down. If anybody saw him in the ginnel, he'd claim to be visiting another house. Nobody knew their neighbours any more. They wouldn't check up on a stranger visiting someone by the back door, not unless he had burglar's tools in his hands.

Within a week, he'd bought a dodgy digital video camera from a man in a pub. Kieran's mum thought that he did an evening course at college, where he was meant to be retaking A levels. In fact, he'd never registered. He spent most of his evenings and weekends in an unheated house on Montague Street.

The beauty of Kieran's job was that he finished in time to get to Montague Street before Jo was home from school. For two months now, he'd been watching her, trying to work out a way into her life.

Maybe he should stop spying on Jo from the house opposite. But it felt so great, looking at her while they were talking on the phone. It really turned him on. Her too, he could tell from the way she was sitting. And the nights without her would last forever if he didn't spend them in Montague Street. He mustn't think of it as *spying*, Kieran decided, but as *protecting*. He was watching over her.

The buzzer rang. Kieran had almost forgotten that he was at work. He looked up to see who it was. There were two police women outside the glass. He panicked. They knew about him spying on Jo. They were going to do him for breaking and entering. They were going to tell Jo and her parents about him.

"Yes?" he said through the intercom. "Who have you come to see?"

"Kieran Manders?" asked the taller and older of the two. "We want a quick word."

He buzzed them in, his hands sweaty and his face, he was sure, beginning to redden.

"It's about the car that was dumped out here yesterday," the younger one said. She had a pretty face, but her black hair was cut far too short, he thought.

"Right," he said, trying to conceal his relief.

"We need to know whether it was here when you arrived at work in the morning."

"That's right. I got here at five to seven."

"Did you touch it?" the older one asked.

"Eh…"

"We only need to know if it was still hot," the pretty one explained.

"I did feel it, yeah. But it was cold. It was a cold night. It had been raining. Isn't this a lot of trouble for a burnt-out car? It was pretty ancient, you know."

"We know," said the taller copper, who wore sergeant's stripes. "But it belonged to one of our detectives. Thanks for your time."

And that was it. They were gone. Two minutes later, Kieran was relieved. He stepped out into the cold, late-November day with a spring in his step, and headed straight for the bus.

He was camped in the front bedroom, camera in hand, ten minutes before Jo got home. He'd meant to leave a decent interval before phoning her, but he didn't need to. The moment Jo sat down, she called him. He answered the phone, focussing his camera on her gorgeous face, which lit up when she heard his voice.

Neil looked in a bad way, Ben thought. His face was pale and pasty. His posture was limp, defeated. And his shirt was badly ironed. The two men hadn't met outside work for months, so they spent their first few minutes in the Grosvenor making excuses to each other without either of them actually apologizing.

"Women," Ben said. "That's what it boils down to. So how is Melanie?"

"She dumped me."

"Ouch."

"I thought it'd be all over the station by now," Neil said.

"Haven't heard a whisper. Who knows?"

"Clare."

"She only started back on Tuesday," Ben said. "And Clare's pretty discreet. Hey, are you and her…?"

Neil shook his head. "That's history," he said,

but something about the way he said it made Ben doubt him. There was history and history, he thought. There was the stuff you just forgot about. Then there was the stuff which never stopped haunting you.

"A bit of history's what I wanted to talk to you about," he said. "You've heard that Charlene's marrying Jagger?"

"It's hardly a secret," Neil replied, avoiding Ben's eye.

He's known for ages, Ben realized. This was what happened when you didn't stay in touch: people avoid telling you things they know you don't want to hear.

"I tried to warn her against him," Ben said. "But she wouldn't listen."

"Charlene strikes me as a fairly astute judge of character," Neil commented. "Maybe you've got Jagger wrong."

Ben shook his head. "Jagger's tied to racist groups. There's no doubt about that."

"As I recall," Neil said. "There's no proof what-soever, only unsubstantiated accusations from Jed Sutcliffe. I'd be careful what you say, Ben. Jagger has plenty of friends in the force. You don't go round slandering lawyers, not if you're wise."

"Fair point," Ben said. "What happened to Jed Sutcliffe?"

"He was in some kind of witness protection

scheme, but I expect that it's winding down now – the prosecutions were months ago."

"Could you find out?"

"I'll ask," Neil promised.

"There was another thing. Didn't CID look into the death of Jagger's first wife during the Scott Travis murder case?"

"We did," Neil told him. "At your suggestion. The theory was that he might be vulnerable to blackmail over it. But there was nothing there, Ben. Pamela Jagger was slightly over the legal limit, driving too fast. She wrapped her Merc around a lamp post in the early hours of the morning. Jagger was home in bed."

"What was she doing out at that time?" Ben asked.

"It wasn't in the report. Working on a case, probably. Or maybe she was playing away. We didn't find out then, so we're not going to find out now."

It was Charlene who'd told Ben about Jagger's first wife. She'd been feeding him information about her boss in order to try and get back with Ben. At the time, she seemed to believe what Ben said about Jagger. What changed her mind?

Neil leant forward. "What is it, Ben? Why can't you let go? After all, you've got Julie."

Ben thought about that while Neil went to get another pint. It was nearly closing time and this would only be their second pint. They would not be getting drunk together, nor putting the world to rights the way they used to.

When Neil returned, he started to talk about Melanie. He went on and on about how she was the only one for him, how he had to change her mind, then invited Ben back for a drink. His small house was a five minute walk away. Ben didn't fancy it. Tonight, they were both obsessive, but about different things. They would only continue to bore each other.

"What time have you got to be at work tomorrow?" Ben asked Neil.

"Half-eight."

"If I were you, I'd get some kip. You look knackered."

"I am," Neil said. "Couple of hours a night, that's all I'm getting."

"Then take the day off sick. See a doctor."

"Maybe I'll do that."

Which meant he wouldn't. The Grosvenor was throwing out. The two men said good night and Ben crossed Mansfield Road to flag down a taxi. Neil, he noticed, didn't head home, but went in the opposite direction, towards town, or towards Clare's. Was that where he was going? There had been that funny look when Ben asked about Clare earlier. Neil was so cut up over Melanie and Clare was grieving over Paul Grace. It would be only natural if...

A taxi stopped. The driver was Asian. White taxi drivers never picked up Ben. The event was so commonplace that he had more or less stopped thinking about it. He gave his address, then returned to the question which Neil had asked earlier, the one he hadn't answered: *Why can't you let go?*

Now Jo was sure. There was somebody squatting in the house opposite, the one that was for sale. Coming home from school today, she'd caught a glint of metal in an upstairs window, a definite movement. Since then she'd kept an eye on the house. She'd left her curtains open to tempt whoever it was to keep looking, to give themself away.

Jo rang Nat from the extension in Mum and Dad's bedroom. Of course, Nat thought that she was phoning to talk about Kieran. She'd been off school today so hadn't had a blow by blow replay of the date.

"Has he called you yet?"

"Noooo. I saw him last night. And I'm seeing him again on Saturday."

"Tell me about it."

Jo told her, finishing with the little kiss he'd given her at the bus stop.

"That was it?" protested Nat, who'd lost her virginity at thirteen. "A peck!"

"It was brilliant."

"Are you sure he's not gay?"

"We're not all like you, gagging for it," Jo ribbed her. "He's dead romantic. I reckon he's the sort of guy who takes things one small step at a time. Anyway, there's something else I want to talk about…"

She told Natalie about the shadows she'd seen in the house opposite.

"It must be a – what do you call it? – a peeping tom."

"Something like that," Jo agreed. "What should I do?"

"Dunno. What do your parents say?"

"I haven't told them."

"Why not?

Because Mum and Dad were so over-protective that if Jo revealed any threats to her delicate, teenage lifestyle, they would probably lower her curfew and insist on vetting her boyfriends. Kieran would be condemned as far too old for her.

"It might be my imagination," Jo conceded at the end of the conversation. "I don't want to freak them out."

When she went back into her bedroom and looked out of the window, a car with bright lights swept down the street. Jo was sure she saw a silhouette. What should she do? Of course, there was one person who she could always talk to, one person whose advice she needed most of all. He had said that she could call him any time. So she went back to her parents' bedroom, and dialled his mobile number.

Kieran answered on the first ring.

"It's good to hear your voice," he said.

"It's good to hear yours. I've really missed you today."

"Me too."

"What are you up to?" she asked her boyfriend.

"You want to know the truth? Sitting in a room, staring out of the window, thinking about you."

"Aaaw. You say the nicest things. Listen, Kieran, there was something I wanted to talk over with you."

"What?"

"It's…"

Jo heard footsteps on the landing stairs. The door burst open.

"Joanne, who are you talking to at this time?"

"It's just Natalie," Jo said, humiliated because Kieran could hear.

"You saw her last night, didn't you? And you know that you're not meant to use this phone without permission. You should be in bed, young lady!"

Jo's face reddened. "Got to go, sorry," she whispered into the phone, then hung up. "OK, OK," she said to her mum. "Can't a person have a private conversation any more?"

She stormed into her room, turned on the light, jumped on to the bed and began to punch the pillows. Then she remembered to close the curtains.

* * *

He had not meant to come here. Leaving the pub, Neil's feet had taken him in this direction, that was all. He'd meant to take a walk around the edge of the forest, maybe, but had cut straight across it. Walking across the forest at night was dangerous, but Neil was past caring. Anyone who tried to mug him would provide Neil with an excuse for a fight. Ideally, Neil would like to beat up Melanie's new boyfriend, but anybody male and under thirty would do as a substitute.

The night was dark and cold. Nobody attacked him. Neil walked fast, head down. He should stop himself when he got to Mount Hooton, turn around, go home. A shadow stepped out from behind a tree.

"Looking for business?"

The boy was twelve, thirteen at the most. Neil stopped, and spoke to him almost tenderly. "Haven't you got a home to go to?"

The boy gave him a withering look, like this was some corny chat-up line, then began to give him a price list. Neil carried on walking. The kid was probably in care, or on the run from a children's home. Handing him over to Vice would only cause aggro for everyone. The lad would be out again by tomorrow, selling his body for pocket money. Meanwhile, Neil would have to explain to his colleagues what he was doing in the forest at a quarter to twelve. Best just to leave it.

He followed Bentinck Road to Alfreton Road,

then cut across to Ilkeston Road. It had just gone twelve when he got to Wellington Square. Mel was home tonight. The light from her bedroom was pale, which meant that Melanie had the reading light on. Often, when Neil had rung her up to wish her good night, Mel would be reading. She'd tell him about whatever book it was: William Shakespeare, John Donne, the Augustan poets…

Her new bloke could not be with her. Melanie would only make love with the lights out. Presuming that they had reached that stage. It had only been a week and a day since, to Neil's knowledge, she first went out with him. Maybe it wasn't too late for her to change her mind.

Neil heard footsteps on the steps which led into the alley, so he walked briskly into Wellington Square, keeping his eye on Mel's bedroom window. He was almost in front of her house when the blind flew up and there she was, looking down on him. Even from this distance, Neil could tell that she was angry. He froze. A dark figure stepped out of the shadows in front of him.

"Good evening, sir."

Neil didn't recognise the bobby in front of him, a tall tree of a man whose helmet made him into a giant. Neil's first instinct was to run, but he glanced behind him and the person coming through the alley was a bobby, too. He'd have to bluff it out.

"Evening," he said.

"Bit cold for a walk," the tall officer, who was thirtyish, commented.

"I've got things to think about," Neil replied, feebly.

"Haven't we all, sir? We've had several calls from residents of this street alerting us to a stranger who's been seen hovering in this dark passageway."

"Oh, right… Well, I understand your concern."

"Two of those calls were from a Miss Melanie Byatt, whose window you were just staring at, sir."

"I see."

The other police officer was standing alongside Neil now – a policewoman, younger than Clare. She was barely out of adolescence, still a little spotty and looked weighed down by all the gear she had to carry.

"The thing is," Neil said, pulling out his warrant card. "I'm with CID. This is a covert…"

The male officer put a finger to his lips. "I wouldn't try that line if I were you, Mr Foster. We know who you are. The night shift have been instructed to look out for you. We'd have had you earlier but, for some reason, you were rather late arriving tonight, weren't you? Now, our Inspector wants a word. Are you going to come quietly, or do we have to arrest you?"

DECEMBER

6

The city was changing. For years, the south side had been a construction site, punctuated by new buildings which fitted uncomfortably with the old. The magistrate's court off Canal Street came first, then the Via Fosse pub, a Jongleurs comedy club and the hi-tech, green, glass-fronted *Evening Post* building. Behind them, the canal still had water in it, but the old factories and warehouses it led to were disused, mostly derelict and awaiting demolition.

The city had expanded. Old buildings in the old centre weren't good enough for the twenty-first century's go-ahead industries. The BBC had followed the *Post*, creating its own small empire beside what used to be called the Boots traffic island. Boots had gone and nobody had a name for this new part of the city, out towards Trent Bridge, though some were calling it Southside.

The area was a triangle, with a science park at one angle, the BBC at another and Notts County football club at the third one. The city's oldest football team were currently languishing at the bottom of the second division, in danger of dropping into the third. Forest, meanwhile, after a bright start to the season, were near the bottom of the Premiership. Somebody had forgotten to tell the football teams that Nottingham was meant to be on the up and up: the third richest city in the country, according to one survey, after Edinburgh and Swindon. *Swindon?*

Yet the city was full of poverty, too. Over the Trent was leafy West Bridgford. People who lived there used the city, but paid their council tax to the Rushcliffe Borough, not Nottingham. The city's other borders held Radford, Lenton, Sneinton, St Anns and, finally, Forest Fields, where Clare lived. These were places so poor that students counted as good earners. There was one exception. Charlene – with whom Clare was on her way to have a drink – lived in The Park, a private estate tucked behind Nottingham Castle. The Park was packed with old buildings. It had wide streets with tall trees and expensive cars outside nearly every house.

Clare was changing. She'd never have made friends with someone like Charlene a year or two ago. Charlene was unashamedly materialistic. She was smart, practical and didn't suffer fools gladly. And she drank in places like this. The Lace Hall was a historic church which had been converted into a museum. It was then sold off to a brewery chain who had spent a million and a half pounds converting it into the Pitcher and Piano. There was a piano in the raised central section, but the music was provided by a tape of vaguely indie music. A sign by the bar said that admittance on New Year's Eve was by ticket only and would cost £10. Clare saw Charlene at the far end of the hall and went to join her.

It was disconcerting, Clare decided, drinking in a place which felt more like a cathedral than a bar. But what were you supposed to do with old churches in the twenty-first century, when hardly anybody believed in God? Within an hour, the place would be heaving. New people would only be allowed in when other people left. Sometimes it felt like night life was the new religion.

Clare and Charlene sat on a sofa in the least formal area, beneath the focal point of the bar/church, which was a huge stained glass window. The window, Clare explained, was by Burne-Jones, a pre-Raphaelite friend of William Morris. Charlene, who had suggested they meet here, wasn't terribly interested in this.

"Wedding plans in hand?" Clare asked.

"We've got a date," Charlene told her. "April. The Saturday after Easter."

"Perhaps you could have it here?" Clare joked.

"It'll be at St Mary's, just up the road," Charlene told her.

St Mary's was the oldest church in the city.

"Am I invited?" Clare enquired, tentatively. "Not that I expect…"

"Course you are," Charlene interrupted. "The question is, will you bring anybody?"

Their drinks arrived: vodka and tonic for Clare, white wine for Charlene.

"Plenty of time for me to find a date," Clare said. "The dress might be more of a problem."

"Why?" Charlene asked, confused.

"I should have taken your advice when I told you about sleeping with Neil."

"You're not…?"

Clare tried not to get emotional. "My period's still not come. I couldn't put off taking the test any longer. It came out positive. I've just made a doctor's appointment."

"Oh, Clare…"

For a few moments, they looked at each other in silence. Charlene was the first person that Clare had told. She'd had to tell Charlene, even though they hadn't been close for long. Charlene was the practical, rational type. She would help Clare to think through her options. Soon, maybe, Clare would have to tell Mum, too. The rest of the world could wait.

"Are you sure it's Neil's?" Charlene asked. "You said you hadn't had a period since Paul…"

"I didn't stop taking the pill until Paul died," Clare said, matter-of-factly. "And I tested myself when I was overdue. Negative. I told the doctor about not having periods when I injured my ankle. She said that the menstrual cycle shutting down was a normal reaction to such a severe shock."

"The test could have been wrong."

"I don't feel three months pregnant," Clare said. "I don't feel anything."

"Are you going to tell Neil?" Charlene asked, gently.

"I haven't decided," Clare replied. Nothing was decided. She began to think aloud. "Neil's been so weird since that night. It's true what they say. If you sleep with a friend, you gain a lover, but lose the friend … and lovers are much easier to come by. If I tell Neil that I'm pregnant, I don't know how he'll react. I'm not sure that I want to know."

"From what Ben used to tell me about Neil," Charlene said, "he'd probably offer to marry you again."

"Yeah, right. That's exactly what I need," Clare said, sarcastically.

"He's a nice guy who cares about you. He'd make a good father."

Clare considered this for a moment. "But I'm not

in love with him. Never have been. And he's not in love with me any more."

Charlene gave Clare a firm look. "There's a lot of nonsense talked about *love*. I'm not *in love* with Ian. But I love him, I enjoy his company. I admire his intellect."

She didn't say anything about fancying him, or having a good time in bed, Clare noted. Without that, what was the rest worth?

"I have to be in love," Clare said. "It'll probably be simplest if I don't tell Neil anything."

"But you intend to keep it," Charlene said.

It was a statement, not a question.

"Why do you say that?" Clare asked.

"Because you're a Roman Catholic."

"Not a terribly good one," Clare pointed out. "I've missed Mass half a dozen times this year."

"Aborting a baby isn't the same as missing Mass," Charlene told her, bluntly.

"No," Clare admitted. "I haven't fully thought it through yet, but I expect you're right. I'll probably keep the baby."

"In which case, Neil will see that you're pregnant and work out that it's his, won't he?"

"Maybe."

"Unless…"

"Unless I let people think that it's Paul's…"

"Maybe it is," Charlene reiterated. "Maybe that first test gave a false result."

"You're right," Clare admitted. "There's a small possibility."

"If you're pregnant," Charlene pointed out, while Clare slurped her vodka and tonic. "You should cut down on alcohol."

"I am doing," Clare said, not entirely convincingly.

They talked for a while about the practicalities of Clare bringing up a baby on her own, but the conversation became uncomfortable. Clare managed to switch it back to the wedding.

"Ian's asked Roger Wellington to be best man," Charlene said. "He sees more of Roger than he does of me at the moment. I don't know what the two of them are hatching."

"Never a good idea to have secrets," Clare commented.

"Solicitors have to have secrets," Charlene said, "even from their life partners. It goes with the job. Ian's having dinner with Roger tonight," she went on. "And they've got some jaunt to Europe planned. I'm not invited, of course."

For her second drink, Clare ordered a pineapple juice and lemonade. She told Charlene about Jan Hunt, whose marriage hadn't survived her having a child and working shifts. Unless Mum helped, Clare would find it impossible to manage, too. And Mum had a nine-to-five job. However, if Clare transferred to CID in March, she would work more regular hours. Could she keep quiet about the baby until then? CID would never take her on if they knew that she was pregnant.

"Pregnancy shouldn't get in the way of promotion," Charlene said.

"It's a transfer, not promotion. And this is the police. People only pay lip service to equal opportunities for women."

"But they'd find it hard to transfer you back after the baby."

"I guess," Clare said. But she didn't like deceit. She didn't like herself very much at the moment, with all these dark thoughts swimming around her head. She felt like she was being punished. But what for? Missing Mass? Having sex with Neil? She didn't know. Clare felt like she didn't know anything any more. And as for her career in the police force, she hardly cared.

"So they let you off?" Ben asked, as they looked around the forecourt of a garage on the Woodborough Road. Ben knew little about cars, but Neil wanted company while he bought a new one – or, at least, a not too old one. This was the first time that Ben and Neil had met since their drink in November. Neil had just confessed to standing outside his ex-girlfriend's house night after night for a week, until two uniformed coppers dragged him away.

"I had to talk to the inspector at Canning Circus for twenty minutes. I swore I wouldn't go near

Wellington Square or contact Mel again, then they took me home. Next day, Greasby had me in and told me that Canning Circus had been in touch. There'd be a note in my file, but it wouldn't count against me as long as I didn't repeat the behaviour. Then he ordered me to take a fortnight's holiday."

"Where've you been?"

"My cousin's. She moved to Birmingham this summer."

Neil's cousin was a nurse, as was Ben's sister.

"She introduce you to any good-looking women?" Ben asked, trying to lighten the tone of their conversation.

"Tried to. Mainly I helped decorate her flat. It was good to be out of Nottingham for a while, to know that I wasn't going to bump into Mel, or Clare, or somebody I'd arrested the week before."

"I know what you mean," Ben said. "I can't tell you what a relief it was when Ruth quit the shift. It means I don't have to avoid her in the parade room, feel guilty every time she passes by. You're not thinking of moving away, are you?"

Neil shook his head. "All I'm thinking of doing is buying another car." He looked inside a Vauxhall Nova.

"You want something newer than that," Ben said.

"I don't like borrowing money," Neil told him. "But you're right. A car less than ten years old would help my image."

"I don't suppose you've had a chance to find out anything about Jed Sutcliffe?" Ben asked. "You remember I asked about…"

"I remember," Neil said, as they crossed the wind-blown forecourt and the prices jumped by two thousand pounds. "I did some checking yesterday. Sutcliffe was in a witness protection programme for three months, given a new name – I don't know what – but he lost touch with his minders back in July. He took his new passport. They think he left the country. No idea where. Sorry."

Ben swore beneath his breath. Sutcliffe was his best hope. Neil looked at a green Fiat Uno.

"You can't have that," Ben said. "Woman's car. Did you find out any more about Jagger's first wife?"

"I've got the name and address of the officer who was in charge of the investigation into her death. He's retired, but he still lives locally. That's all."

Neil paused and gave Ben a worried look. "Don't you think that you should leave it? Isn't what you're doing with Jagger what I was doing with Melanie – prolonging the agony?"

Ben thought about this. "If I'm right about Jagger, I owe it to Charlene to prove it," he argued.

"And you think she'll thank you?"

"Probably not," Ben admitted.

"Hey, how about this?" Neil said, pointing at a black Rover Metro. "Is that a woman's car, or could I get away with it?"

"In black, definitely," Ben said.

Neil poked around for a minute. He seemed excited that the car had a good stereo. Then he went to arrange a test drive.

Ben could do with a car himself. He would be able to take Julie and Tammy places. Trouble was, the area they lived in, any car that wasn't already a wreck soon would be. They needed to move first. Somewhere slightly larger. Tammy would need her own room in a few months. Maybe Curt would move out in June, when he finished school. But Ben doubted it. And Julie was making none too subtle hints about having another baby soon, so that the age gap between Tammy and the next one wouldn't be too big. Ben didn't know how he felt about that.

Neil came back with the smiling salesman. He was going to buy the car. Ben knew it and the salesman knew it. Neil was so transparent. He would never make a good deal. Ben decided not to stick around.

"Have you got that name and address?" he asked, and Neil handed it over. "Sorry," Ben told him. "I ought to be somewhere else."

"Can we drop you anywhere?" Neil asked.

"You're all right, there's a bus stop across the road."

While he waited for a bus into town, Ben glanced at the scrap of paper that Neil had given him. John Parker lived in Lowdham, a smart village several miles from the city. Ben hoped that there was a bus which would take him there. He had a bunch of Christmas presents to buy and didn't want to fork out a small fortune on a taxi each way. Neil drove past in the shiny black car, smiling salesman by his side. Ben hoped his friend wouldn't be ripped off, yet knew that he would be. And, Neil being Neil, he'd hardly mind.

Kieran had never looked forward to a Christmas so much in his life. Jo was coming over to spend the evening of Christmas Day with him. Provided, that was, he got over the hurdle of meeting her parents tonight. They had to approve him before they'd let their daughter spend an evening at his house. What her mum and dad didn't know was that he'd been seeing Jo at least twice a week for five weeks now. He'd been a bit shocked when she'd told him how old she was. He'd guessed, from her hints, that she was fifteen, but she was fourteen, and only in Year Nine. Whereas Kieran was twenty-three. He'd told Jo that he was twenty, in case a nine year age difference freaked her (or her parents) out.

In a way, Kieran liked that she was fourteen. Age had nothing to do with true love. The younger Jo was, the less likely it was that some other bloke had corrupted her. Kieran would be her first, her last, her everything. He had bought Jo two presents (more might look over the top). There was a small silver ring for her to wear as a token of their love. But the other present was the clincher. Once she had it, they would never truly be apart. He couldn't wait to see her face when she opened it.

Even though he was seeing Jo on a regular basis, Kieran kept returning to the house on Montague Street. It had become a habit. But he had cut down. He didn't use the camera any more, not since Jo mentioned on the phone that she thought some-body was watching her. After that, he'd stayed away for a week. Kieran had enough film already. On Christmas Day, he planned to pretend that he'd just got the video camera as a gift. He'd get Jo to pose for him. Nothing naughty – he didn't want her to think that he was like that. For Jo was pure and precious. That was why he was here, after work, week after week – not to spy on Jo, but to watch over her until her parents came home.

He let himself in through the back door as usual. No hurry. It would be ten minutes before she got home. The house was cold, but he'd left a blanket upstairs which would ward off frostbite. Kieran shut the door behind him and was halfway across the small hall when he realized that he wasn't alone.

"Who the hell are you?"

The guy was an estate agent. Kieran had never met one before, but, even so, he knew the type: smart suit, plain tie, expensive haircut, a shallow dimple in his well-shaved chin. The guy only looked a year or two older than Kieran, but probably earned five times as much.

"I came to look at the house," Kieran said. Maybe he could bullshit his way out of this.

"Yeah? How did you get in?"

"The door was open."

"No, it wasn't. You're the guy who's been hanging out here, aren't you? I found some stuff last time I came: biscuit wrappers, empty cans. That's you, isn't it?"

Kieran tried to think of a way to stall. "I didn't do any damage," he said.

Not unless you counted the window he'd broken to get in the first time.

"You must have a key. Let's have it."

Kieran handed over the key he had had cut.

"Is that the only one?"

"Yes," Kieran lied.

"What's your game? Have you been living here?"

"On and off," Kieran said, adding, in a whiny voice, "I've had some problems at home."

"I'll bet you have. You'd have some more if I called the police out, wouldn't you?"

"Please don't do that."

The estate agent looked at his watch.

"I've got some clients coming in five minutes. If they find out the place is being squatted, I've got no chance. Have you left anything here?"

"There's a blanket in the upstairs bedroom."

"Take it and go. If I ever find you've been here again, I'll make sure you get done for burglary."

"I haven't taken anything."

"Breaking and entering, then. You'll be put away. Got that?"

"Yes."

"Go and get your blanket."

Kieran hurried upstairs. At least the guy hadn't realized why he was using the upstairs room. He folded the blanket quickly and made sure that he'd left nothing else which could identify him. The tiny pair of binoculars he always carried was still concealed in his jacket pocket.

"No, you're not going out the back," the estate agent ordered, as Kieran tried to escape by the way he'd come in. "Leave by the front."

"I'd rather not."

The estate agent reached into his pocket for a mobile phone and Kieran felt like hitting him. The smart young man pressed the "nine" button twice.

"All right," Kieran said. "All right. I'm going."

He rushed out into the street, blanket under his arm, and looked around. No Jo. He turned left and began to walk quickly. A hundred yards and he'd be round the corner. A cold wind blew. Rain began to spit. Was that the wind howling? No, it was her voice, calling him. Kieran stopped and looked around. Jo waved. He waved back. He prayed that the estate agent wasn't looking out of the window.

But it wasn't the estate agent he needed to worry about.

Kieran tried to think of a way to dump the blanket. He could just drop it over a wall. But Jo was bound to see whatever he did. Now she was running towards him. He had to think very, very quickly.

7

"You're not meant to be here till eight," Jo said, confused by the sight of her boyfriend so early in the day. Worried, too. Seeing her in school uniform might put him off. "What are you doing with that blanket?"

"Long story," Kieran told her. "I'll explain inside."

He seemed in a hurry, so she crossed the road and Kieran followed her into the house.

"You said you always had an hour on your own before everyone else got home," he explained as she let him in. "So I thought I'd join you."

Jo was confused. If Kieran was coming to see her, why had he been walking away from the house? And why did he look so furtive? But Kieran could be odd sometimes, evasive even. Jo was learning to handle him. She would work out what was going through his mind later. Right now, she had to make sure that he was out of the house before Mum got home at five-fifteen.

"Why aren't you at work?" she asked, after putting the kettle on.

"I'm working new hours," Kieran said. "I finish at three."

He smiled nervously. Jo smiled back, seeing immediate possibilities – two hours together every day before Mum got home. They could have almost as much freedom as Curt and Natalie.

"It means getting in for seven in the morning," Kieran went on, "but I don't mind getting up early."

"Does everyone finish at three?" Jo asked, taking off her school jumper. It made her cold, but at least the blouse beneath looked OK. She was grateful that she was wearing her black wool tights, rather than the black trousers which kept the cold out better.

"No, there's a late shift, too. Three to eleven."

"We couldn't have that," Jo said, pouring hot water on to coffee granules. "I'd never see you."

She reached up and kissed him. It was a wet, wonderful kiss.

"Let's go upstairs," she said.

He didn't need telling twice.

They were never alone together, not really. She had been to Kieran's house a couple of times, but his mum was always in the background. It didn't feel like they could get intimate. Now, Jo realized, they had over an hour. Anything could happen.

"This is my room," she said, flinging open the door. "Like it?"

"It's very … really nice."

She would make him turn his back while she got changed, Jo decided. That would be seductive, but not too forward. Then she saw something which made her change her mind.

"Oh God, he's there!"

"Who?" Kieran stood, put an anxious arm around her shoulder.

"Across the road, look. That's the window I was telling you about!"

The voyeur had got more daring, Jo realized. The light was on and the curtains had been opened. She could see him, clear as day – a dark haired bloke in a suit, medium height and build, twenty-fiveish. Not her idea of a peeper, at all, but she'd be able to describe him to the police.

Then she realized that the man wasn't alone. There was a couple with him. They were Mum and Dad's age, maybe older. One of them glanced over the road, straight at them. Kieran let go of her and went to the side of the curtains, which he drew.

"You know what they are, don't you?" he said.

Jo immediately realized that she's made a fool of herself.

"They're looking at the house, to buy it. Sorry, I feel like an idiot."

"Don't be silly."

He came over and hugged her. A moment passed and his hands were in her hair, then moving down her back. She put her hands inside his shirt and stroked him. It felt fantastic. They kissed.

"I love you," she said.

"I love you too."

Later, when he had gone home, Jo realized that she had forgotten to ask him about the blanket.

Retired police officers weren't meant to hang on to files or photographs, but it was difficult to stop them from taking copies. Many meant to write their memoirs, though only one in a hundred got round to it. Still, they took the files. Some were souvenirs of triumphant cases to show the grandchildren. Others were jigsaw puzzles without the central pieces, held on to in the hope that, one day, the missing bits would show up.

Once Ben had won John Parker's trust, then told him all he knew about Ian Jagger, the retired detective agreed to help. He went upstairs and spent some time rooting about in a boxroom. While waiting, Ben looked at the photos on the sideboard. There was Parker's retirement do and, next to it, his marriage. Parker's wife had died of cancer just months after he left the force. Further along were six-by-four photos of two children, both of whom had long since left the city. A life. Ben wondered if his would amount to more. The former chief inspector returned to the room.

"This is what you want," Parker said, then poured them both another drink.

The Pamela Jagger folder was a slim one. She had done Law at Nottingham University, then articles at a leading Nottingham solicitors'. She had met Jagger when she was twenty-five and newly qualified. He was ten years older and not yet a senior partner. Jagger and Co didn't exist then. They married a year later. In the same year, the senior partner at Jagger's firm had a heart attack and retired. Jagger took over, changed the firm's name and hired his wife. The marriage, from what the police could find out, was a very happy one. There was, however, some jealousy at the firm over Pamela's privileged relationship with the new boss.

Jagger and Co thrived. Ian and Pamela Jagger began to deal with more and more important clients. The couple moved in the highest ranks of provincial society. The week before Pamela's death, however, they were overheard arguing in the office. Later, when the police asked what the row was about, Ian Jagger said that it was a minor matter, to do with his not spending time visiting her relations.

Ben broke off reading for a moment. He wondered how Ian Jagger would get on with Charlene's parents, who were the same age as him. Carlton Harris was a doctor, a family practitioner. Charlene's mother, Netta, taught in a primary school. Both were lifelong socialists, even though that was an unfashionable word these days. They were disappointed that their only daughter didn't share their politics, expecting her to come round in later life.

How did Carlton and Netta feel about Charlene marrying a fascist? Jagger might not reveal his politics to the Harrises, but he couldn't deny his close friendship with Roger Wellington, or the signed photo of Margaret Thatcher he kept in his office. It showed him as a younger man, accompanying the then prime minister to a Nottingham coal mine which had stayed open throughout the miner's strike.

"Found anything you can use?" Parker asked.

"There's nothing here," Ben replied. "An unexplained row, a few hours in his week which he couldn't account for fully. But there's no motive and nothing to indicate that Jagger hired somebody to kill his wife. Nor is there any suggestion of how they might have done it. The coroner's court makes the accident look run of the mill. It was late at night and Pamela fell asleep at the wheel. The only mystery was what she was doing out at that time."

Parker nodded. "Off you go then, son. Looks like you've had a wasted visit."

"What I don't understand," Ben said, as he began

to put the papers back in the file, "is why you made copies of everything."

Parker didn't comment. Ben paused to look again at the photos of Pamela Jagger. She was a very striking woman. More so, possibly, than Charlene. One picture was torn from a newspaper.

"Who's this bloke with her?" he asked, pointing at a black guy with a broken boxer's nose. The man was standing with Pamela outside a police station.

"Dexter George. She represented him in an assault case. It didn't go to trial."

The papers wouldn't quite fit in the folder.

"There's something else in here," Ben pointed out.

"I wondered when you'd notice that."

Ben held the envelope upside down. A green labelled micro-cassette fell out.

"What's this?"

"An answering machine tape. It was obtained illegally, so we could only use it for background."

"Where's it from?" Ben asked.

"Dexter George's flat in Leicester. A bright young boy of mine pinched it while George was making him a drink."

Ben ignored the illegal seizure and tried to work out what Parker was hinting at. "Why was Dexter interviewed?" he asked.

"We were trying to find out if Pamela Jagger had been to see him the night she died. Dexter was the only client whose address tied in with the road she was driving on. George said that he hadn't seen her since his acquittal and stuck to his story. The answering machine messages suggest otherwise. You know how those tapes work?"

"They record a message and, once you've listened to it, they rewind."

Parker nodded. "However, unless you deliberately erase the messages, some of the old ones stay on until a longer message records over them. With me?"

"Yes. So…"

"This tape was taken two days after Pamela Jagger died," Parker explained. "There are a couple of fresh messages on the tape, but after that, there are the remnants of two messages from Mrs Jagger. They make intriguing listening."

Parker wasn't going to tell him everything, Ben realized. He wanted Ben to hear the messages for himself. "Do you have a machine here?" he asked.

"No," Parker said. "But I'm sure you can find one. Take it with you. Be careful, though. It's the only copy. I think I can trust you to return it to me."

Ben took the tape and the photograph of Pamela Jagger with Dexter George.

"Once you've heard that," Parker told him, "you'll know nearly as much as I do. Give me a ring if you want any more information. Or you might want to talk to Dexter, if you can find him. He got into trouble again after Mrs Jagger's death. I've no idea where he is now."

Ben left in time to catch the last bus back to the city.

Tonight would be the first time that Jo had brought a boy home to meet her parents. She was nervous, but not *that* nervous. Kieran was presentable and had a good job. He was older than her, but the age difference was more or less the same as that between Mum and Dad. But Mum and Dad might still object to the six years between her and Kieran. Really, they ought to be grateful. In Jo's experience, sixteen-year-old boys only wanted one thing, whereas Kieran was a gentleman. This afternoon, for instance, when they'd fooled around, Kieran had held back. If he'd pressed Jo, she might have gone all the way. Not that she could tell her parents that side of his character, not in so many words.

Now he was late. Jo began to worry. Had he bottled out? That would be so humiliating. Had something happened to him? At five past eight, the doorbell rang. She heard Dad letting him in.

"You must be Kieran."

"It's a pleasure to meet you at last, Mr McCord."

Jo watched from the top of the stairs. Kieran took his overcoat off. Beneath it, he was wearing his suit, like on their first date, but with a shirt and tie instead of a T-shirt. He looked a little like the estate agent across the road this afternoon. He looked like a grown-up. Jo bounced down the stairs, wearing jeans and her nicest, tightest top. She kissed her boyfriend on the cheek. That was a mistake. Dad looked livid.

"Your mother's just making a brew," he told Jo, without looking at her. "Or would you prefer a beer, Kieran? You're old enough, after all."

Jo winced. "Tea or coffee would be fine," Kieran said.

Dad went to talk to Mum while Jo and her boyfriend sat down in the front room.

"He doesn't like me," Kieran whispered.

"You're the first bloke I've brought home," Jo said. "That's all it is."

"Is it?"

Then Mum came in with the tray and a face immovable as marble. Mum said, "Call me Marcia," but it was Dad who did all the talking. He began to fire questions at Kieran: school, job, home life, interests – it was like a careers interview. Jo felt sorry for her boyfriend. At one point, Kieran got his dates confused and Dad jumped on him like it was a police interrogation. Kieran tried to be as nice as possible. The only thing he didn't mention was that he finished work so early. They'd agreed that it wasn't a good idea for Mum and Dad to know that the two of them could have an hour and a half to themselves every single day.

"And your mother's … a widow, is that right?"

"She's a single parent. I never knew my father."

Jo began to be frustrated. She wasn't being brought into the conversation at all. It was time, surely, for her and Kieran to go up to her room. But Kieran kept answering questions. He made polite enquiries about holidays, Dad's job, why the family had ended up settling in Wilford. It was half an hour before Dad dropped the fatal question, the one which Jo thought he'd be tactful enough to leave unsaid.

"Don't you think that you're rather a lot older than our Jo, Kieran?"

"I know," Kieran said. "When we first met, I assumed that Jo was older than … she is. But Jo tells me that you're six years older than Marcia, Mr McCord, so you'll understand that a few years difference isn't necessarily a bad thing."

"But we met when we were in our twenties. Jo's never had a boyfriend before."

This wasn't strictly true, as Mum knew, but both Dad and Kieran seemed to want to believe it.

"Believe me, sir," (that was the first time he had used the "sir") Kieran pleaded, "I treat Jo with the greatest respect. I'm aware that she's very young, but I also think that she's very special. I care for her a great deal, and I would never do anything to harm her. I hope that satisfies you."

Dad grunted. There was nothing much he could

say after that, though Jo didn't like the speech much. Kieran sounded like he agreed that his girl-friend was still a child. When they were eventually allowed upstairs to listen to some music, it was all Jo could do to get him to kiss her. Kieran was gone by nine-thirty. Within a minute of his leaving the house, Mum was in Jo's room.

"You didn't like him, did you?" Jo confronted her.

"Are you sure that he's only twenty?" Mum asked in her cagiest voice.

"Of course I'm sure. Are you saying he's a liar?"

"He looks older, that's all. Your father thought so too."

Dad, thankfully, had gone to the pub.

"Can I go, then, at Christmas?" Jo asked, plaintively.

"As long as his mother really is there, and you get a taxi back by twelve."

"Thanks!" Jo said, hugging her, though Mum did not return the hug as warmly as she usually did.

Nottingham Playhouse was just round the corner from the offices of Jagger and Co, Solicitors. Ian Jagger had been on the board for several years. It was a good space, with great acoustics. Local legend had it that the theatre put on good productions in the nineteen-sixties and -seventies. These days, however, it rested on its laurels, relying on pantomimes, crowd pleasers and copious grants. Even Ian agreed that the million pound lottery grant the board had spent on an obelisk by Anish Kapoor would have been better devoted to building a studio space, or commissioning new writers. But the theatre frontage looked wonderful. That was what mattered these days, the front you showed. All surface, no feeling.

Attendance tonight was an obligation. A bearded board member was interviewing Roger Wellington, Ian's best friend. At nine-forty-five, the paunchy, pompous politician (a distant descendant of the Iron Duke and Lord High Constable after whom two city streets were named) stepped on to the stage to scattered applause. This interview was one of a series celebrating the Playhouse's twenty-fifth (or was it thirtieth?) anniversary. Roger – "Welly" to the tabloid press – was Nottingham's most famous MP. He lived in the city, which was solidly Labour, but represented a safe area of Conservative villages just beyond it.

Despite the tickets being free, there were only a hundred people or so in the theatre, which held seven hundred. Many of them appeared to be members of the MP's constituency association. The atmosphere was cosy. The questioner cracked jokes about his own Labour background but made no attempt to raise difficult subjects, like the scandal involving Wellington's daughter the year before.

Because of that, Roger Wellington had agreed to stand down at the next election. But this was not common knowledge, and he still had time to change his mind.

Wellington had his rabid supporters in the audience. One wanted to know whether he would be tempted to stand again for the party leadership.

"We've had enough ditherers," the questioner asserted. "What we need is somebody who can take a strong line over Europe, defence, law and order. That's what'll bring the party back to power!"

Wellington demurred. "To be honest with you," he said, adding the questioner's name, "when I look at the way things have gone lately, I'm rather glad that I didn't win the leadership. Opposition must be very frustrating after such a long period in office. I'm enjoying my golf, my directorships, catching up with friends, long holidays." He grinned, before adding, "But never say never…"

A worthy-sounding woman asked the former home secretary a question about recent nail bomb attacks in London. They were rumoured to be the work of the far right group, Combat 18.

"Are the racists making a comeback?" she concluded.

"I don't think so," Wellington replied. "Britain is the most tolerant country in Europe. That's because of the Race Relations Act, which makes it an offence to incite racial hatred. Because of the Act, we've avoided the poisonous politics you get in mainland Europe and elsewhere. As for Combat 18, the British National Party – I'm glad to say – made a huge mistake when it disowned them. What happened was that the main racist organization in this country became old and unfashionable, while the younger racists in Combat 18 are poorly organized and heavily monitored. Combat 18 don't do anything which the security forces don't know about. I'd be surprised if these horrific attacks in London are down to them."

He went on to give token praise to the country's rich, multi-ethnic traditions. Charlene bristled. Racist incidents in the city were up twenty per cent this year. These platitudes were coming from a man whose policy on asylum seekers made the present Home Secretary look like a fairy godmother.

Ian seemed uncomfortable too.

"How do you think he's doing?" he asked her.

"He comes over a little … smug," she whispered back. "How can he be so complacent about racism?"

Her fiancé agreed. "Complacency's a bad thing for a politician," he murmured, as the questions moved on to the fate of the local football teams.

"As long as Forest hang on to Umberto Capricio, they've got a chance of staying up," the MP insisted.

This brought the loudest applause of the evening.

8

Doctor Khan was way behind and the waiting room was heaving. Clare's appointment was for two-fifteen but she finally got to see her at ten past three. The doctor did a cursory examination, then confirmed what Clare already knew. She was pregnant.

"What do you want to do?" she asked.

"I guess I want to keep it," Clare said, softly.

"You *guess*?"

As a teenager, taking risks, Clare had wondered how she'd cope with this decision. She used to have a fantasy, straight out of a romantic novel, where she went to see a handsome young priest who talked her into keeping the baby, then left the priesthood to marry her, be the baby's father. But there was no handsome young priest, no one to talk to except Mum, Charlene and the young doctor opposite, who was impatiently pressing her for an answer.

"When do I have to make up my mind?" Clare asked.

"You say your last period was in September, so the baby should be due in May," the doctor said. "Though you don't feel three months gone to me."

Clare ignored this last remark. "When do I have to decide by?" she asked.

"You should make up your mind by the end of January."

It was early December now.

"But it's not a decision you want to put off," the doctor said. "It can take a toll on you."

"I know," Clare said. "That's just beginning."

Doctor Khan went through some more things but Clare hardly took any notice. When it was over, she shook the doctor's hand and left the surgery in a daze. Clare walked along Gregory Boulevard, head bent to avoid the biting wind, trying to decide what to do. Abortion was wrong, but so, in Clare's mind, was being a single mother by choice. Her mum would say that having a termination was a kind of murder. Maybe it was. Clare remembered girls at schools who'd got rid of their babies. They weren't murderers. They'd had to choose between a greater and a lesser evil.

Clare wished she could go and see her own mother, just up the street, but Mum would be at work. So Clare went back to the house, where Sam sat at the dining table, smoking.

"There's tea in the pot."

Clare poured herself one. It was stewed.

"You look like crap," Sam said.

"That's how I feel."

The morning sickness had started, only it came in the afternoons.

"Not going to work today?" Sam asked.

"I was on earlies."

"Oh… I didn't hear you going out."

They lapsed into silence. Clare wondered how those girls at school would feel in five, ten years time, if it turned out they could no longer have children, for whatever reason. She wondered how she would feel if…

"Penny for them," Sam said. "What's on your mind?"

Clare didn't answer at first. She and Sam were friends, but they still had a sort of tenant-landlady relationship. She couldn't easily confide in her, never had, really. It was the same with Jan Hunt, at work. They were friends, but Jan was also her boss. True, Jan had told Clare about the marriage break-up, but the sarge was also close to Neil. Clare didn't want Neil to find out from someone else.

"Do you think that you and Steve might have

children?" Clare asked, aware as she said it that the question would seem to come out of the blue.

Sam looked aghast. "Steve's far too self-centred. And he's only twenty-three."

"Plenty of men become dads in their twenties."

"Not so many these days. He wants his fun. I'm not going to ask what he gets up to while he's on the road with this play."

Steve was doing a stint with Red Shift Theatre Company, performing in a modernized *Taming of the Shrew*.

"But what about you…?" Clare asked.

"My biological clock hasn't turned into a time-bomb yet. I'm only thirty-one. What's brought this on, anyway?"

For a moment, Clare nearly let it slip, so strong was the urge to talk to someone. But then she changed her mind.

"It's my friend, Charlene. She's only twenty-four, but she's marrying a bloke in his forties."

"Her boss. Gary told me. And he wants her to reproduce, pronto."

"Right."

"That'll teach Charlene to stick to blokes her own age. By the time she gets her life back, she'll be stuck with a pensioner."

"It doesn't seem to bother her," Clare said.

"It will," Sam said, and Clare guessed that she was right.

"Think I'll call her up," Clare said. "Arrange a drink."

When Clare finally got through to her at Jagger and Co, Charlene said she couldn't see Clare until the following night.

"But tell me, Clare. Is it…?"

"It's definite," Clare replied.

"I don't know what to say."

"Me neither."

"I'll be thinking of you. Till tomorrow. Bye."

Sam gave Clare a funny look as she put the phone down. Did she suspect? Clare was suddenly too tired to care. She went upstairs and slept until seven.

Julie was going out of her mind. Ben had finished work at two, but he still hadn't come home. She'd rung the station twice. They said they had no idea where he was, but cops covered for each other all the time. Ben hadn't said that he'd be late, hadn't said anything when he left the house at five-thirty. Was he going off her? For the last couple of weeks, Ben had been out of sorts – brooding about something, Julie guessed, though he denied it when she asked.

Was there someone else? Ben had become tired of his previous girlfriend, Ruth, after a few months. He'd been with Julie for nearly the same amount of time. The sex had started to drop off, but that seemed natural to Julie. Things couldn't stay so intense for ever. They were gentle, relaxed together, something which Julie had never had with a bloke before. They had even skirted around the subject of having children. Ben had helped out her brother, Curt. He had moved in with her. They felt like a family. She was probably worrying about nothing.

Only he was late. And Julie had to put up with Curt's girlfriend, Natalie, who was going on about her mate Jo's new boyfriend, who was nearly *twenty-one*.

"They're not doing it yet," Natalie said. "Can you believe that?"

"Jo's only fourteen," Julie said. "I didn't do it until I was nearly sixteen."

And got pregnant the second time, more fool her.

"Yeah, but he's *twenty*!"

"Maybe he doesn't want to break the law."

"You coming upstairs?" Curt asked, and Natalie went. No need to guess what they would be up to. Julie had nagged Natalie into going on the pill the day she found a condom beneath Curt's bed. You couldn't rely on condoms, as Julie had found to her cost. You couldn't rely on Curt to keep using them either. And the last thing the world needed was another little Wilder coming into it. A baby Shipman, though … that might be another matter.

She heard the sound of a key in the front door and breathed a sigh of relief. Then she went through to the living room and began to yell.

"Where the hell have you been?"

"Leicester," Ben said. "I had work to do."

"Then why didn't you tell me? I rang the station, they said they had no idea where you were."

"What the hell do you think you're doing, ringing the station?" Ben exploded. "They'll think that I'm playing away."

"And are you?"

He looked angry until he saw the tears roll down her face. Then he held her.

"I was scared," she whispered.

"I should have called. I'm sorry."

But he didn't explain what he'd been up to and Julie didn't pursue the question.

9

Had anyone told Jed, a year ago, that he would be hiding out in Holland, actually living in Amsterdam, the situation would have seemed glamorous, exciting. But this small city's charms faded fast when you had no money, no job. Not only that, but a couple of weeks had stretched into a couple of months, and more. The people whose floor Jed was kipping on were beginning to lose patience with him.

Now Jed waited for Simon in the café where they had met five weeks before. Simon lived in France, which was too dangerous a country for Jed to visit. Simon was a freelance writer, who had done work for major British and international newspapers. Would Simon have finished the story that he and

Jed were collaborating on? Jed wasn't naive. He knew that these things took time. His own GCSE English grade-B prose would need a lot of polishing up, improving.

But the book would be worth nothing without proof. Jed had some embarrassing photos of Jagger. He had a tape of an ambiguous conversation. But they needed more. Had Simon really found it? Had he managed to get evidence which could put Jagger in jail? The message he'd sent to Jed had been oblique.

Tuesday. Same time. Same place. Be packed.

Did that mean they had a result? Or did it mean that Combat 18 were on to him, that Jed should be ready to move on? If so, which city would be next? Munich again? Cologne? Oslo? Bremen?

The café door opened and Simon walked in. Simon looked smarter than when Jed first met him (Simon had provided Jed with a safe house after his police protective custody ran out). His curly hair was cropped short. He wore a casual woollen suit with a T-shirt beneath. The journalist sat down beside Jed.

"Dressed for the occasion?" Jed asked.

"I've been seeing publishers. They take you more seriously if you're well groomed," Simon replied, with a smile.

"You've finished?

Simon nodded.

"That was quicker than I expected."

"I know the subject inside out," Simon said, "and I had a good first draft to work with. You put a lot of atmosphere in there, Jed, a lot of telling details. I had to restructure a bit, tidy up the prose, add a lot of background information, but – overall – it was a piece of cake. The only thing missing was the evidence."

"*Was*?" Jed asked, urgently.

"I saw my friend yesterday. She couldn't get everything, but she got enough: statements showing big money going into a Swiss bank account. There's another document which establishes without doubt who the account belongs to."

Jed hardly dared ask the question. "Ian Jagger?"

Simon smiled more widely, showing bad teeth. "We've done it, Jed. Jackpot!"

In the end, Ben had to buy a micro–cassette recorder to play the tape. He'd asked around at work, but no one used them there. Someone suggested that it was the sort of thing a journalist would have, but a journalist was the last person Ben wanted to discuss this with. He'd trudged round the city after getting off work at two. Eventually he'd picked up a dictaphone in an office supply store near the ice stadium. It ran at two speeds, which was handy, because Ben didn't know at what speed the tape was recorded.

Ben ought to go home. Julie worried. He hadn't

been giving her enough attention lately, he knew that. But he couldn't tell her that this was about Charlene. Women, in his experience, got jealous easily. So Ben walked up to the Central Police Station, found a spare interview room, then sat down and listened. Mickey Mouse said something about rearranging a dentist's appointment. Ben changed the speed.

The second message was from a male police officer. Ben didn't recognize the voice.

"… have to talk to you about Pamela Jagger, who, as I expect you've heard, was tragically killed in a traffic accident two nights ago. It's just routine, but if you can make sure that you're in at 10 am tomorrow, the seventeenth."

That call dated the tape. Pamela Jagger had been killed on February the fourteenth, nearly seven years ago. There was some banging before the tape cut into an earlier message. The voice was female, educated and Afro-Caribbean.

"… the other night. He's off again, up to something in the South of France. So you can come here, lover. But not before seven. Park in the same place as before. Bye." She blew a kiss, then there was more banging.

The message that followed was from the same voice, but it sounded slurred, less coherent. The tape was about three minutes in, which meant that Pamela had probably been talking for that length of time already. Ben couldn't make out all the words: "…missing, but it's not that simple … never that simple. He didn't need to be like that, and nor did you. Call me on my mobile. I'm waiting. Call me, Dexter. I love you."

Lover. I love you. As simple as that. Motive for murder, if Jagger knew about it. Charlene was seeing Dexter George. From the desperate sound of her voice on the second message, she might even have been thinking of leaving her husband for him. Ben was getting somewhere at last. To get any further, he had to find Dexter George.

Charlene was in the bath with her fiancé. Ian's flat had a huge bath, which required large quantities of Molton Brown foaming bath oil to fill it with bubbles.

"Stay in tonight," Ian begged. "I'm off tomorrow, and we haven't had a quiet night in for weeks."

Ian was going on one of his European jaunts with Roger Wellington. He was vague about what these trips involved. Charlene got the impression that they were fundraising for European conservative groups. Roger made the speeches, while Ian dealt with the red tape, negotiating grants, tax breaks and the like.

"I can't," Charlene said. "I promised Clare. She's got this problem she needs to talk over."

"Serious?"

"Very."

Ian didn't inquire further. He was the soul of discretion.

"I've got something I want to talk over," he said. "Something serious."

She looked straight at him. His face, so often a mask, had softened, so that he looked more like a priest than a lawyer. "What is it?" she said.

"I was thinking… Why wait until the wedding?"

"Why wait for what?" she asked, though she knew what was coming.

His voice became as vulnerable as the expression on his face. "Why don't we start trying to make a baby straight away?"

She reached over tenderly and held his hand.

"I know that you're not in as much of a hurry as I am," he said, "but … why wait?"

"I don't want to talk about it now," Charlene said, preoccupied with Clare's problem, "but I'll think about it."

Ian got out of the bath and Charlene began to do what she'd just promised. When she and Ben had discussed having kids, they'd figured they'd do it when they were both about thirty and established in their careers: Ben, an inspector, maybe; her, a partner. Well, Ian would make her a partner tomorrow, if that was what she wanted. They'd discussed it. Jagger and Co would become Jagger and Jagger. But Charlene felt she ought to earn her name up there. And if she had a baby, Ian wouldn't let her work full-time for years. He was old fashioned that way.

"You look glum," her lover said, as he towelled himself dry. "I don't want to pressure you."

"Not glum, just thoughtful," she replied, getting out of the bath herself. "But I'll bet you could cheer me up."

And he did.

Neil knocked on Clare's door at seven. Gary answered.

"How's it going?" Neil asked, as he was invited inside.

"All right," Gary said. "You come to see Clare? Only I think she's going out."

"Oh. Right."

Gary called upstairs, but there was no answer. "Probably in the bathroom. Give her a minute."

Neil nodded. "How're you and Ben getting on?" he asked. Ben was Gary's tutor officer and partner.

"Good," Gary said. "Though Ben's a bit … quiet, sometimes. Did you find that?"

"I did," Neil agreed. "He broods."

"But never tells you what he's brooding about."

"Hardly ever," Neil agreed.

Gary's mobile rang. He began talking to Umberto. Neil signalled that he was going upstairs, then did so, knocking gently on Clare's door. The last time he'd been on this landing, Neil reflected, they'd just slept together. He'd been avoiding Clare since, partly because of that, partly because he'd been trying to get his head straight after making a fool of himself with Melanie. He wasn't sure if he'd got his head straight yet. He wasn't sure if it'd ever be straight again.

Suddenly Clare emerged from the bathroom, wearing only knickers and a bra.

"Uh. Sorry," Neil said. "Gary called, and I knocked."

Clare wasn't embarrassed. "Nothing you haven't seen before," she said. "Come in, if you want. But I'm getting ready to go out."

"A date?" Neil asked, following her into the bedroom. She'd put on weight. Her stomach, never flat, was rounded with flesh. It suited her, actually. Neil tried not to watch as Clare chose a silk top from the wardrobe, put it on, then inspected herself in the mirror.

"Just a drink with Charlene," Clare said.

Neil had forgotten that Clare and Ben's ex were friendly.

"You invited to the wedding?" he asked.

"I am," Clare replied. She wasn't usually so monosyllabic. It occurred to Neil that she might think he was angling to go as her date. This was the last thing on his mind.

"I shouldn't have called round out of the blue," he said.

"Don't worry. I like it that you can do that. Not many people do. It's been a while, that's all."

"I know." They had never discussed what happened. Now, Clare was looking in a mirror and Neil was looking at her bottom, unsure whether to talk to her or to reach out for her. Then she put on her jeans and the spell was broken.

"Why don't we arrange a drink ourselves," he said. "This weekend?"

"I'm working," Clare told him.

The following weekend was Christmas. They discussed their plans. Neil would be at home with his mother and sister. Clare would be at her Uncle Angelo's with his family, her mum and, for the first time in ages, her father.

"Are you working New Year's Eve?" Neil asked.

Clare nodded. "No leave."

They agreed to meet on New Year's day and go for a pub lunch, followed by a walk if the weather was good. Neil offered Clare a lift into town in his new car, which she accepted.

"What do you think of her?" he asked, finally, as they turned down George Street.

"It's … nice. I preferred your old Cortina."

"It was a rust bucket!"

"But it had a good retro look."

Retro. Neil wasn't into that. Clare was probably comparing his car with Paul Grace's flashy red Mazda, an expensive sports model which Neil couldn't compete with. Even so, what was he thinking of, buying something as boring as a Metro?

"Oh, what a shame!"

"What?"

"Stop a moment. Look." Clare pointed at the building on their right. It was an ancient gothic building, with ornate carvings above the leaded glass windows, two of which had been smashed.

"This is my favourite building in Nottingham," Clare said. "See the plaque? An architect called Fothergill Watson designed it. He used to work there, over a century ago."

Clare and her buildings. Neil sometimes wondered why she hadn't stuck with architecture, instead of joining the police.

"Hold on a minute." She got out of the car, read a notice on the door.

"Is it being demolished?" Neil asked, as she returned.

"I don't know. All the notice says is that the solicitors who used to be there have merged with another solicitors and moved out."

Behind them, a taxi sounded its horn. Neil was blocking the road.

"I'll walk from here. Thanks for the lift." Clare left without offering him her cheek to kiss. Neil put his foot on the accelerator.

Clare was out of his league, Neil reflected, always had been. So was Melanie. If he spent his life pursuing women like that, his heart would keep getting broken, and the pieces would become harder and harder to glue back together.

Neil wasn't ready to go home. He pulled out his mobile and gave Jan Hunt a ring. He hadn't seen Jan for ages. He needed Jan's respect and worried that she would have heard gossip about the way he'd made a fool of himself over Melanie. But he also needed a woman's company, her friendship and counsel. Hopefully, Jan's boring husband would be working.

Neil's old sarge seemed pleased to hear his voice. "Have you eaten?" she asked. "No? Me neither. Come over and I'll fix us some pizza."

Neil accelerated out of the city, stopping only to buy red wine. Jan was the one he should have called in the first place, he realized, the one woman he could see without sex being on the menu. Maybe Jan would tell him what to do with his life.

Dexter George did not have a criminal record. He owned a car, but the address it was registered at was three years out of date. He had not left a forwarding address. Jagger and Co might have details of his current residence – George was one of their clients – but Ben could hardly ask Charlene to look it up.

Ben had called up the details of the assault case in which Pamela had represented George. He could see why it hadn't gone to trial. After Pamela's death,

Dexter had been done for fraud, selling timeshares in high-class villas in Spain which didn't belong to him. It was a quality scam which had netted well over a hundred grand. But the case against George consisted of contradictory statements from two guys who each had a string of convictions. The only physical evidence was an airport surveillance video-tape. The tape supposedly showed George taking money off a punter, but might have shown any five-foot-ten black man with a goatee and a puffa jacket. Nor was there any way of proving that the large manila envelope he was taking contained cash.

The case never came to trial. It looked like Dexter, pressured by the investigation, had left the country. With all this in mind, Ben rang John Parker. He explained what he had found out so far.

"I get the impression that the police wanted him for something more serious, but the timeshare scam was all they could find to do him for," Ben concluded.

"You're right," the retired DI said. "Leicester CID did suspect him of drug dealing. George had a lot of money. It had to come from somewhere. But that ties in with the Spanish properties. George spent a lot of time over there. The timeshare stuff might have been a cover, the real money coming from dope, brought in on boats from Morocco. George claimed that the timeshare con had nothing to do with him. Thing was: two blokes he employed casually did the scam."

"You think that George might have been innocent?"

"Nobody's innocent," Parker said. "Not you, not me. The question is, what was he guilty of?"

"I spoke to CID in Leicester. They think that George might have gone back to Spain, settled there."

"It's a possibility," Parker replied.

Ben thanked the former chief inspector, then walked into the Market Square for a bus. He kept passing travel agents' windows. This time of year, they were full of cheap flights to Malaga, trying to attract pensioners. It might not be hot over there, but it was a hell of a lot warmer than here. He rang Julie.

"Where are you this time?" she asked.

"I'll be on my way home in half an hour. I need to call in somewhere first. Do you like Spanish wine?"

"Spanish. Why?"

"I've been thinking. We could do with a proper holiday. You, me, Tammy and Curt. How do you fancy going to Spain for Christmas?"

"Brilliant!" Julie said.

"I'll get it sorted," Ben told her. "See you in an hour."

10

Christmas Day. It hadn't snowed and it wasn't going to. The sky was overcast, threatening rain. Yet it was still the most romantic day of Jo's life. Christmas at home was nice. She got good presents. Grandma and Grandad came over for Christmas dinner. Jo was allowed a glass of wine with the meal and the whole family collapsed in a heap with a Steven Spielberg film afterwards. Yet the day seemed to pass in slow motion. What Jo was waiting for was five in the afternoon, when Dad would drive her over to Kieran's. Seven hours later, when Jo got a taxi home, she might look the same on the outside, but she would be a different person.

Dad had had his doze during the film and now looked at his watch.

"You ready to make a move, young lady?" he asked.

She was, but Dad was also going to run Grandma and Grandad home and they took ten minutes to get ready. That meant she would be late, would lose a precious few minutes with Kieran. God, she hoped he liked the shirt she'd bought him. What if it was too big, or he didn't think the colour suited him?

Dad dropped her off first, and didn't insist on seeing Jo to the door. There were lights on all over the small house. It was obvious that Kieran was home. As he let her in, Dad drove off.

"Come in quietly," Kieran said. "Mum's got a migraine. She's gone to bed."

Kieran's mum needed a chair lift to get upstairs and spent most of her time in bed. Jo hadn't explained this to her own mum and dad, who assumed that Mrs Manders would be around all evening.

In the living room, beside a slim, plastic tree, they exchanged presents. Kieran loved his shirt and insisted on putting it on then and there. Then he gave Jo a tiny box with a beautiful ring inside it. Jo would have been delighted with just that, but Kieran had another surprise for her. From behind the sofa, he produced a box with something rattling around inside it. Jo ripped off the polka-dot paper.

It was a mobile phone, a pay as you go one, like Kieran had, in her favourite colour, lime green.

"I've bought you a year's worth of vouchers,"

Kieran said. "That includes line rental and an hour of calls every week. So we'll be able to call each other wherever we are. And you won't have to worry about your mum and dad nagging you for hogging the phone, or running up the bill."

"It's wonderful!" Jo said. "I love you."

"I love you, too."

A year's worth of vouchers – that meant he thought they would still be together in a year's time. Jo was sure now, sure as she ever would be.

"Let's go upstairs," she said.

They hadn't specifically said that today was the day that they were going to do it. Still, it was on both their minds. In their snatched afternoons together, Kieran had explained how much he respected her. Jo didn't want him to respect her too much. When they were both ready, it would happen. She had been ready for a while, but her boyfriend, she'd come to realize, was shy. Maybe he didn't have much experience. So what? She had none at all. They would work it out.

"I'll just go and check on Mum," he said.

"OK. I'm going to try out my phone."

It was already connected. Jo rang home, where her mum and her sister were tidying up.

"That's a very extravagant present," Mum said, when Jo told her about it. "Still, I suppose Kieran has a good job. He can afford it.'

"It's the best present I've ever had," Jo

exclaimed, then realized that this was a little tactless.

"You have a nice time," Mum said, ignoring the comment, "and don't do anything you'll regret, Jo. You know what I mean."

"I won't," Jo said, as Kieran came downstairs and signalled that the coast was clear for them to go upstairs. "Love you, Mum. Bye."

She followed her boyfriend upstairs, sure that she wasn't going to regret anything at all.

Julie found Spain in December disappointing. First there'd been the palaver about the room. The tour rep had objected to Curt and Natalie sharing a bed, because they were both only fourteen – an issue which hadn't occurred to Ben. So they had to put on a pretence of Ben sharing with Curt; Julie and Tammy with Natalie.

Then there were the amenities. Julie didn't know why Ben had chosen this particular resort. There were no amusement arcades. Some decent bars, but they were occupied by ex-pats and pensioners on extended cheap breaks. Hardly anyone else was under thirty. There was one disco, but it only seemed to play music from the seventies and eighties. Who wanted to hear that?

As for the weather, it was better than Nottingham, but not exactly hot. The beach was too windy to sit out on, the sea not warm enough to swim in. They had hired a car and found some interesting, authentically Spanish villages a few miles away. However, because it was Christmas, the shops were all shut.

Ben was bad company. All he wanted to do was read his OSPRE book. This was the sergeant's handbook. Ben's sergeant's exams were in April and he needed an 80% mark to pass. Even so, this was meant to be a holiday. Ben had yet to make love to Julie once. He had only rented the car grudgingly. Julie didn't mind reading. She'd brought a bunch of magazines and a couple of Ed McBains with her. But what kind of person went on holiday and did nothing but read? If Julie wasn't so in love with Ben, she'd be giving him a really hard time about it.

"Why this particular bar?" Julie asked, as the pair of them walked along the wind-swept beach, hand in hand, looking for the Rio Grande.

"It's supposed to be the best one," Ben promised.

He'd checked it out the day before, but it had been closed. Curt and Natalie were back at the hotel, looking after Tammy. They'd brought Natalie along after Curt offered to pay for her from his reward money. He'd also pointed out his girlfriend's babysitting capabilities. Curt and Natalie had already been out for Christmas dinner on their own, at lunchtime. Ben and Julie had opted to leave their meal until early evening.

The Rio Grande, when they got to it, looked

unpromising, just another concrete box with plastic chairs outside and tinsel sprayed on the window. Inside, it wasn't crowded. A scribbled sign promised a traditional Christmas dinner with turkey and all the trimmings. Ben ordered two dinners and a bottle of champagne, then disappeared to the loo for ten minutes. On return, he seemed distracted, kept glancing over Julie's shoulder towards the back of the bar.

Julie tried to make conversation, but Ben was hard work. Julie had planned to use this special time to discuss their having a child. But Ben would only talk about how many hours a week he was going to have to devote to studying for his sergeant's exams.

"Have you considered going to college?" he asked her. "Now that I'm not paying rent on my flat, we can afford child care."

Julie had considered it. The way things were going, by next August, Curt would have a few GCSEs, putting her to shame. She'd messed up her exams because of being pregnant with Tammy.

"I don't know what I want to do," she said.

This wasn't true. She wanted to have another child, or two, with Ben. Then she would start a career when all three were at school. She would still be only twenty-five or -six, after all. But this no longer seemed the time to say that.

The food was only so-so. Julie couldn't understand why anyone would recommend the place to Ben. They'd soon eaten as much as they could manage. There was a long wait for the plates to be cleared.

"I shouldn't think they'll mess up the Christmas pudding," Ben said.

Julie didn't care. She watched her figure, so rarely touched puddings. What were they doing here? The other customers were middle-aged, garishly dressed and drinking heavily. When she pointed this out, Ben said, "At least it's not full of senior citizens."

A thirty-something black guy with a shaved head and a faint beard came in. He was greeted extravagantly by the barman. Ben's eyes followed the guy around the room.

"Do you know him?" Julie asked.

"I think I might do," Ben replied. "Excuse me a minute."

He got up and went over to where the guy was sitting. He would be more than a minute, that much was obvious. What the hell was he playing at?

Jan was woken by the phone and didn't know what day it was. This morning, Henry hadn't known what day it was either, and woke at six. He'd been fractious ever since. Jan's mum and dad had come at noon. They'd spent the day avoiding any discussion of divorce, so that Jan finally brought it up herself. Kevin would have Henry one evening a week, she'd told them, every other weekend and for two holidays a year. This was what they'd agreed.

Jan needed a life of her own. She wouldn't get one unless Kevin did his bit with child care. So she'd arranged for Mum and Dad to drop off Henry at Carol's on their way home. Let him fret his way through their Christmas, too.

She'd run herself a bath after her mum and dad left, then fallen asleep within minutes of getting into it. Now the phone was ringing, and she nearly let the machine take it. But then she realized that it might be her pal, Marie, who'd invited her over for a drink tonight. Jan, tired, had been in two minds about going, but the sleep had refreshed her. She was ready to say, "Yes, I'll come", so hurried, dripping, to the hall, and picked up just as the machine was cutting in.

"Hello."

"Jan, it's Neil. Merry Christmas."

"Same to you. How's your day been?"

Neil's mum was asleep in front of the telly, he said.

"I'm looking for someone as bored as I am. Fancy a bit of company?"

Jan hesitated. She'd half promised Marie, but there would be loads of other people at her house. Jan preferred conversations which were one to one. The last time Neil had been round, they'd had a really good time together.

"I'd love you to visit," she said. "But I'm in the bath. Give me an hour, OK?"

She got a towel, then rang Marie to say that she wouldn't be coming.

"I've had another offer," she said.

"A bloke?"

"Just Neil."

"The cute kid who used to be your partner? You cradle-snatcher, you!"

"It's not like that. He's lonely. His girlfriend chucked him. His best friend's on holiday."

And Clare was in Bedford, Jan remembered. She was probably third choice.

"He hasn't had any in months and it's Christmas," Marie pointed out. "If I were you, girl, I'd take advantage."

Jan giggled and arranged to see Marie the following day instead. She thought about getting back into the bath, but it was cold, so she pulled the plug and began to dry herself, thinking about what Marie had said. Neil was only twenty-four. He went for younger women. His last two girlfriends had been nineteen when he got together with them. Jan was only eight years older than Neil – the same gap as between Clare and Paul Grace. But it was different for women.

There'd never been a hint of flirtation between her and Neil. This might be because of the age gap, or because she'd been his tutor officer and, later, his boss. Their friendship had matured since Neil had left the shift. Now it was more like a younger brother/older sister thing. They could confide in each other. When he last came round, two weeks before, Neil had confessed to making a fool of himself over Melanie, standing outside her house for hours. He'd nearly been arrested. Jan told him not to be too hard on himself. She'd described how she found out about Kevin, how she'd gone through everything that Kevin left behind when he left her for Carol, things he'd meant to come back for, and made a big bonfire.

"Mad, I know. You should have seen his face when he saw what I'd done."

They both had a good laugh over that. But if they were going to get off with each other, that was when it would have happened.

When Neil got up to go, a drink or two over the limit, they'd had a kind of cuddle, their bodies pressed together for a moment and he had patted her back, as if she were a child. There was nothing sexual about it, no desire – not on his part, anyway. Even so, Jan wanted to look her best for him. It was Christmas, after all.

She inspected herself in the mirror. She was too tall, too skinny, but she had always been that way and had learnt to be be relaxed about her body. The lines around her eyes were faint, and easily disguised. Since Kevin left, she had been letting her hair grow.

Jan was trying to regain some womanliness. She was fed up with being a practical, working mother. That was what had cost her her husband.

Jan put on a black cashmere jumper which was heaven to touch, then chose a long grey skirt which was slashed to just above the knee. Then she felt a fool. If Neil realized that she was dressing seductively, he would run a mile. He wanted her friendship, not her body. And, surely, that was what she wanted, too? Suppose they had a drunken fling? Their friendship would be over.

She was about to go up and change when the doorbell rang. He was early. Neil apologized. "Taxi came twenty minutes before they said it would."

"You caught a taxi?"

He held out a bottle of wine. "Can't afford to risk being over the limit."

"You're right."

"You look … great," he said, kissing her on the cheek. "Merry Christmas."

Jan felt embarrassed. "Kevin was coming round for Henry," she lied. "I wanted him to see what he was missing."

"I'll bet he was kicking himself," Neil told her. "You really do look great."

"Thanks," Jan said, taking his coat and resisting the urge to tell him that he looked pretty damn good himself.

*　　*　　*

The whole thing was a disaster.

"I'm just going to the bathroom," Kieran said, and Jo, humiliated, pulled the sheets up around her. This was not how Natalie, or other girls at school had described it. There'd been talk about lads who didn't know what to do, but they'd been fifteen or sixteen, not *twenty*, for crying out loud!

It wasn't her fault, she was sure of that. She'd been gentle and patient, but everything she'd done had only made things worse. Now Jo didn't know how to behave. When he came back, would he want to try again? Did she want him to?

Jo decided to get out of bed and dress. Maybe her nakedness had unnerved him. Did she look too young? Surely not. It had to be about lack of experience. They were both virgins. Each had been waiting for the right person. Now they'd found each other, but didn't know how to make their bodies fit together.

It was all right, Jo reasoned as she dressed. They were in love, and would work it out in time. Now she had all of her clothes on but for a sock, which seemed to have rolled beneath the bed. She felt for, but couldn't find it. Then she did. It was entangled with something else, which Jo pulled out. A canvas bag, with *Sony* written on the side. Jo didn't know that Kieran owned a video camera. Was it a Christmas present? If so, why was it under the bed?

Still no sound of him coming back. Maybe he'd

looked in on his mum. Jo put on the sock and wondered what kind of camera it was. She unzipped the top of the bag. The camera was a pretty new model. Maybe they could have some fun, playing with it. She pulled out the machine for a closer look. *80x digital zoom*. Beneath it, she noticed, there were four tiny tape cases. They were clearly labelled: *Jo, September; Jo, October; Jo, November*.

At first she didn't know what it meant. Jo might be her name, but it could also stand for something else. After all, the labels said September and October. Jo hadn't even met Kieran until November.

The case with *Jo, December* written on it was empty. It must be inside the machine. Suddenly anxious, Jo worked out how to switch the camera on. It had one of those flip-out screens which allowed you to view the tape as you were shooting it. She rewound for a few seconds, then pressed *play*.

What she saw was her bedroom window. The lamp lit her desk. She sat at it, doing homework. Jo felt sick to her stomach. It was him she'd seen. It was Kieran, watching her from the window opposite. And since September! That explained what he was doing walking near her house. It explained the blanket, too. For the house opposite had been sold. He must have had to get out.

On video, Jo switched off the light. The picture cut to static for a moment. It was replaced by Jo clad only in a towel. She'd just come out of the bath. She walked into the room, then, worried that she was being watched, opened her bedroom wardrobe. Hiding behind it, she put her dressing gown on before closing the curtains. If she hadn't hidden he would have been able to see her, as he doubtless had many times before, catching her nakedness on tape. Watching this, thinking about this, Jo lost control of herself. She vomited all over the machine and the bed. There was vomit everywhere. She didn't hear Kieran come back in.

"Jo. What's wrong? I heard… Oh, Jo!"

Kieran was wearing a dressing gown. The look on his face, the sound of his voice – both were full of concern. Jo's eyes flooded with tears.

"Don't be upset," he said, softly. "We tried to take things too quickly, that's all. Everything will work out, I promise. I'll just get a cloth."

She couldn't look at him. Kieran left the room to get the cloth. Jo stood. At least she'd hardly got any sick on her clothes. She found a tissue,wiped her mouth and face. Jo wanted to get out before Kieran came back. All she had to do was put on her shoes. As she was lacing up the second one, Kieran returned, cloth in one hand, washing up bowl in the other. He came round to her side of the bed.

"I'll get this cleaned up in no time."

Then he saw the camera.

"Oh. You found that."

He began to wipe the machine, his face becoming a furious red.

"Did you…?"

"I looked," Jo blurted out.

"I'm sorry."

"Sorry? Is that all you can say?" Jo was hurt, confused. She was also angry. "How could you?"

"I'm … crazy about you," Kieran said, speaking quickly but still not looking at her. "I have been since the first time I saw you. That was months before we met. I bought the camera because…" Now he turned, put down the cloth and looked at her, pleading in his eyes. "I know this will sound stupid, the way things turned out, but I needed to have you near. I didn't dream that you'd go out with me, so I…"

"You videoed me with no clothes on!"

"It wasn't about seeing you naked," Kieran said. "You've got to believe me – it was always about love."

"*Love?*" Jo couldn't believe what she was hearing. She began to cry again. "I thought I was falling in love with you," she said. "I must have been mad. There's a word for people like you." Jo couldn't remember what the word was. She picked up her bag. "Give me them. The tapes. Give me all of them."

Reluctantly, Kieran did as she asked. "This isn't as bad as you think," he pleaded, as she put them into her bag. "I love you, Jo. I only wanted…"

"I don't care what you wanted!" Jo said. "To think I nearly…" She had to get out of this house, immediately, or she would lose it altogether.

"Wait!" Kieran said. "We have to talk."

For a moment, she thought that he was going to grab her, but Kieran wasn't the violent type. He was a sad, pathetic *voyeur* … that was the word she'd been after.

"Jo, I worship you. I live for you…"

"Drop dead," Jo told him. "I never want to see you again."

Now Kieran was crying, but Jo had used up her tears. She left the room, swang her bag over her shoulder and was about to run downstairs when she realized that somebody was blocking her way. Kieran's mum. Jo had never seen her standing up before. She was leaning against her chair-lift, looking frail and concerned.

"I heard shouting. Is something wrong, Jo, dear? You don't look well."

"Yes. No." Jo was flustered. She didn't want to upset this ill old woman. "I've been sick," she said. "I've got to go home."

"Can I get you…"

"No, really." Jo needed to get past the old lady. From the bedroom behind her, Jo could hear Kieran pulling on his clothes. In a moment, he would come out after her. Then it would be much harder to get away. "I really need to go home."

"Has Kieran called you a taxi?" Mrs Manders asked.

"Yes," Jo said, glad to be given the idea. "It's just come. I'd better go down now, or the driver might go to another call. You know how busy they are at Christmas."

Slowly, Mrs Manders began to move away from the top of the stairs. "If you're sure that you're…"

"Thanks very much for having me," Jo spluttered, almost pushing the old lady aside in her hurry to get down the stairs. "Bye."

As she was opening the front door, Kieran called her name, but he couldn't get down to her in time. Jo ran all the way home, passing endless houses with their Christmas trees and lights, all of them blurring into a garish stain across her tear-soaked eyes.

She paused only once, at the footbridge across the Trent. Jo took out the filthy, filthy video tapes that Kieran had made of her, and threw them all into the middle of the muddy river.

11

By nine, Neil and Jan had got through the best part of a bottle of wine. They were conducting character analyses of everyone they'd both worked with. John Farraday was all right, they agreed, but Tim Cooper was a waste of time. Gary Monk, both agreed, was a diamond geezer.

"If he wasn't gay," Jan said, "I could really go for him."

Neil smiled uncomfortably. Jan didn't usually discuss stuff like that. But Jan, suddenly single, was changing. She had dressed to kill tonight. Supposedly, it was for Kevin, but Jan had been in the bath when Neil phoned and Henry had already gone to Kevin's, so that didn't ring true. She hadn't dressed that way because of him, had she? Neil didn't know how he felt about that.

They avoided discussing Clare and moved straight on to Ben.

"He's got a chip on his shoulder about not getting on the graduate fast-track scheme," Jan reckoned. "He thinks that's down to racism and he's probably right. So he's determined to be the youngest sergeant in the county. That would prove he's better than anyone else."

"He might do it," Neil said, agreeing with her analysis.

Jan had made sergeant at thirty, which was good going, especially for a woman with a kid. Ben aimed to do it by twenty-five, but Neil didn't tell Jan this.

"If his love life doesn't screw things up," Jan said. "He should have stuck with his lawyer, the one who's marrying Jagger."

"Ben's pretty upset about that," Neil told her, then added, in a confidential tone, "I reckon Ben always meant to end up with Charlene. I think, deep down, Ben thought they could take a break then come back together."

"Maybe he's not the only one who thinks that way," Jan said. "Charlene knows how much Ben hates Jagger. Getting engaged to him is a sure way to make Ben jealous. The only way he can stop it happening is to marry Charlene himself."

"You think Charlene would marry Jagger just to spite Ben?" Neil asked.

"Not consciously maybe, but it makes a lot of sense, doesn't it?"

Neil agreed that it did. Then they both had a good laugh, like old mates. Neil told himself off for thinking that Jan might be up for it. Then he found himself looking at the stretch of thigh which her split skirt revealed and tried to concentrate on gossiping about his old shift, instead.

"So what's Inspector Winter like?" he asked.

"Careful career man. Not in a hurry, like Paul Grace, but just as meticulous. Friendly enough, reasonable sense of humour, wife and two kids. Shall I open another bottle of wine?"

"Why not?"

While Jan was opening the bottle and had her back was turned to him, she asked, "So what about you and Clare? You're both free agents now. Any chance that you'll get back together?"

"I don't think so," Neil said. "Although..." he almost told Jan about their one night stand, but it was awkward. Clare was Jan's partner. From the way that Jan was talking, Neil was sure that Clare hadn't confided in her about what happened. So he shouldn't either.

"Although what?" Jan asked.

"Nothing. Clare and me, that's in the past. Melanie's in the past, too. I need to look to the future."

Jan poured the wine. "I'll second that. To the future!"

"The future!" Neil echoed.

They drank.

"Why do you want to know about Pam?" Dexter George asked Ben as they stood in the Rio Grande. "We're talking – what? Seven years ago. It's Christmas Day, man. What's so important? Are you a relative of hers?"

"That's right," Ben said. Dexter was unlikely to co-operate if he knew that Ben was in the police. How big a lie dare he tell? "She was my sister," he said.

Dexter put an arm around him. "I'm sorry. I didn't know she had a younger brother." He paused. "I don't remember you at the funeral."

It had never occurred to Ben that Dexter George would have attended Pamela's funeral. He had to think quickly.

"I was in Jamaica then," he said. (That was where Pamela's family were from, like Charlene's). "Couldn't get back in time."

"I'm sorry to hear that," Dexter said. "Listen, Ben, there are some things that were never explained about her death, but now isn't the time to talk about them. I'll be back tonight, late. Come and see me, any time after twelve. I'll tell you everything I remember."

"Thanks. I really appreciate it."

The two men shook hands. Ben returned to Julie.

"What was all that about?"

Ben couldn't be bothered to act. "Police work. I know him from Nottingham. He might have some information about a case, so I'm meeting up with him tomorrow."

"Ben, we're on *holiday*!"

"Yeah, I know. Sorry."

Julie's eyes narrowed. "We didn't come here because of him, did we?"

She was sharp, Julie. It didn't do to try and fool her. Still, Ben tried.

"No, of course not," he said. "But he'd mentioned this bar and…"

"That's why we came here for Christmas dinner," Julie filled in for him. "You could have said."

The atmosphere was frosty for a while. Ben ordered another bottle of wine, ate humble pie. He asked Julie about her plans for the coming year. That got her going. Ben began to relax. He had escaped that awkward moment easily. Now he had to decide exactly what questions to ask Dexter.

"…before Tammy's two," Julie was saying, and Ben nodded. They'd been having these theoretical conversations about having children for a while now. There was no rush. Julie hadn't even turned eighteen yet. She was talking about coming off the pill.

"It sounds like a good idea," Ben said, without actually committing himself to a time scale.

"I love you," Julie said, reaching over to kiss him. "Let's go back to the hotel."

"You bet."

Ben didn't know what he had done right, but he was happy that he had. They paid the bill and walked back along the beach, hand in hand.

"This is my best Christmas, *ever*!" Julie said.

"Same here," Ben replied, squeezing her hand.

"Jan?" She was asleep and it took him a couple of goes to get through. "Jan?"

She was in a warm, cosy place and, for a moment, thought that she was in bed with her husband. "Wake up, Jan."

"Uh?"

Jan lifted her head, which was on Neil's shoulder. The two of them were snuggled together on the sofa. The Janet Jackson CD had long since finished.

"How long have I been asleep?" Jan asked.

"About half an hour."

"You should have woken me before."

"No," Neil said. "It was nice. I nodded off myself. But I guess I ought to call a taxi."

"Of course."

While he phoned, Jan popped upstairs to splash water on her face. She smoothed her hair and wiped off mascara where it had smudged. She thought about fixing her face, but there was no point. His taxi would be here soon.

"They say fifteen, twenty minutes," Neil said, when she returned.

"Sorry. I dozed off. Henry had me up at six this morning," Jan explained.

They stood awkwardly. "There's a drop of wine left in the bottle," Jan said. "Or would you like coffee?"

"A quick coffee would be nice," Neil said, but the kettle hadn't boiled when Jan heard a car pulling up outside. In the hall, Neil was putting on his coat.

"They always come quickly when you don't want them to," he said. "Sorry."

"It was really good to see you," Jan told him. "I've had a lovely evening."

"Me too."

They were close together now. He leant forward to kiss her on the cheek, but Jan needed more than that, so darted her head beyond his and put both arms around him. They hugged tenderly. As their bodies parted, Neil kissed her on the lips. It was a soft, moist kiss. Both their mouths were partly open. It was a kiss which might have led somewhere, had the taxi not sounded its horn.

"Better go," Neil said. "Merry Christmas, Jan."

"Merry Christmas," she said, as he slipped off into the night.

Ben had left Julie asleep before setting out. The Rio Grande, by the time he got to it, was quiet. Only a handful of drinkers remained, one of whom wished

Ben a merry Christmas. Ben returned the greeting, then asked after the owner.

"Who wants to know?" The barman asked, pressing something concealed beneath the *Cruzcampo* beer pump.

"He's expecting me," Ben said.

As he spoke, Dexter George's head poked through the back door behind the bar.

"Ben? I'll only be a minute."

Someone dodgy was in there, Ben guessed, as he was poured a beer that he hadn't asked for. Somebody who would leave by the back way. The door opened again.

"You want to do this in private?" Dexter asked.

"I guess."

"Come on through."

The barman lifted the counter and Ben took his beer through. Dexter George sat in his bar's ill-lit, cramped back room. There was space for two chairs amongst the clutter of crates, boxes and cleaning materials. The former boxer was smoking a fat, six-inch spliff, which he offered to Ben.

"Can't touch the stuff," Ben lied. "Asthma."

He needed his brain sharp for the discussion which followed.

"You wanted to talk about Pam."

"That's right," Ben said. "I was wondering, how did you meet her?"

"It was six months before she died. I was a young

black guy driving a Ferrari in those days. You know how the police treat a black guy in a car like that?"

Ben knew. "You get stopped every other week."

"Try twice a week. I got put in the cells twice, charged with stealing my own car. The second time they arrested me, kept me in overnight, I sued them for harassment. They settled out of court – five grand – but that was when the real trouble started. I'd been in the papers. Every cop in Leicester knew who I was. They were just waiting to fit me up for something. But they were clever. Instead of fitting me up in Leicester, where their motive would be obvious, they got the boys in Nottingham to arrest me. I was supposed to have beaten up this white woman in an alley after following her out of a club."

"Did they have much evidence?" Ben asked, being careful not to sound like a policeman.

"The woman was drunk and suggestible. All she remembered was a big black man, but they showed her my photo, convinced her it was me. They even had two witnesses say they saw me leaving the club just after her. Best of all, they had an off duty cop who said he saw my car driving away from the scene at the right time."

"Were you at the club?" Ben asked.

"Not that week. I'd been there before, but I was still fighting then. I had a big bout coming up, so it was healthy living, an early night. I was in bed, alone. I could have faked an alibi easily, if I'd known that I needed one. Anyway, I decided to get a Nottingham solicitor. Jagger had a good reputation. When they offered me his wife, instead, I was insulted. But then I met her. Well, I guess she had that effect on everyone she met."

Ben remembered that he was meant to be Pamela's brother, so he'd better start acting. "Ever since she was thirteen," he said.

"But it wasn't her looks, man. A good boxer can always get fine-looking women. It was her brain. She was so smart, so funny. She got the case thrown out at committal. I didn't even have to stand trial. I took her out for a drink to celebrate, and I got the vibe that she was interested. So I gave her two tickets for my next fight. She came with a girlfriend, but visited the dressing room on her own and didn't go home until very, very late – you know what I'm saying? No disrespect to your sister, man."

"It's OK."

"After that, I saw her maybe once, twice a week. When she died, I was talking about moving to Nottingham to be nearer her."

"Would she have moved in with you?"

Ruefully, Dexter shook his head. "She made it clear from the start that she was never going to leave her husband."

"Did Jagger know about you?"

"I don't suppose he thought that she was playing bridge with her buddies until two or three in the morning every week. She gave me the impression that he was cool with it."

"Tell me about the accident."

"Nothing to tell. I still don't understand it. The crash was at two in the morning, but she wasn't coming back from my place, she was driving towards it. I was in, but I wasn't expecting her. She hadn't called."

"Had Pam been acting strangely before it happened?" Ben wanted to know.

"There was something on her mind. When she was down, she smoked too much of this stuff." He pointed at the joint he was stubbing out. "Which her hubby didn't like. It led to rows."

"They argued a lot?"

"He kept secrets from her," she said. "Used to go to France a lot. Maybe he had a mistress there. Just before she died, Pam started telling me she loved me. She'd say it on the phone. She didn't love me. We weren't like that. It was like he was listening in, and she was telling him, not me, to make him jealous."

"You think that Jagger had her killed?" Ben asked.

"For seeing me? I don't think so. Look, I can understand that you were upset, your sister dying, missing the funeral and all that. But it was an accident. The road was icy. She lost control."

"Why was she coming to see you?" Ben asked. "Why not call first?"

"I've often wondered that myself," Dexter said. "Maybe she wasn't on her way to me. Maybe she went for a drive in order to think. She used to do that sometimes. She told me once she was happiest on her own, driving in the night, a little jazz on the stereo. So, yeah, maybe that's what she was doing."

"You've been very helpful," Ben said, though he hadn't learnt anything useful. "I appreciate it."

"You're welcome," Dexter said. "By the way, how did you find me?"

"Coincidence," Ben said. "We're on holiday here and somebody mentioned your name. It rang a bell."

Dexter seemed to accept this. "That's a fine look-ing young woman you were here with the other day. You don't want to neglect her, chasing after your sister's ghost. Do you hear what I'm saying?"

"I hear you," Ben said.

Dexter began to roll another one. "Say, how's your sister, Dawn? She must be in her twenties now."

"That's right," Ben said, getting up to go. "She's well."

Suddenly, the former boxer jumped up, his large body blocking the door back into the bar.

"Wrong answer," he said. "Pamela didn't have any sisters. She was very clear on that, what it was like being brought up as the only girl with four brothers. So, tell me, before I break your neck, who the hell are you?"

JANUARY

12

"New Nottingham. Impressive, isn't it?" Charlene said to Clare.

"I guess." The two women were walking from Jagger and Co, which was near the Playhouse, past the old General Hospital site which was full of glitzy bars and offices, all freshly built, yet designed to look vaguely Victorian. It was unseasonably warm for January. Both women were lightly dressed. They walked by Nottingham Castle into The Park. Charlene had a small flat there, which she'd just put on the market. Property was booming. She'd already had an offer thirty per cent higher than she'd paid nine months before. As they headed downhill, Clare felt her side.

"Are you all right?" Charlene asked.

"I dunno," Clare said. "It's a burning pain, a kind of cramp. I've had it before. Mum says it's common to get discomfort in early pregnancy." She sighed.

"You told your mum?"

"On Boxing Day, yes. On the way back from Uncle Angelo's."

"How did she take it?"

"Surprisingly," Clare said. "I thought she'd go crazy, then start making plans for me to move back in, for the two of us to bring up the baby together."

"That's probably what my mum would do," Charlene said.

"Mine didn't. I asked for her advice. She told me that I ought to tell Neil. Said that we either ought to get back together, or I ought to have an abortion."

"I thought your mum was a Catholic?"

"She is," Clare said. "That is, she converted when she married my dad. I haven't told *him* yet, of course."

Clare knew what Dad would say. She hadn't told him for the same reason that she hadn't gone to a priest. They would both have the same message: *Abortion is a sin. It's murder*. Clare didn't believe this, not in all cases. She'd never criticize anybody for having an abortion. But that wasn't the same as having one yourself.

They reached Charlene's flat. This was the kind of place Clare would like for herself, if she had the money: a one bedroom flat on the first floor of a grand old house. The flat was spartanly furnished with framed prints on pale walls. No place to bring up a baby, though. Where would Clare bring up *her* baby?

"Have you told them at work yet?"

"No," Clare said. "It's bound to get back to Neil if I do. So I have to decide what to tell him."

She and Neil were meant to be having lunch on New Year's Day but she'd made an excuse and cancelled.

"I thought you were going to let people think the baby's Paul's," Charlene said.

"I was," Clare said. "But I don't like lying and I'm not sure if I could stand all the sympathy I'd get."

Then she had another pain in her side and had to sit down.

Jo spent her lunch hour in the library, on her own, pretending to read. Natalie had wanted to talk to her, but Jo didn't fancy telling her about it at school, where anyone could overhear. Natalie was too excited about her own holiday to notice Jo's reticence. According to her, it had been all sun, sex and drinking. Oh, and Julie's boyfriend had got himself beaten up. Very mysterious. Julie was worried that Ben had been seeing someone else's woman. Ben claimed the beating was because somebody found out he was police. They thought he was spying on them.

Today was the first day of the Spring term. Jo was

relieved to be back. Hanging about the house all the time had never been her style. Since Christmas, she'd felt like a prisoner in her own home. This wasn't because it was cold, or because Natalie was away. It was because of Kieran.

The first time it happened was on Boxing Day, the day after she'd dumped him. The McCords had gone to visit Jo's aunt and uncle in Birmingham. They didn't get back until nine. Nobody mentioned Kieran Manders, but Jo thought about little else. The day before, she'd been in love with him.

As they'd pulled into Montague Street, Jo had glanced at the house opposite theirs. It had been sold, but wasn't yet occupied. How did Kieran get in? Had he got a key? The house was dark. The curtains of the room he had used were drawn. It was over, she thought.

Only it wasn't. There were two messages from Kieran on the machine. The first was polite, anxious. "We didn't work things out yesterday," he said. "I'd like to come round, explain properly. Call me."

The second was more wretched. "Jo, why's your mobile turned off? I need to see you, Jo. You're making a terrible mistake. We can work this out. Call me."

Mum and Dad looked at Jo as the tape rewound. They knew that Jo had finished with Kieran, but had been too relieved to ask many questions.

"Are you going to call him?" Mum asked.

"No," Jo said. "I'm going to bed."

In her room, she'd closed the curtains carefully, leaving a tiny gap that she could see out of. Nothing. Before turning in, Jo looked through the gap in the curtains a second time and there he was. Not in the house across the street, but on the street itself, watching. And he had seen her. Kieran reached into his coat and pulled out a phone, gestured. Jo couldn't see his face, only a silhouette. For a fleeting moment, something about the way he was standing looked so forlorn that it touched her.

What should Jo do? Have Dad chase him away? No. She ought to be able to handle this herself. Jo picked up her phone, switched it on, and pressed the code for his number. Kieran answered immediately, his voice soft and sweet.

"You didn't call me back, so I came over."

"We've been away."

"I know. We need to talk, Jo."

"There's nothing *to* talk about," she told him. "I haven't told anybody what you did, but if you don't leave me alone, I will."

"There's no need to talk like that," Kieran said. "We love each other. We can work this out."

"I don't love you any more," Jo told him.

"We're meant for each other, Jo. I can't live without you."

"Don't talk daft," she'd told him, trying hard to be grown up, to talk common sense. "Find a girl your own age. But don't spy on her first."

"I only did it because I loved you," Kieran said. He sounded like he was crying. Jo resisted the urge to look out of the window. Something in her still wanted to look after him. She must be mad.

"If you love me, leave me alone," she said softly, kindly.

"I can't do that," he told her. "You need protecting, Jo. I'm the only one who can make you happy. Whatever you do, wherever you go, I'll watch out for you. That's all I was doing before."

"*That's all*? Kieran, you were acting like a … a … pervert! I can't go out with you. I don't want to see you. Leave me alone, or I'll get Dad to call the police!"

Jo hung up and switched off the phone. When she got up the nerve to look out of the window again, five minutes later, he wasn't there.

But he had been there the next day, and the one after. On the Monday, he must have gone to work, but had appeared afterwards, wearing a long coat, collar turned up, a scarf and gloves. He hadn't tried to ring her, but he was there.

Yesterday, the day before term started, when Kieran should have been at work, Jo thought that she was safe. She went into town to spend her Christmas money. Coming home on the bus with a new CD, a video and lip gloss, she hadn't noticed him. She'd nearly screamed when a voice whispered from the seat behind.

"I'm here, Jo, just waiting for you to change your mind."

She couldn't change seats. The sales were on and the bus was full. She didn't look round, either. How long had he been following her? The journey home seemed to last hours. She got off the bus without looking back, but there he was at the window as she walked away, waving.

Who should she tell? Mum would spill the story to Dad, who would blow his top, probably go to the police, which – despite what she'd said to him in their final phone conversation – was the last thing that Jo wanted. Maybe the best thing to do would be to wait for him to get bored, give up.

Lunch hour was almost over. Jo was putting her book away when she heard a familiar voice.

"Hey, Jo!"

It was Martin Todd, the boy who'd asked her out the summer before then stood her up. What was he doing here? This was Year Nine's day for using the library at lunchtime.

"Did you have a good Christmas?" he asked.

"All right, thanks."

"You're looking great!"

Despite her depression, Jo smiled. Martin appeared to take a deep breath.

"Look, I know I messed you around before. It was a misunderstanding, honest."

Mrs Franks, the librarian, came over to tell Martin

to get out. This was a Year Nine only session. For a moment, Jo thought that he was going to leave without saying what he had to say.

"I'll only be a minute, Miss, *please*!"

"One minute," the librarian said, "then *out*."

Martin spoke so quickly that he almost garbled his words. "Thing is, it's Gary Turner's sixteenth on Saturday. He's having a party. Would you go with me?"

Jo, flattered, didn't know what to say. Gary Turner's folks had a big house on the river. It would be a good party. And she knew better than to bite Martin's hand off. "I'll think about it," she said. "Ask me again tomorrow."

Martin grinned nervously. She had him where she wanted him, Jo realized. It was a new feeling.

"I'll do that. Happy New Year, Jo."

She grinned back. Maybe things were looking up after all.

13

"What time'll you be back tonight?" Julie asked, as Ben left the house.

"Late. I'm meeting Neil for a drink after work."

"Oh. OK." She kissed him on the left cheek, the one that wasn't bruised.

"Don't be too late," she said, to which Ben didn't reply.

Truth was, Ben realized as he walked up the street, Julie had begun to bore him. He'd had this happen before, when he was on holiday with Ruth. See too much of a person and you ran out of things to say to them. Sometimes, even sex became a chore. In Spain, Julie kept wanting to push their relationship further: move house, have a baby together. There was an unspoken codicil: get married. But

Ben's mind was on someone else's marriage. He hadn't told Julie about Charlene marrying Jagger. But he couldn't stop thinking about it.

He'd had to take some stick over his bruised cheek at work. Escaping the Rio Grande on Boxing Day night after Dexter caught him out hadn't been easy. Whatever Ben said to Dexter, the former boxer was bound not to believe him. At first, he'd just tried to leave. That was when Dexter had cracked him on the side of the face. Ben was no fighter. He'd gone down, lost consciousness for a few seconds. When he'd come round, he'd had no choice but to tell Dexter the truth.

The truth stopped the former boxer from hitting Ben again, but Dexter found Ben's behaviour hard to fathom.

"You came all this way to find me because Jagger's marrying your ex-girlfriend? You expect me to believe that?"

"I know Jagger's a racist. He may even be a murderer. But I've no proof."

"Listen," Dexter said. "As far as I know, Jagger's clean. He's no racist – why would he marry Pam, tell me that? As for killing her … forget it."

"What if I got proof?" Ben asked. "Proof that Jagger had his wife murdered. Would you help me?"

"Sure I'd help you," Dexter said. "I cared about Pam. But you didn't even know her. You're just another black guy got a chip on his shoulder because a rich white guy is giving it to the woman he wants. Learn to live with it, Mr Whatever-your-name-is. And get out of here."

So Ben had left. He'd had some explaining to do when he got home to Julie, and he'd had a hard job explaining the state of his face when he got back to work. After all that trouble, John Parker's leads had taken Ben nowhere. There was only one person who could help Ben now: Jed Sutcliffe. But Ben had no idea where to find him.

A well dressed, thirty-something woman was waiting opposite the desk when Jan came on duty at two.

"It's about my daughter," she said. "I think she's in trouble."

Jan took a few details and showed the woman to an interview room. She had to start the shift before going back to her. It was tempting to let Clare deal with the woman, but Clare had been out of sorts lately, so Jan left her doing paperwork, then joined Mrs McCord.

"You say this man's been following your daughter?"

"Following her, standing outside the house. He keeps ringing, too. Jo never answers the phone herself. At first, I tried to reason with him, but I've given up. There are often long messages on the ansaphone when I get in from work. We've had to get a new machine, cuts people off after two minutes."

"How long has this been going on?" Jan asked.

"Since Boxing Day."

"Ah." It was only the second week of January. As harassment went, this was pretty small beer. "Does she know this man?" Jan asked.

"Yes, she used to go out with him."

"I see. How long for?"

"A couple of months. They broke up on Christmas Day. Jo said he was getting … too intense, something like that."

"And your daughter's fourteen, while Mr Manders is – did you say twenty?"

"That's what he says. He looks older than twenty to me. I've never liked him. Even the way he met Jo seemed … strange. It sounded to me like he might have been following her."

"You say your daughter isn't aware of how often he's outside the house?"

"I don't draw it to her attention, in case it scares her, but she must notice."

"In cases like this," Jan said, "openness is often a good idea. I think you should talk to your daughter about it. But let me go and check something."

Jan ran Kieran Manders' details through the police national computer. There was nothing known about him. Then she went back to the interview room.

"I realize that this is a worrying situation, but I don't think it's too serious. He'll probably get bored pretty soon, give up. If you like, my partner and I will go and see him, warn him off. What's his address?"

Marcia McCord gave her the man's home address and the place where he worked. Jan wouldn't embarrass him by going to his work. What Kieran Manders was doing was no more serious than what Neil had confessed to doing after Melanie chucked him. Neil had lost the plot for a couple of weeks, that was all. A broken heart could do that to anybody. A quiet, sympathetic word should be enough to sort the situation out. Jan wondered how Neil was. She hadn't seen him properly since Christmas Day.

"I'm sure there's nothing to worry about," Jan reiterated, handing Mrs McCord a scrap of paper with the station number on it, "but if he's outside the house when you get home today, call this number – they'll get hold of me, wherever I am – and we'll pick him up. Otherwise, we'll visit him in the next day or two."

"That's a great weight off my mind."

Jan showed Marcia McCord to the door, then went up to join Clare. Her partner was talking to Neil.

"I'm too tired after work," Clare was saying. "But I'm off tomorrow. Come round the house about eight. I'll cook for you."

"Great," Neil said, with his youthful grin. "See you then."

He greeted Jan on his way out. "We must get together again soon," he said.

"Let's do that," Jan muttered, yet, suddenly, she felt shot through the heart. Neil was trying to get back with Clare. Of course he was. Clare was younger, prettier than her. She and Neil were single, child-free. Why would Neil be interested in Jan, except as surrogate older sister? Yet Jan had found herself thinking of Neil in a new way since Christmas. She couldn't help it. He was the only man who had shown any interest in her since Kevin left. *Don't be ridiculous!* she told herself. You're a grown woman, getting jealous of your partner, who used to go out with him. Nothing would be more natural than the two of them getting back together. She ought to wish them luck.

"You ready?" she asked Clare.

"Yeah. We're in a car, aren't we?"

"I thought so. Cold out."

"Good," Clare said. "I'm not on top form today. Indigestion, or something."

They set out to patrol the city.

When Ben and Gary returned to the station after their first patrol at four, Inspector Winter was waiting.

"My office, please, Ben."

What was this about? Ben wondered. His first thought was that it had something to do with Julie's family. His girlfriend's mother was living abroad with a suspected murderer. They were probably in South America, some country that didn't have an extradition treaty with the UK. Then there was Curt. Julie's younger brother had been in plenty of trouble with the police when he was younger. But since Ben moved in and Curt got that reward money, he'd been on the straight and narrow. He was even working well at school, or so the teachers said. Maybe Winter wanted to talk about promotion. Ben had just put in for his sergeant's exams, though he hadn't been revising as hard as he could because of the Ian Jagger business.

"Come in, Ben, would you?"

Ben entered the inspector's obscenely neat office. His boss wasn't alone. With him was DSI Petit, Head of Major Crimes, the most senior police-woman in the county. Ben waited until he was told to sit down.

"It's about a case you were involved in nearly a year ago," the DSI said. "Jed Sutcliffe."

A bolt of electricity shot through Ben's body.

"What happened to him?" Ben asked, keeping his voice calm.

"We don't know," DSI Petit said. "Sutcliffe was in protective custody in the period immediately after the riot in the city centre, but his evidence wasn't needed and he was released to the care of a worker from an anti-fascist group."

"He wasn't offered a change of identity?" Ben asked.

"Do you know how much that costs?" The DSI asked. "It isn't as if Sutcliffe was ever working for us. Had he been, a major riot could have been prevented, as could the embarrassing press conference where he attacked senior local figures."

Meaning Ian Jagger, though Jed's accusations against the solicitor had been covered up, never reported.

"So why are you asking about him now?" Ben asked. "Has somebody got to him?"

He could think of half a dozen notorious racist activists who would happily murder Jed without counting the consequences. No matter how naively Jed had behaved, the police ought to have offered the lad protection.

"Rather the other way round," DSI Petit said. "We have reason to believe that the youth is involved in a blackmail plot. We're trying to locate him."

"I see," Ben said.

"You're the one member of the force who he had a relationship with."

"I wouldn't go so far as to call it a relationship," Ben said.

"Perhaps not, but he gave you vital information."

"Yes," Ben said, remembering that Jed had also allowed a load of racist thugs to beat him up. "I guess he trusted me."

"So I want to hear straight away if he contacts you again."

"I see. Do you think that's likely, ma'am? If he's really involved in blackmail?"

The DSI pursed her thin lips. "He's the sort of lad who thinks that the means justify the ends. You know what it's like when you're young. You see everything in black and white terms."

Ben winced and the DSI added, "Please excuse any unfortunate connotations which that phrase has. We're not looking to persecute Sutcliffe. He's always been in over his head. But he could cause damage."

Damage to whom? She was being very oblique, Ben thought. How much was the DSI actually going to tell him?

"So if he gets in touch, you'd like me to…?"

"Arrange to meet him, then get in touch with me immediately, whatever the time or place." The DSI handed Ben a card with her office and home phone numbers. "I hear you're putting in for your sergeant's exams. The right move here could considerably aid your career. We're looking to promote officers like you."

She meant officers *of colour*. But Ben wanted to be promoted on his merits, not because he was black.

"This blackmail plot you mentioned," Ben said. "Would it help me to know what it involves?"

"I don't think so," DSI Petit said. "You're really better off if you don't get involved. Believe me, Ben, we have your best interests at heart."

Ben didn't believe that for a moment, but she had used his first name, so he had to sound appreciative.

"Thank you, ma'am," he said. "I'll be in touch if I hear anything."

When he left the room, he found that he was sweating heavily. Ben hoped that DSI Petit hadn't noticed. She and Winter were probably too busy looking at the bruise on his right cheek.

In the parade room, Gary was putting down the phone.

"That was Jan," he said. "She wants us to pick up some bloke who's been pestering a fourteen-year-old girl on the edge of our beat, bring him back here for her to talk to."

"All right," Ben said. "Let's get over there."

Jo had her curtains closed, though it was still daylight. Now and then she glanced out of the gap in the middle. He was still there: her stalker, or guard. Kieran hadn't tried to talk to her since term started, but he had always been in the background. Today she had sensed him at the end of the road when she got off the bus. He'd know that she was in the house alone. That scared her a little. Jo resolutely refused to look out of the window, to acknowledge him. But nor did she dare have a bath, because she'd feel too vulnerable. He could break in, trap her somehow.

Mum had just come home, so Jo was no longer worried, only irritated. She tried to make Kieran's presence into a kind of joke. After all, Jo had a new boyfriend. She'd gone out with Martin twice since the party ten days ago. Nothing much had happened. After Kieran, she was playing it cool. Martin was hard-working and a little shy. He would let her set the pace.

Martin was the kind of boy she needed. They had lots of stuff in common – not just school, but music and films, stuff like that. They talked about all sorts. Whereas Kieran was soppy all the time. He went on and on about his job, which she was sure he exaggerated. The way Kieran used to talk, if it weren't for his invalid mum, he'd be living in a penthouse flat in the city centre.

Jo heard a siren and glanced out of the window again. Was there a fire? No. The sound came from a police car, pulling up opposite the house. Jo saw Kieran walking away in his long, dark coat. But a tall, handsome police officer got out of the car and called to Kieran. Her ex-boyfriend stopped, turned round. It was starting to get dark, so Jo couldn't see the expression on his face. Kieran let the police officer lead him to the car, put him in the back. Then the police drove off.

One of the neighbours must have reported him. What was it they called it? *Loitering with intent*. This time, hopefully, Kieran Manders was gone for good.

14

On Saturday, Ben didn't get up until twelve. Julie was especially loving in the morning, so much so that he regretted his mood of the day before. Of course he still loved Julie. His obsession with Charly marrying Jagger was to do with pride, not love. But pride was a powerful force.

Maybe he'd taken it as far as he could. He'd been to Spain. What had come of it? Nothing. Maybe it was time to give up, make a baby with Julie, marry her even, if that was what she really wanted. Study hard, keep his nose clean, and he'd be an inspector by thirty, maybe even a superintendent by forty. Ben had the brains. Also, for the foreseeable future, being black was an advantage where the top brass were concerned. They were falling over themselves to show that they weren't racist.

Julie shouted up to say that breakfast was ready. She'd done poached eggs the way he liked them, and had even started buying the lean-cut, un-smoked, dry-cured bacon which he preferred. A half pint of orange juice was already poured. Ben sat down and tucked in.

"There's a letter for you," Julie said, as she poured boiling water into a coffee filter. The coffee tasted better if you let the water cool for a few seconds first, but Ben was sensitive enough not to mention this.

"Thanks. Nice breakfast."

He looked at the envelope. It was addressed in unfamiliar handwriting and had been redirected from his old home in Mapperley Park. The post-mark was a week old, the place it had come from, illegible. Ben finished his eggs and bacon before ripping it open. Inside was a postcard which showed the famous photograph of the five young racists believed to have murdered Stephen Lawrence in the 1990s, waving their fists at a camera: *THIS IS WHY YOU HAVE TO JOIN US* was written beneath the picture. Ben turned the card over.

The flip side of the card had a message recruiting members for an anti-racist organization. Scribbled in the white space below it was a message.

Hi. Remember me? Still after Jagger? Give me a call before next Saturday. J.S. Beneath the message was a mobile phone number.

"What's wrong?" Julie asked, as she began to pour the coffee.

"Got to make a phone call," Ben said.

"Go ahead," she said, handing the coffee to him.

Suddenly, paranoia gripped Ben. The person he ought to be calling was DSI Petit. He had her home number in his wallet. If he was going to call Jed, it mustn't be from here. He thought about this, but not for long.

"Got to go out for a couple of minutes," he told Julie.

"What about your coffee?" Julie asked, but he was already through the door.

He had to wait five minutes for the phone box to be free. Jed answered on the second ring.

"What took you so long?" the youth asked Ben.

"I've moved. Your letter only reached me today. Where are you?"

"In Nottingham. I decided to go ahead without you. But I could still use your help."

"Go ahead with what?" Ben asked.

"I think we ought to meet," Jed said. "Soon. Can you get into town in half an hour?"

"Just about."

"There's an Amnesty International bookshop on Heathcote Street, next to where the Independent Bookstore used to be. I'll be waiting for you there."

"I'm on my way," Ben told him.

He shouldn't be meeting Jed, not without phoning

DSI Petit first. Her card was burning a hole in his wallet. But he had to hear what Jed had to say before involving anybody else.

Jed was already waiting when Ben got to the bookshop, lingering over the poetry books in the centre of the narrow shop. The lad had changed in the months since Ben had last seen him. His hair had grown, for a start. It was surprisingly curly and blonde. His face was softer than Ben remembered. He was wearing a skull cap and baggy clothes. If Ben hadn't been expecting to see Jed, he wouldn't have recognized him. Which was probably the exact effect that Jed intended.

Before Ben could speak, Jed acknowledged him with a wave. A moment later, they were on their way out of the shop.

"Where to?" Ben asked.

"Somewhere empty or somewhere noisy. Any suggestions?"

Ben took him to the Bunker Hill Inn, a popular pub on the end of Hockley where the crowd were mostly older and nobody would take any notice of them.

"A lot of people want to know where you are," he said, after buying drinks.

"And you're the only one who knows," Jed said. "Well, you and one other person. Take a look at this."

He handed Ben a set of A4 papers.

"What's this?" he asked.

"The proofs of my book."

The A4 pages looked more like a magazine than a book, but Ben let that pass. He read the title, *I was a Teenage Racist* by Jeremy Sutcliffe and Simon Shaw.

"Who's Shaw?" he asked Jed.

"A journalist."

Ben nodded and began to flick through the pages. At university, he'd developed a technique for skim reading without missing anything of significance. It involved checking out the subtitles, the beginnings and endings of paragraphs and, if they existed, careful perusal of the bullet-pointed conclusions at the end. This book didn't have bullet points, but it did have photographs. *I was a Teenage Racist* described how Jed infiltrated Combat 18, the neo-Nazi organization. It detailed the history of many prominent British fascists and Jed's dealings with them. And then, in the final chapter, it dealt with Ian Jagger.

Jed alleged that Jagger was one of Britain's most senior racists. He had direct knowledge of how Jagger funded racist groups, providing stolen cash cards and getting jobs for potential recruits like himself. He went on to show how Jagger had managed to keep himself out of the press despite Jed's accusations, using his relationship with the former Home Secretary, Roger Wellington, to have a D notice put on them, which meant that the press weren't allowed to print any story which alleged that Jagger was a racist.

"I didn't know about the D notice," Ben said.

"You're not meant to. That's the whole point of them."

Jed described how he had followed Jagger to Europe late the year before. Included in the book were fuzzy photos of Jagger with people who Jed claimed were leading members of the French far right.

"None of these prove anything," Ben said. "Not for sure."

"Turn the page."

On the next page were detailed descriptions of bank transactions – money which had been transferred via a French bank to accounts held in Jagger's name.

"It's still circumstantial," Ben told Jed. "The money could be for legal work."

"Over two million pounds' worth?"

"Maybe not."

Ben closed the book. "When is this going to be published?"

"It isn't," Jed said. "Not here. Not yet. No British publisher would touch this. They're all afraid of being bankrupted by Jagger. So this is coming out with a small Amsterdam publisher which has no money, and, therefore, nothing to lose. But the main impact will be through the press. Once we send copies to all of the radio stations, TV, newspapers."

"But what about the D notice?" Ben asked.

"That only covers the bank card fraud. These are new allegations. But I need a bit more proof. Simon and I are meeting Jagger tonight. Simon thinks that Jagger's going to offer to pay us off."

It was as Ben had guessed from the start of the conversation. This was the blackmail which DSI Petit was concerned about.

"And where do I come in?" Ben asked.

"We want a policeman there in case any of this comes to court. We need you to be able to overhear the meeting in case the tape doesn't record properly, or is tampered with. You're the only police officer I trust, Ben."

"That's flattering," Ben told him. "But it's also mad. Your scheme's full of holes, Jed. You think that Jagger's foolish enough to incriminate himself on tape? He might not even turn up. If you're right about him – and I think you probably are – you're likely to get arrested. Jagger's out of your league, and mine."

"I wanted to talk to you earlier in the week," Jed said, "to consult you, see if you had a better idea of how to do this. Maybe it's not too late. If you've got a better strategy, I'll listen to it."

"Let me think," Ben said. Do the wrong thing here, and his career was over.

"The aim is to get Jagger, right? You won't take any money off him, even if he tries to hand it over there and then?"

"That's right," Jed assured him. "If he offers the money, that's proof, isn't it?"

"And what about your journalist friend? How does he fit into this?"

"He'll be with me."

"Watching? Or with you at the meeting?"

"Jagger's meeting both of us. Simon's the one who's been negotiating with him. I wanted Simon to go alone, but Jagger insists on me being there too."

What was Jagger's game? Ben wondered.

"Are you still interested?" Jed asked.

"Yes, I am. You see…" Ben explained about Charlene marrying Jagger. "I want to stop it. The only way I can do that is to expose him, make her realize what he's like. But what you're doing – blackmail, concealed cameras and a tape – it's too risky. You've already failed once. The only way I can get involved is if we do this legitimately, with police involvement. Delay the meeting, give me a copy of the evidence you've garnered and I'll go to someone senior in CID."

"How do you know that they won't be working with Jagger?" Jed asked. It was a sensible question.

"I don't," Ben said, "but I'll take safeguards."

"I'll have to discuss it with Simon," Jed said.

"Do that. And keep well out of sight. There are plenty of people looking for you … and I don't just mean skinheads."

"All right," Jed said. "How shall I contact you?"

"Easiest if I call you," Ben said. "How long do you need?"

"I'm meeting Simon at seven. We're supposed to be seeing Jagger at eight in the big back bar at The Trip. Call me just after seven."

"All right," Ben said. "But I'll be lucky if I can talk to anyone from CID tonight. You'll probably need to delay the meeting with Jagger until Monday evening at the earliest."

"Maybe," Jed said. "If Simon agrees. I'll talk to you later."

Once Jed was gone, Ben looked through his personal organizer. He didn't have a home phone number for DI Greasby, Neil's boss at CID. Now he thought about it, Greasby had warned him off pursuing Jagger in the past, pointing out that Jagger had powerful connections. The person to go to would be DSI Petit. There would be trouble if he didn't go to her. But the super was a friend of the solicitor's. She was probably in contact with Jagger already. Also, Petit was bound to see the story from Jagger's side, no matter what picture Ben painted of Jed.

If Paul Grace were still alive, it would be easy. Inspector Grace knew the full story and he didn't trust Jagger. But what about his replacement? Winter had been there when DSI Petit talked to Ben about blackmail earlier in the week. If Ben spoke to

Winter, there was a chance that he would go straight to Petit, even after Ben pointed out that she might be on the solicitor's side. But Winter *ought* to go over her head. Moreover, if anything went wrong, it would be his problem, not Ben's. There might even be a chance of Ben both nailing Jagger and getting himself promoted into the bargain.

Ben had never called the inspector at home. He didn't have his number. But he knew where he lived. He went to the bar and asked to borrow the phone book. There were three and a half inches of Winters, but only one who lived in Woodborough. Ben took down the number and went to find a phone box. He ought to get himself a mobile one of these days. Or maybe not. Occasionally it was useful if people couldn't find you. And there were some calls, like this one, which it would be better if nobody had a record of.

The inspector was in.

"I need to speak to you privately, in person," Ben said. "It's urgent."

"You'd better come over then," the inspector said, then explained how to find his house. Ben set off for the taxi rank in Market Square.

"I'm out again tonight," Ian told Charlene as they finished eating lunch at Sonny's restaurant.

"Sorry. What was that?" Charlene had been distracted. Ben Shipman, her former boyfriend, had just walked right past the window without looking in. This was the first time she'd seen him since that day outside the court, when she told him that she was getting married. Ben looked preoccupied, wound-up about something. But he wasn't in uniform, so it would be something other than work. Funny how she could tell what he was feeling even from fifteen feet away, while Ian, her fiancé, remained a mystery to her.

"I was just saying that … are you all right, darling?"

"Yes, I'm fine. You said something about going out… I thought we were going to that Swedish film at Broadway."

"I might be done in time. Otherwise, would you mind going alone? I could meet you at the end."

Charlene frowned. She indulged Ian's liking for arty foreign films, but would never go to one by choice, and certainly not on her own, though she didn't say this now.

"I think I'd rather rent a video," she said.

"Maybe that's a better idea," Ian said. "Then I wouldn't have to rush."

"I'll call Clare if you're not back by eight," Charlene told him. "She was complaining about spending Saturday night in on her own."

While Ian paid the bill, Charlene recalled that Clare had said she was seeing Neil on a Saturday night. Was that this week or next? Things were coming to a head there. Charlene was starting to learn how Clare's mind worked. She sensed that, once Clare definitely decided to keep the child, she would feel bound to tell Neil. And then, who knew what would happen? There could be worse fates for Clare than marrying Neil Foster, who was kind, honest and reliable, if a little lacking in the charisma department.

But there could be better fates too. If Clare could bring herself to terminate the pregnancy, maybe she would work up the nerve to leave the police as well. For Clare, like Ben, was wasted in the Notts Constabulary. And Clare, unlike Ben, probably had enough sense to see that.

"Ready to go?"

As they walked through Market Square, hand in hand, Charlene saw Ben getting into a taxi. Ben had always insisted on using buses when he went out with her. What, Charlene wondered, was so urgent?

15

Inspector Winter's was a three-bedroom detached house on a wide street which wound its way uphill to Woodthorpe Park. It had glass double doors, which were open. A child's plastic, mechanical crane lay just inside them. Ben rang the doorbell and was greeted by an ebullient five- or six-year-old.

"Don't take my crane!" were the first words he said.

"Ethan, who is it?" called a female voice from inside.

A slim, tall woman hurried into the messy hall. "I'm Jane. Tony's just taken Tom to a party. He didn't think you'd get here so quickly. He won't be long."

Jane showed Ben into the living room, which appeared to be the one part of the house where children weren't allowed. There was a pile carpet, framed pictures on the mantelpiece and a neat pile of CDs on top of the sound system, behind which were two shelves of books and videos. Ben collapsed into a large, comfortable settee.

"What can I get you to drink?" Jane asked, as, elsewhere in the house, a baby began to cry.

"I can wait till … Tony gets back," Ben said. "Please, see to the baby."

Jane smiled. "She's only nine months. You know what they're like. Tony tells me that you've got one that age yourself."

"No, I…" Ben realized that she meant Tammy, but before he could correct himself, Jane had gone to see to her child. Almost immediately, Ethan poked his head around the door. He seemed nervous of Ben. Was it his colour, or merely that Ben was a big, strange man?

"You gonna show me your crane?" Ben asked. "I used to have one like that myself. What can you lift with it?"

By the time that Tony Winter returned, ten minutes later, Ben was playing happily with his son. The inspector shooed the lad away.

"You'll make a good father," he told Ben, matey in a way which he never was at work. "Have you and Julie got any plans in that direction?"

"It's under discussion," Ben told his boss. Actually, he'd thought about it a lot since Christmas, decided that he felt far too young to be a dad. He wasn't sure whether Julie would accept this, so hadn't explained his feelings to her yet.

"All right," Tony said, when Jane had come in with a cafetière of strong coffee. The wife, Ben realized, was at least two inches taller than the husband. How did a bloke deal with that? The inspector waited until she'd poured them each a mug, then spoke again. "What's urgent enough to bring you over here on a Saturday afternoon?"

"That conversation we had with DSI Petit yesterday," Ben said.

"About the Sutcliffe lad?"

"Yes. I've just been to see him. He contacted me this morning."

Winter nodded, his expression blank. The Sutcliffe case probably meant little to him. He had been working in Mansfield when it all happened.

"So why have you come to me with this?" he asked. "Weren't you supposed to go straight to DSI Petit?"

"I need to talk it over with someone first," Ben told his boss.

"All right," the inspector said, with raised eyebrows, as, upstairs, the baby began bawling again. "Talk."

Ben told the inspector about Jed and Jagger: how

the solicitor had got Jed out of jail, fixed him up with a job, encouraged him to engage in bank card fraud and racist attacks, then help organize a riot. He explained how Jed had turned the tables, tape-recording Jagger, informing the police about the intended riot, then calling a press conference to expose the solicitor.

"I don't remember reading any of this," Tony Winter said.

"The press didn't print it. Jagger's got connections. He's very friendly with Roger Wellington, the former home secretary. Wellington arranged for a D notice on Jed's allegations about Jagger. They were never published."

Tony Winter's eyes widened. "Now hold on, Ben. I'm way out of my depth here. D notices? Former Home Secretaries? I can see why DSI Petit is involved. Let me ask you again. Why haven't you gone straight to her?"

"Because I got the impression that she's on Jagger's side, that he'd gone to her with the black-mail story as a way of finding out where Jed Sutcliffe is hiding."

"What are you saying?" Winter asked, jokingly. "Jagger will have the lad beaten up? Or do you mean murdered?"

"Not as such, but…" Ben decided not to mention the death of Jagger's wife. That would stretch the imagination too far. Instead, he told Winter about his meeting with Jed, how the youth and a reporter intended to entrap Jagger that night and wanted him along as a witness.

"You weren't thinking of going and not telling anyone until afterwards, were you?" Winter asked.

"No, sir." Ben chose that *sir* carefully. "I tried to persuade him to delay the meeting. I wanted to do the correct thing. That's why I called you."

"You did right," the inspector said. "Have you got DSI Petit's home number on you?"

Ben got out his personal organizer. He had a number that his boss didn't. What did that tell him? He handed it over. A minute later, Winter was talking to the Detective Superintendent.

"He's in town, ma'am, and he's been in touch with the officer you saw yesterday. I know you told PC Shipman to call you directly. That's what he's doing, through me. He came straight here from meeting Sutcliffe. All right."

He put the phone down and turned to Ben.

"I think I got you off the hook for not going straight to her, but she doesn't want me involved. She's sending a squad car to pick you up and take you to Century House, where she'll meet you. Want my advice?"

"Yes, sir."

"Do exactly as you're told and don't proffer any opinions. This case could make your career, Ben. It could also break it. Understood?"

"Yes, sir," Ben said, adding, insincerely, "thanks for talking it over with me."

"Any time," Winter told him, equally unconvincingly.

Kieran finished work at three and was at a loose end. The night before, he'd gone to see the new Bond film. The movie was good fun, but only made him feel bad because Jo wasn't there. He kept imagining her next to him, holding his hand, her warm body pressing against his. Today was a Saturday. He ought to be spending the rest of the weekend with Jo. Instead, it would be just him and Mum, like it always used to be.

If Kieran called a taxi, he could be outside Jo's house in five minutes. Only he couldn't go to her street, not after what had happened the day before. The police had kept him in the station for hours. Then he'd been given a lecture by some tall, dried-up female sergeant who he'd taken no notice of at all. Instead of letting him go, she'd made him wait another half hour, which was when the inspector turned up. The inspector, a small bloke with a big voice, had given Kieran the same lecture but with added macho bits.

"A bit young for you, wasn't she? Take my advice and get over it. Plenty more fish in the sea. They have laws against this sort of thing now. It's harassment."

"Then maybe I should have a solicitor," Kieran interrupted him. "Because there's no evidence against me and I have a disabled mum at home who doesn't know where the hell I am."

"You can ring your mum if you like," Inspector Winter said, matter-of-factly, "but we'll be letting you go soon, provided you show some understanding of what you've done wrong."

"I told you I've…" But by now Kieran had worked out that he ought to show some remorse, just to get out of there. "Listen, she's making up most of it. She's the one who did all the chasing, the hanging around near *my* house. I felt sorry for her, but I didn't really encourage her. On Christmas Day, I told her that there was no chance, I just wanted us to be mates. She took it badly."

This threw the inspector, so Kieran carried on. "She's a nice kid, but she wanted me to … you know, and she's too young. I told her to choose a guy her own age. She took it the wrong way. That's why she called you."

"It wasn't her who called us," the inspector revealed. "It was somebody who'd noticed you on her street, several times."

"Montague Street's on my way home from work," Kieran lied. "And, sure, I've called by a couple of times. I wanted to let her down gently. She's only a kid, after all. I thought staying friendly was the best way to keep from hurting her. But I've learnt my lesson. I'll walk home a different way in future."

"All right," the inspector said. "Make sure you do that."

Kieran didn't know what to do with himself. He couldn't stop seeing Jo. He needed to make some new tapes of her. He missed the old ones, which she'd taken away. At least he still had his hidden highlights tape, the stuff he'd transferred on to VHS. But it wasn't enough.

Kieran didn't want to go home just yet so, despite the cold wind, he walked into the city. As he passed the magistrates' court, a woman coming out gave him the eye. Kieran wasn't interested. Too old. And what was she doing in there if she was a decent person? Kieran liked women who were innocent, uncorrupted. Which meant girls, really. Like Jo. How could he carry on seeing her without getting hassle from the police? He stared at the traffic, all four lanes of it flooding Canal Street. Then, suddenly, he hit upon the answer.

DSI Petit wasn't very patient with Ben. He told his Jagger story in rather less detail than he'd told it to Winter but she just kept repeating, "Yes, yes, I know all that". When he'd finished, she said, "Why did you see Jed before calling me, as I requested yesterday?"

Ben had no answer to this, so he lied. "I mis-understood," he said.

"I hope that I can rely on you to follow precise instructions in the rest of this case."

"Of course," Ben told her, "but there is one thing I'd like to be assured of."

"It's not my job to give assurances to junior officers," the DSI snapped.

"Just tell me this, then," Ben said. "Who are we after – Jed Sutcliffe or Ian Jagger?"

"We are *after* whichever of them commits a criminal act," the DSI said. "And that answer had better satisfy you, *officer*."

Ben knew better than to say any more. DSI Petit began to detail the steps they were taking to mount a surveillance of Jed's meeting with Jagger that night.

"I suggested that they delay it," he said. "To give us time."

"Not necessary," the DSI said and Ben's brain clicked.

"You already had this organized," he said. "Jagger's told you about the blackmail attempt, and the meeting."

She didn't comment, but Ben could see that he'd hit upon the truth. Jed knew the risks they were running. He had come to Ben for reassurance, for back-up. But this was beginning to look like a stitch-up.

"Listen," Ben said to the DSI, taking a risk. "I know Jed. I've seen his book. He's one of the good guys, out to expose racism. He's not a blackmailer."

"He's obviously convinced you of that," the DSI said. "Tonight, we'll see whether he convinces us. What time did he say for you to call?"

"Seven-fifteen," Ben said, adding a few minutes.

"Use the phone in your house. That way, we can listen in."

Ben ought to be angry that they were tapping his phone, but found he wasn't. It was only what he'd expected.

"One of the squad cars will drive you home, then pick you up at a quarter to eight. We can't have you late for the meeting, wherever it is."

Ben was dropped off twenty minutes later. When he got in, Julie was out. She and Tammy had gone to visit a friend. Curt, Natalie and Natalie's friend Jo were watching a video.

"Julie's really hacked off with you," Curt said. "Where you been?"

"Work. Got to go out tonight, too. Whose phone is that?"

"Mine," Jo said.

"Mind if I borrow it?" Ben asked.

"What's wrong with the phone in the kitchen?" Curt asked.

"Maybe he wants more privacy," Jo said. "Yeah, course you can. As long as it's not another woman you're calling."

"It's not, I promise," Ben said.

He took the phone upstairs and dialled Jed's number. Ben wanted to make sure that the youth knew exactly what the situation was before walking into the meeting tonight. But after he dialled, all Ben got was a long silence. Jed's phone was switched off, or disconnected. The mobile company's answering service kicked in, but Ben didn't dare leave a message in case it was traced. What was Jed up to? The more Ben thought about it, the more obvious it became: Jed was walking into a trap.

16

Neil got to Clare's early and nearly walked over to Asda to buy her some flowers. But then he'd be late. Anyway, he already had wine, and flowers might be over the top. It was hard to know what tone to set with an ex-girlfriend, particularly one who you had slept with for the first time two months ago, but had hardly seen since. He walked to the end of the street then retraced his steps.

Neil knew that Clare wasn't for him, but he was anxious to maintain his friendship with her. It was hard for a bloke to have female friends. Neil got on well with his sister, but she was a lot younger than him. He went back even further with Jan Hunt than he did with Clare, but recently his relationship with Jan had become … complicated. Maybe things always got too complicated between men and women. Maybe he shouldn't have come here tonight at all.

Two minutes to eight. That'd do. He rang the doorbell and waited. No one came. That was odd. There were no lights on in the front of the house. Had Clare forgotten? Neil rang the bell again. As he waited for an answer, the phone rang. That would wake Clare, if she'd dozed off. Still, no one came.

The phone was in the hall. It kept ringing, which meant that the answering machine wasn't switched on. If no one answered, Neil knew from experience, the machine activated itself after fifteen rings. This was what happened now. He could hear every word.

"Clare, it's Charlene. Are you there? I'm just calling on the off chance that you're free. Was tonight when you were seeing Neil? Anyway, I'm at Ian's. He's had to go out and might be gone all evening. So I wondered if you'd like to bring a video round. Or I could come to you. Give me a call if you're back at a reasonable time. Bye."

Clare must be out. Either she'd forgotten, or something had come up. Neil nearly left. But it wasn't like Clare to stand him up, so he thought he'd just go round the back, see if anything was wrong.

The back alley wasn't used much. It was dark and icy. Before he got to the back gate, Neil slipped and nearly broke the bottle of wine. Then he found that the back gate was bolted from the inside. Neil couldn't get in. But he saw something which worried him. Clare's light was on. Clare wasn't the sort of person who left the house without turning off her light. What was wrong?

He called her name. No response. Clumsily, Neil fumbled around on the ground, looking for something to throw at her window. He'd done this once at a friend's and managed to crack the glass. He didn't want to do that again. He went back to the street, tried the doorbell again. Nothing. In the gutter, he found a scrunched up aluminium can. That should be all right. Neil returned to the alley and took careful aim. The can hit the glass just below the frame of Clare's window. The glass didn't crack, but it made enough noise to wake Clare if she was sleeping. Nothing happened. Once more, Neil called her name. There was no response.

He should have gone then. For the rest of his life, Neil would wonder about what sixth sense led him to stay, made him decide to vault the gate, then call Clare's name a final time. Again, there was no reply. Neil took a deep, anxious breath then began to kick at the back door, praying that neither Clare nor Sam had slid the bolts at the top and bottom across.

They hadn't. The door gave way on the third kick. Neil ran through the house. Downstairs, the only light was the winking green dot on the answering machine. Neil hurried up the creaking stairs to Clare's room, the door of which was ajar.

Clare was on the floor, her body bundled up as

though she were in great pain. She looked deathly pale. Something was very wrong. Neil slapped her face, trying to wake her. There was no response. Then he began to panic. Clare didn't appear to be breathing. He felt for a pulse. It was there, but very, very weak.

"Clare! Wake up! Clare!" he shouted and shouted, but knew it was no good. If he had his car with him, he would take her to the hospital himself, but he was on foot. He rushed downstairs and phoned for an ambulance.

Jed made the short walk from the hotel to The Trip To Jerusalem ten minutes late. This was deliberate. Simon, his journalist partner, was to get there first. Simon would have time to phone Jed if there was a reason to back out.

Ben Shipman had called earlier. "Listen, Jed. I'm calling from a box, so that no one can listen in. If you mention this call, I'll deny it took place, all right?"

"Why the secrecy?" Jed asked.

"I think you'll be walking into a set-up. The police aren't interested in Jagger, they're interested in you."

"I know that. It's a risk I'm willing to take. Will you be there?"

"You won't see me until afterwards, but I'll be around."

Afterwards. That was something which Jed had

been looking forward to for a long time. If he proved that Jagger was corrupt – even if the solicitor was not prosecuted – he would feel like his job was done. He could get on with his life. Not in England, maybe, where he had too many enemies, but somewhere.

"If you're there, you'll be a witness if Jagger does anything dodgy, won't you?"

"I can't guarantee anything," Ben said. "Look, call your journalist friend. Get him to give Jagger some excuse, put him off. Take the time to think about this."

"I've done all my thinking," Jed said. "I'm taking a tape recorder with me. This time, I'm going to get Jagger to incriminate himself."

"Don't bet on it," Ben told him. "Listen. I'm going back to the house. I'll call you again in five minutes. Act as though this conversation didn't happen. If you decide to cancel, say so. If not, just tell me where the meeting is and I'll get there."

"I won't change my mind," Jed insisted.

"Remember," Ben had said, in parting, "if you take the money, you're as guilty as he is."

"Don't worry," Jed had told him, "I'm no fool."

"I know that, but Jagger's very, very clever."

When Ben called back, five minutes later, Jed had said the time and place, as instructed. Had Ben got here in time? Jed looked around the crowded pub. The Trip was on the site of the oldest inn in

England, and hence attracted a lot of tourists. It was always crowded but people seldom stayed long, so it was usually possible to get a seat sooner rather than later. Jed walked through the first bar. Before he got to the second, there was a small, dark alcove with one tall table in it. Standing there was Ian Jagger, who had his back to him. Where was Simon? Where was Ben? Jed was summoning up the courage to approach Jagger when someone tapped his shoulder.

"Jed, isn't it? This is my round. What can I get you to drink?"

Jed's mouth opened and closed without any sound coming out. The speaker was Roger Wellington, the former Home Secretary. Wellington was (as Jed's book hinted but didn't try to prove) the man behind Jagger. What was he doing here?

"I'll have a pint of Pedigree," Jed managed to reply.

"Fine." Wellington ordered and they stood in strained silence while the drink was poured. "Help me carry them over, will you?"

"Jed!" Jagger said as Jed and the politician joined him. Where was Simon?

"So this is what you really look like. A vast improvement on the skinhead garb, I must say."

The solicitor looked younger than Jed remembered, less demonic.

"I hear you've written a book," Jagger went on.

"That's right," Jed replied. "Would you two like to see some of it?"

"Why not?" Jagger said, calmly.

Jed handed them the set of proofs which he'd shown Ben earlier. The book was complete except for a post-script which, if things went according to plan, would chronicle this meeting. The page the two men were looking at gave a detailed list of funds which had been transferred from European banks to Jagger and Co.

"Where did you get these financial records?" Jagger asked, as he flicked through the rest of the pages.

"It hardly matters," Jed said.

"Oh, but it does," the solicitor said. "If they're freely available, I'm hardly going to pay you to suppress them, am I?"

"Somebody photographed them for me. Your accounts aren't freely available … yet. That's all I'm telling you."

Jagger raised an eyebrow as he looked at the photo of himself embracing Jean Marie Le Pen. "You took this?"

"Yes."

"Not the best camera-work in the world," Jagger commented, "but somewhat embarrassing all the same."

"Can I ask a question?" Jed said, taking a sip of his drink for confidence before he continued. "What I've never understood is *why*? You're not prejudiced against black people, Mr Jagger. Not black women, anyway."

Wellington laughed. "You have a lot to learn about the world, young man. One has to keep sex separate from politics, or trouble will follow."

"This is about politics, then?" Jed asked, turning to Wellington. "Is that why you're here?"

The former cabinet minister shrugged and reached into his pocket. "Politics is about power. Power, for the most part, is about money. You want some, I believe…"

He pulled something out of his pocket. This was going too fast. "Hold on," Jed said.

"Too late," Jagger told him.

Jed stood up and, suddenly, two men who'd been sitting at the bar leapt from their seats. Jed looked back at Wellington, then at Jagger, then at the thick brown envelope which the former MP was pushing across the table towards him.

"I don't want it!" Jed pushed it back. "I never wanted it!" Too late, he realized that he had touched the envelope. His fingerprints would be on it.

"Ben!" he called out.

But the black policeman was nowhere in sight. Other officers were everywhere. They were all in plain clothes but as soon as they stood it was obvious that they were coppers. Bemused tourists looked on as Jed was handcuffed. Meanwhile, a medium height, middle aged woman with short dark hair walked over to the table he'd been sitting at. She was, Jed noticed, wearing plastic gloves. The woman picked up the brown envelope and put it into a clear plastic evidence bag. The last thing Jed saw before being roughly dragged away was the woman taking off her gloves, smiling, then shaking hands with both Ian Jagger and Roger Wellington.

The ambulance came in eight minutes. The journey to the hospital took a little longer.

"What's your relationship to Clare?" one of the paramedics asked, as they took her downstairs on a stretcher.

"Friend," Neil said. "Close friend."

With Ruth gone, there was no friend closer, Neil guessed, unless you counted Charlene Harris, who Clare had only known for five minutes. Neil had already phoned Clare's mum. She was out, but he had left a message on her machine. He'd said that Clare had collapsed, but not explained how serious her condition was.

Neil travelled with Clare in the ambulance. They were giving her oxygen.

"It looks like she's bleeding internally," the para-medic said. "Could be a burst appendix. Has she been complaining of pain in that region?"

"I don't think so," Neil said, not sure which region he was talking about. He'd seen so little of Clare lately. He could call Jan, or Charlene, see if they knew whether Clare had been ill. She'd looked a little knackered at work yesterday, that was all he could think of.

Outside, the siren sang. Neil hadn't done any driving with a siren on for quite a while. He used to enjoy it, getting a little adrenalin rush from the speed he was doing, from the traffic nervously edging out of his way. But, today, the ambulance seemed to be going at a snail's pace. The paramedic was radioing ahead. An operating table had to be ready. She turned to Neil.

"Any idea if she's pregnant?"

Pregnant? Neil's mind went back to October, that drunken night. Had he used a condom? Neil didn't carry them on the off chance. They'd both been very drunk. So probably not.

"She could be," Neil admitted aloud. "You think this is a miscarriage?"

"More serious than that," the paramedic mumbled. "We can't be sure."

At the hospital, Clare was taken straight to the operating theatre. Neil had to wait near reception. He went to the phone and left a message on the machine at Clare's house, explaining what had happened, why the back door had been kicked in. When he returned to reception, Maria Coppola was running through the door like a madwoman. Neil called to her.

"What is it? How is she?" she yelled.

"Probably internal bleeding, they say. Possibly a

burst appendix. Or it could be…" Neil saw the answer in her eyes before he even asked the question. "Maria, is she pregnant?"

Clare's mum nodded and her expression told Neil all he needed to know.

"It's mine?"

Small, frail Maria took his hand. "She wasn't going to tell you. I said she should, but…"

Neil had never felt so bewildered.

"Neil, I'm sorry. I don't know what to say. I'm so scared."

"Me too," Neil said, feeling faint.

"She's all I have," Maria murmured.

"She'll be all right," Neil said, quietly, not even convincing himself.

He and Maria stood, both of them trembling, and did the only thing that they were able to do. They waited.

Ben watched as Jed was dragged out of the pub. Where, he wondered, was Simon Shaw, the journalist? Jagger and Wellington, of course, had been left behind. As Jed reached the front door, his young eyes swung frantically around and caught sight of Ben.

"I didn't take the money!" Jed yelled, or that was what Ben thought he heard as the lad was dragged away. The next words were clearer. "Listen to the tape!"

Then Jed was gone.

In the back bar, Jagger and Wellington appeared to be celebrating. DSI Petit sat between them, looking pleased with herself. Ben couldn't help but feel that he had played right into Jagger's hands.

Or had he? One thing was clear. DSI Petit had known about this meeting before she spoke to Ben yesterday. The purpose of her conversation with Ben wasn't to get information, it was to make sure that he didn't get involved and mess things up. If Ben had met Jed without telling her, he would have lost his job. However, his unexpected presence might also have prevented what went down tonight.

As soon as Ben had agreed to come here in his official capacity, he was ineffectual. He'd been made to stand where he couldn't hear anything and could barely tell what was going on. All Ben had seen was a brief conversation which ended abruptly. Roger Wellington, not Jagger, had pushed a large brown envelope across the table to Jed. Jed seemed to push it back again. In the same instant, plain clothes officers were arresting Jed.

Already, the order of what had happened was confused in Ben's mind. In the normal way of things, Ben and the other officers present would confer, agree the way in which things occurred and stick to it. But this hadn't been the normal way of things.

DSI Petit was on her way out of the pub. She stopped by Ben at the bar.

"Well done, Benjamin," she said. "Those two got what they deserved. It was straightforward black-mail, I'm afraid. They were threatening Mr Jagger with tax evasion rather than racism, you'll be pleased to know."

"Jagger set them up," Ben said and the super-intendent smiled.

"He's a sophisticated man. But he's no racist, as I'm sure your ex-girlfriend could tell you. Best to have him on your side, don't you think? I told him about your part in tonight's little affair. He's very grateful."

Ben couldn't help himself. He spat on the floor. The DSI looked mildly disgusted.

"I suppose I understand your feelings."

"Did you record the meeting?" Ben asked.

"We didn't, no," the DSI said, looking away. "The acoustics in here are very poor." She turned back to him, her face a pale mask. "Now, there's no need for you to hang around. We have enough witnesses with-out you bothering to make a statement. Thanks for your help. It won't go unrewarded."

Burning with anger, Ben left the pub. Both he and Jed had been used liked fools. Even if Jed had succeeded in taping the meeting, Ben realized, Jagger and Wellington would have said nothing incriminating. What happened to Simon Shaw? he wondered. Whose side was he really on?

Jed might be beaten but Ben still had one card left

to play. He had to tell the story to Charlene before she threw away her life on Jagger. The Trip was only a few minutes walk from Charlene's flat. Ben strode uphill through The Park's ill-lit streets. There was a light on in the flat, but it might only be there to deter burglars. Still, Jagger was out tonight. Where else would Charlene be but home?

Ben knocked on the door. He'd do anything he could to stop this wedding. He'd even tell Charly that he still loved her. He knocked a second time. No one came. Ben knocked again. No answer.

Probably she was already on her way to The Trip, anxious to join Jagger and Wellington in celebration. Ben had been a fool, he realized, as he stood on her doorstep in the cold: a fool to let her go, a fool to take on her fiancé and think he stood a chance. What did Ben know about Jagger? Only what Jed had told him. Now Jed was thoroughly discredited. Maybe the youth *had* made it all up. Ben was past caring. This time, it really was over. Jagger had won.

17

Jed was shown into an interview room at eleven on Sunday morning. The police had not questioned him overnight. Nor had they had mistreated him. They had merely left him in a cell on his own, to stew.

Jed already knew the solicitor. Julian MacKeith had a strong anti-racist background. *Searchlight* had hired and briefed him, so he already knew the whole Jagger saga. Jed expected Julian to be sympathetic. Mr MacKeith, however, was not impressed with Jed's defence.

"Even if the financial papers are genuine," the goateed solicitor said, after listening to Jed's account, "it wouldn't justify blackmail."

"I wasn't there to blackmail Jagger," Jed corrected. "The tape would show…"

"*What* tape?" MacKeith said. "You claim that you were secretly recording the conversation, yet no tape recorder was found on you when you were arrested."

"It must have been taken off me."

"*Must have?* You don't remember?"

"It all happened in a rush. I was being man-handled. My bag was taken off me – that's where the tape recorder was. Maybe Simon got hold of it. Have you seen him?"

"No. The police don't know where Shaw is or why he didn't turn up at the pub. Anyway," the solicitor went on, "I'm not representing Shaw, I'm representing you. And our best bet is to depict you as Simon Shaw's unwitting stooge. Why did you throw your lot in with him, Jed?"

"He was one of the people who minded me when I was on the run. I told him that I wanted to write a book. He said that he was a journalist and could help."

"Did he say what kind of journalist?" MacKeith wanted to know.

"Freelance. But he said he'd written for the *Financial Times*."

"I checked that," MacKeith said, in a sour voice. "Evidently the *FT* published a letter from Shaw once, as a kind of joke. It was about how international socialism would inevitably destroy the stock market. Shaw used to write for a weekly paper called *Socialist*

Worker. They stopped taking his articles because his facts were too unreliable. When you came along, Shaw must have seen you as his way back to publication. Shaw was a failed journalist, Jed, not a real one."

Jed put his head in his hands. "I never asked for money," he reiterated. "The police must have been taping our conversation too. Their tape will prove that."

Julian MacKeith sighed sympathetically and shook his head. "The police say that the pub was too crowded for any taping device to be effective. Also that, though they offered to wire up Mr Jagger and Mr Wellington, both men refused, fearing that any device might be spotted."

There was a cast-iron conspiracy against him, Jed realized. Even his own solicitor was buying into the police story.

"You've got to believe me," he pleaded. "I had a tape recorder in my bag. The tape would show that I didn't ask for money."

"I'm bound to believe you," the solicitor said. "But no tape recorder has turned up. Meanwhile, the police have a tape recording of a telephone conversation where Simon Shaw asks Ian Jagger to bring two hundred and fifty thousand pounds to the meeting at The Trip. In the absence of your tape, there's that one. Then it's your word against a leading solicitor and a former Home Secretary about what happened in the pub. Your fingerprints are on the envelope with the money in it. Who do you think a jury's going to believe?"

Jed didn't answer. The solicitor stood up.

"Act contrite and I might be able to get the charges against you reduced, provided you agree to plead guilty. But I warn you: repeat these allegations about Ian Jagger and the police will make sure you're put away for a long time. Your story has to be that Shaw put you up to it and you were taken in by him."

"But that's not how it was," Jed said. "If anything, Shaw was taken in by me. He wanted to help me prove the truth about Jagger."

"That's as may be," Julian told him. "But he's free and you're under arrest. Your only hope is that neither Wellington nor Jagger will want the publicity that this case will bring. The police might agree to reduced charges if you agree to plead guilty."

"But I'm not guilty of anything!" Jed pleaded.

"There are at least half a dozen witnesses who will say otherwise."

Neil drove back to the hospital, his mind going over the events of the night before. The surgeons had operated on Clare for nearly three hours. She'd had something called a laparotomy and a blood transfusion. Neil and Maria had still been waiting for the operation to finish when Clare's father arrived, at two in the morning. He'd driven over from Bedford as soon as he heard.

Nick hugged his estranged wife. Neil backed away to give the couple privacy, then watched as Maria explained that Clare had been pregnant, which Simon hadn't known. Clare's father looked crushed. Neil felt to blame, though Maria had not once criticized him. Now Nick came over and embraced Neil. Clare's father had lost weight and looked older. Had Maria told him that Neil was the father of Clare's lost baby?

"You found her, Maria says. Saved her. We can never thank you enough."

No, she hadn't told him. Neil felt awkward. If he was going to take the credit, he must also take the blame. He had been drunk, irresponsible. But before he could say anything, the surgeon came out. He addressed Maria and Nick in a calm, measured tone.

"Your daughter had an ectopic pregnancy which her doctor failed to detect. The baby formed in the left fallopian tube, eventually rupturing it. There was a great deal of internal bleeding. If this young man hadn't got to your daughter when he did, she wouldn't be alive now."

"But she is safe?" Nick asked, his voice child-like, pleading.

"Yes. Clare lost a great deal of blood and was in danger for several hours. But she's no longer critical."

Nick crossed himself and began a prayer of thanks in Italian. The doctor finished.

"She has, as I explained to your wife earlier, lost the baby. That was inevitable from the start."

"Can she have more children?" Maria asked.

The doctor was evasive. "I will discuss such matters with Clare when she's conscious and after we've done further tests. But that won't be for some time. You can see Clare if you like. She's sleeping. Then I suggest that you all go home and get some sleep yourselves."

Now it was twelve hours later, nearly two in the afternoon. Neil reached the ward where Clare was recuperating. Nick was by her bed. Maria, he explained, had gone home to sleep. Clare, too, was asleep.

"I won't disturb her," Neil said. "I'll just sit with her."

But Clare began to stir. She opened her eyes and, seeing Neil, smiled. She even managed to crack a joke: "Shouldn't you be at work?"

Neil kissed her pale cheek. "I spoke to Jan this morning. She sends you all her love and'll try to come to see you tomorrow. I haven't tracked down Sam yet."

"She and Steve went away for the weekend', Clare said, then turned to her father. "Dad, you could do with some fresh air. Neil'll stay with me for a while, won't you, Neil?"

"As long as you want."

Obediently, Nick Coppola left. Now that he was

gone, neither of them knew what to say to each other. Neil reached out and took her hand.

"You saved me," she said.

"I'm sorry the doctors couldn't save the baby, too," Neil told her.

"It never stood a chance," Clare said, looking away from him.

"Do they know how it happened?" Neil asked. "I mean, why it happened?"

"I had symptoms," Clare said. "Pain in my shoulder, faintness, a burning in my side. But I put the symptoms down to different causes: pregnancy, carrying awkward equipment, whatever… An ectopic pregnancy's easy to miss, they say."

"What caused it?" Neil asked.

"The doctor said one of my fallopian tubes was badly scarred. I'd had some kind of inflammatory disease in my pelvis. I don't know how I caught it."

Neil held her hand. "You're safe, that's the main thing."

"I know," Clare said, opening her eyes, which were very sad. "I'm sorry I didn't tell you about the baby."

"I think I understand why," Neil told her. He didn't explain what he meant.

Clare knew what he was like. If she'd told him the baby was his, he'd have offered to marry her. But Clare had already turned him down once.

"I hadn't decided," Clare said, quietly, "whether to keep it or not. I wanted to, but… "

223

She was crying. He held her, gave her a tissue to wipe her face. When she spoke again, her voice was calm. "Maybe it's better this way – that's what Mum says. She wanted me to have an abortion. But it was my baby, Neil…"

"Our baby," he corrected her, and now he began to cry too.

They held each other for a long time, until a doctor came. Neil left, promising to return the next day.

In the pale-coloured, over-lit corridor, he met Clare's father once more.

"The baby was yours," Nick said, sadly.

"Yes. I didn't find out until last night."

"I know you would have done the decent thing," Simon said, quietly, before walking on, returning to his daughter.

I would, Neil thought, pressing the button for the lift. *Only I know that Clare wouldn't have let me.* Around him a stream of people were arriving to visit relatives, partners, friends. Ordinary people, nearly all of them with fear lurking behind their eyes. That was because of where they were, this place where we all expect to end up, terrified.

But Neil didn't feel afraid. He felt guilty. Guilty and… The lift was slow in coming. He realized that the main thing he felt was relief. Clare was safe, and she was no longer pregnant with his child. They had had a lucky escape. The cost to him had been minimal. The cost to Clare he wasn't so sure about.

With a metallic *ping*, the lift arrived. Neil stepped lightly into it, pressed the button for the ground floor, descended.

MARCH

18

Gary looked around the parade room to see if Clare was in. She was meant to be back from sick-leave today. They shared a house, but he hadn't seen her for weeks, not since she'd left the hospital. She'd be staying with her mother, he supposed.

There was no sign of Clare. He wondered if she'd decided to jack it in. She'd dropped a hint or two. He wouldn't blame her for wanting a big change, not after all the things that she'd been through.

Gary enjoyed being a copper, but was sometimes tempted to jack it in himself. He hated the casual homophobic comments that other officers made around him. Several people on the shift knew that Gary was gay, but he didn't advertise the fact, so it wasn't common knowledge.

It would be nice to have a job where he could be out, but at least his situation wasn't as bad as Umberto's. Calling a footballer gay was a way of creating aggro on the field. No player in his right mind would admit to being queer. Only Ben, Clare, Sam and Ruth knew about Gary's relationship with Umberto. They were the only ones Gary trusted not to tell the press.

Forest were virtually relegated now. Only a miracle would save them. Gary prayed for one every night. If Forest stayed up, Umberto would stay here. If not...

"We've got a call," Ben told him. "Wordsworth Hall. It's meant to be boarded up. Kids possibly trapped inside."

Jan Hunt hadn't done the briefing yet, but Gary was kitted up, ready.

"Let's go," he said.

Just before Gary joined the force, there had been a series of nasty rapes at Wordsworth Hall, which was on the edge of the Forest recreation ground. The old building was, until recently, a student hall of residence. There was a glut of student accommodation in the city right now, while there was a shortage of high quality real estate. So the students were moved on, while the hall awaited redevelopment.

Ben and Gary sped down Mansfield Road and turned on to Gregory Boulevard, where Wordsworth Hall came into sight. The place had only been closed for a matter of months, yet, already, it was being allowed to go to ruin. Security cameras, installed the summer before, had been vandalized or stolen. Windows were boarded up. Who knew what it was like inside? The hall didn't have a caretaker. What would be the point, when it was sure to be demolished? Signs on the red brick walls advised parents not to let their children go inside. The signs warned of (now non-existent) security devices and threatened that trespassers would be prosecuted.

The hall might be empty but the car park was crowded, full of cars owned by students attending nearby New College. Ben and Gary had trouble finding a space. As they got out of the car, a woman rushed over. She was thirtyish with heavy lines beneath her eyes and a silver nose stud. She must be the one who'd phoned the police.

"I saw two kids going in through that window nearly an hour ago," she told Gary and Ben, pointing at a window where two out of the three boards covering it had been removed. "I'm pretty sure they haven't come out. I called out to them. No reply. I'd have gone in after them myself only I've got a bad hip and…"

"You did right not to go in," Ben told her. "This is our job."

Gary took down the woman's address while Ben approached the window. Probably a false alarm. The kids would have found another way out. Their parents hadn't reported them missing, which was a good omen. Why weren't the little buggers in school, Gary wondered? Silly question. This area had the lowest school attendance in the whole country.

The window was quite high. The kids would have needed a bunk-up to get in. So did Ben. To protect himself, Gary put on his heavy police-issue gloves. Even then, when Ben stepped on them, he felt like his hands were on fire. Ben tried to get through the window and swore.

"There are splinters everywhere! This is too tight."

Ben came down, hurting Gary's hands again.

"Let me have a go," Gary said, glad that he was wearing gloves.

Ben was taller than him but Gary had the bigger build. Getting inside was no picnic for him, either. One board remained in place at the left of the window. Gary punched it so hard that his right hand hurt again. The board gave way. Gary grabbed the top of the window frame and pulled himself inside.

The air was dank, fetid. Gary sensed that he was at the end of an unlit corridor. As he took out his torch, he heard an unsettling noise. Turning the beam on, he saw several large rats, scuttling away. It never took vermin long to get established once a place had been abandoned.

Gary retched, sickened by the rats, the smell. Then he recovered himself and called out, keeping his voice warm, friendly.

"Anyone in here? This is the police. We're not looking to get anybody into trouble, just want to make sure you're all right."

He listened. The rats were quiet now. The kids were probably long gone. Yet Gary could hear something. Breathing? Sobbing?

"Who's there?" Gary called. "Do you need help?"

No reply. He walked carefully along the corridor, listening, looking out for obstacles. When he got to the doors at the end, he listened more closely. The crying – if that was what it was – seemed to be coming from the floor above. Gary pushed open the safety doors and directed his torch beam upwards.

Scavengers had been busy. The carpet had been ripped from the stairs. There were gaps in the wood-work. Gary reached for the railing to steady himself, then realized that the railing wasn't there. He nearly tripped. From the floor above, he heard a child's voice, distinct this time. It sounded like a boy.

"Help!" he was calling.

"You're looking well," Jan told Clare.

"Thanks." Clare felt better than she'd any right to, considering. Six and a half weeks had passed since she had nearly died. The doctor had offered to sign her off for another week, but Clare was ready to get back to work. No, that wasn't quite it. Clare knew that, if she didn't go back to work now, then she never would.

"How's Ruth?" Jan asked.

"Good. Back in her old job and enjoying it."

Ruth was a police radio operator in Halifax. Clare had stayed with her mother in Bobbers Mill for two weeks while she recuperated from her ectopic pregnancy. Then, once she'd stopped feeling so wobbly, she'd gone to stay with Ruth and her mother. It seemed important to get out of Nottingham. Clare had read a lot of books, gone out for short walks when the weather allowed and had a lot of long talks with Ruth. She had nearly decided what she was going to do.

While she'd been away, Clare had stayed in touch with her parents, but not with her friends. Charlene had sent flowers, Mum said. Sam and Gary had sent her a get well card, as had her shift, but Clare had not spoken to any of them. However, there was one person who Clare had had to talk to. Neil.

Her ex-boyfriend had driven over one Sunday afternoon. Ruth and her mum had made themselves scarce so that they could talk. It was the single most difficult conversation of Clare's short life.

"When we slept together," Clare had had to tell Neil, "you might have caught an infection from me."

"What kind of infection?" Neil had asked, with concern.

"Chlamydia," she'd said, trying to keep her voice steady. "It's a sexually transmitted disease. I probably caught it when I was sixteen, from the first guy I slept with. He was … promiscuous, and care-less with condoms. I've always been careful since, until that night when we … forgot."

"I see," Neil had said. He sounded shocked. Clare didn't know whether this was because of the disease, or because he thought Clare was a virgin until she went out with Paul Grace. There had been a long, increasingly awkward pause.

"You didn't know you had it?" he'd asked, eventually.

"No. At the time, sex sometimes … hurt a little. But I'd not done it before and assumed that was natural. Then nothing." Clare had spoken in a rush, trying to get it over with. "There are often no symptoms, for either sex. The doctors say it does no damage if you find it early on: a few antibiotics and it's gone. But if it's left, it can scar the fallopian tubes, cause tubal pregnancy. That's what happened to me."

Neil had taken a few moments to take this in, then asked the inevitable. "Will you be able to have children?"

"Probably. They say the other tube is OK. My chances are down around fifty percent. It'll make it harder, but not impossible. There's another thing…"

Neil had guessed what she was going to say. "I'll take a test," he'd said. "Get it sorted."

"You haven't…?"

"…with anyone since? No."

"I'm glad we got that conversation out of the way," Clare said, a little later. "I was dreading it."

After that, there hadn't been much to say, but they'd gone for a drink, said it anyway.

"I'll always be there for you," was the last thing Neil told Clare before he drove back to Nottingham. He'd meant it, too. But Clare knew it wasn't true, that Neil would find somebody else who'd come first. Maybe Clare would too. As long as whoever-he-was didn't expect her to sleep with him. Clare was off sex for life.

"Ah, Clare, there you are. Good to have you back." It was Inspector Winter. Everybody was being unnaturally friendly because of what had happened to her. They all assumed that the baby Clare had lost was fathered by Paul Grace, their former boss. Simplest to let them believe it, though Clare found it painful. Paul was the love of her life, yet they'd only had a few short months together before he died.

"There's a young lady here wants to say hello," Winter added.

For a moment, Clare didn't recognize her. The tall, pretty, assured-looking seventeen-year-old was Hannah Brown ... no, Hannah *Knight* now. She had taken back her real father's name. Hannah had run away from home eighteen months before. Finding her had been Clare's first case as a probationer.

"You look great," Clare told the girl. "What are you doing now?"

"A levels," Hannah said. "I'm here on a work experience placement."

"Sixth formers on the beat?" Clare asked, jokily.

"That's right. Getting a taste for the life."

Hannah's father had been a copper, Clare remembered.

"The inspector said you'd not been well," Hannah said.

"I'm better now," Clare told her. "Want a word of advice? If you're thinking of joining the force, get a degree first. I'm sure you're clever enough. They'll respect you more."

"Thanks," Hannah said. "You're right. I am thinking about it. Perhaps we could meet up for a drink while I'm here, talk it over."

"Not today," Clare told her. She wanted to be generous to Hannah, but the timing was wrong. "Another time," she added. "Right now, I'd only put you off."

Jan interrupted them before Hannah could respond. "I need you in a car. There's a little boy's trapped on the top floor of a derelict building."

The boy's name was Ryan Harper.

"What happened, Ryan?" Gary asked the small voice which was coming from the floor above him.

"We were playing hide and seek," the boy's voice said. "I came up the stairs. The railing came off in

237

my hand. Then I lost my balance and my foot went through the floor. I can't move."

Gary pointed a torch in the direction of Ryan's voice. Some of the wood from the stairs was hanging loose. Sections of the stairs had been removed by scavengers. There would always be people who needed wood to burn. Gary flashed the light around some more. He still couldn't make out the boy.

"Do you see my light?" he asked.

"Yeah."

"I can't see you. Direct me."

He pointed the light into the darkness above.

"Up a bit," the boy said. "Left a bit. No, I mean right. Now go left. Up some more. You're pointing straight at me."

Gary saw the side of a leg, poking through one of the holes in the stairs. It was too dangerous for Gary to get any closer. He would have to wait for the fire brigade to arrive.

"How did you manage to get up there?" he asked.

"I thought that Tom must have come up here," Ryan said, adding, almost proudly, "I can see well in the dark."

"Your friend," Gary asked, urgently. "Where is he?"

"I don't know," the boy said. "I shouted, 'Coming, ready or not', then I started looking. After I fell through here, I called out for him, but he didn't come."

"Have you hid in here before?" Gary asked.

"Once."

"Do you know your way around?"

"Sort of.'

"Does Tom?" Gary asked.

"No."

"How did you get in?"

"There's a fire door at the bottom. It looks boarded up, but one of the boards just lifts off."

That was how the scavengers got stuff out, Gary realized.

"All right," he said. "Let's hope Tom went for help after hearing you shout that you were trapped."

He took the boy's details, then those of his friend. Ben came through on the radio.

"The fire brigade's just arrived," he said. "There's a fire exit at the side of each floor. They can get to Ryan through there."

"The other boy could still be in here," Gary said. "I need you to check if he's gone home. He's a ten-year-old, Tom Johnson, wearing a red T-shirt and jeans. Tom could be anywhere. He thinks he's playing hide and seek, but he's been hidden the best part of an hour. He might be in trouble."

Gary gave Ben Tom's address.

"I'll send someone," Ben said, "but we'd better start a full search anyway. Back up's just arriving."

"Be careful," Gary warned. "The stairs are full of holes. There may be other hazards, too."

"OK," Ben told him. "Stay where you are."

As he disconnected from the radio, Gary heard Ryan moan. There was a crunching noise. Gary's torch light picked out the shadows of falling splinters.

"I think I'm going to fall through!" the boy cried out.

"Don't worry," Gary said, weighing up the risk. Should he wait for the fire brigade to get in or could he help the boy himself? He took a deep breath, knowing that hesitation might be fatal. Then he called out.

"I'm coming to get you."

The police car belted along the ring-road, its siren blaring. Hannah hid her excitement. The only pause was when they had to wait at traffic lights by the junction with Nottingham Road.

"Look," Clare said, pointing at the former Futurist cinema, a beautiful Art Deco building which had long been converted into a carpet warehouse or similar.

"What?" Jan said.

"It's got the 'u' back. For as long as I can remember, there's been a 'u' missing in the Futurist sign. They've finally fixed it."

"Great," Jan said, as the traffic cleared. Hannah couldn't understand how Clare could be distracted like that when a boy's life was in danger. The car sped up Nottingham Road, down Sherwood Rise and turned right onto Gregory Boulevard. They parked in front of Wordworth Hall.

Not sure if she was really meant to be there, Hannah followed Jan and Clare out of the squad car into the car park. She listened as Ben Shipman briefed both them and the firefighters. Two of the firefighters went back to their engine for a battering ram. Their chief, meanwhile, argued with Ben about whether the police should go in or not. Firefighters were trained to work in the dark. Police weren't.

"We've got torches," Ben said, "and my partner's in there. I'm not staying outside."

"We know the hall layout," Clare added. "Do you?"

That shut the fire chief up. By the time that Clare had explained what was where, the hall's front door had been demolished. Hannah trailed behind the three police officers and two firefighters as they marched in. Jan took the ground floor. Without asking, Hannah followed Clare up to the first floor, dodging gaps in the stairs. When Clare stopped to look in the first room, Hannah came in behind her.

"What are you doing here?" Clare asked. "Didn't Jan tell you to stay outside?"

"Not that I heard."

"You shouldn't be here," Clare said.

"I haven't got a torch," Hannah pointed out. "It's safer for me to stay with you than it is for me to go back."

Clare swore beneath her breath. "In that case, stick close by."

They went from room to room, calling out the missing boy's name.

"Tom? Tom?"

There was a radio message to say that there was nobody in at the boy's home. His school had him marked down as absent for the day.

"You know your way around here," Hannah commented, as Clare shone her torch on a cupboard which Hannah hadn't noticed, and checked that it was empty.

"There were some burglaries here last year," Clare told her, the tone of her voice suggesting that there was more to the story than that.

The place had an eerie feel, the stuff of nightmares. Hannah heard crunching and squealing noises. Animal squeaks. There were weird echoes. Then she heard the fire engine being brought into position, drowning the other sounds, making her feel safer. Even so, time passed terribly slowly. She and Clare had covered just one side of the corridor. They were nearly at the stairwell.

Despite the noise from the fire engine outside, Hannah thought she heard a moan. She summoned Clare, who was looking beneath a bed-frame. The room's sink and wardrobe had been ripped out. The bed only remained in place because it was bolted to the floorboards. Clare and Hannah returned to the dark corridor. Hannah held the fire door open. She heard a deep groan.

"Tom?" Clare called into the darkness.

"No. It's me, Gary. I'm stuck. This stair could give way any time."

"How's Ryan?"

"I'm holding on to him."

Clare and Hannah gazed up to where the voice was coming from. There was no way that they could catch Gary. If the staircase gave way, and he fell, the drop would be nearly thirty feet – enough to kill a child, even a grown man, if he landed badly. There was more noise above.

"That's the fire brigade," Clare called out. "There's nothing we can do, Gary, but they'll have you in a minute."

"I hope so," Gary said. "Any sign of Tom?"

"No," Clare said. "No sign."

They ought to start looking again, but neither Hannah nor Clare moved, not until the firemen had got hold of Ryan and began to put a brace around Gary. Then the two women began to search the other side of the corridor, looking as meticulously as they could, finding nothing. Where had the boy gone?

On the floor below, Jan searched alone, dreading what she might find. You could cosset children all you wanted but, if they liked, they could always get away from you. A Victorian death-trap like this would always tempt a boy's curiosity, his sense of adventure. In three or four years, Henry would have to be allowed outside on his own. The thought terrified her.

"Tom? Tom Johnson! Where are you?"

On the radio, Ben informed her that Gary and Ryan Harper were safe. The fire brigade were searching the second and third floor while Clare and Hannah (Hannah! She shouldn't be there – what would the boss say if the work experience girl had an accident?) finished the first. Did Jan need help?

"Send Clare and Hannah down when they're done," she said.

The rooms, only recently occupied, seemed spookily empty. Some still had posters on the walls: *Demonstrate!*, a boy band, a poor reproduction of a Van Gogh. Now and then Jan felt rats running over her feet. She reached the stairwell and looked up. The stairs from the ground floor looked pretty intact – safer than the ones at the other end. Maybe she should radio Clare and Hannah, tell them to come down this way. Most of the brass railings had been removed, but otherwise...

What was that? Jan, flashing her torch around, observed something shiny poking out beyond where the railing should be. It was a large section of brass. Why hadn't intruders taken it with them? Brass must be worth something, melted down. Otherwise, why would so much of it have been taken? This section must have fallen of its own accord. Jan moved closer, lifted the heavy pole as much as she could, pointed her torch. Then she gasped.

The missing boy was beneath the railing, knocked out. The heavy brass pole had fallen on him. It probably happened when part of the staircase collapsed on Ryan, two flights above. Jan could see that Tom had a serious head injury. She couldn't get close enough to tell if he was still breathing.

Jan's first impulse was not to pick up her radio, but to pull out her whistle, which would alert everybody at once. She blew with all the breath in her body, then began to speak to the unconscious boy.

"Tom, Tom?"

There was no response. With every second, Jan became more sure that they had arrived too late.

19

Jo was coming out of school with Martin when it happened. They were hand in hand, looking like the young lovers they had recently become. Martin was making plans for the weekend while Jo was umming and aahing about whether to go along with them. It was only a game she played. They were at a stage where they did everything together, and the only thing that got in the way was Martin's impending exams.

"Look out!" Martin exclaimed, and suddenly the hand–hold became a tug. A dark car mounted the pavement, heading directly at them. Jo screamed as the car hurtled past, bounced back on to the road and skidded off. She'd only had a fleeting look at the face behind the wheel, but knew who it was. Kieran.

"Are you all right?" Martin helped Jo to get up.

"Fine." Jo got out her mobile, dialled 999.

"You think that was deliberate?" Martin asked when she'd finished the call.

"Dunno." Jo hadn't told her new boyfriend much about Kieran – just that she'd seen an older guy a few times and he'd turned out to be a creep. Now, while they waited for the police, she blurted out more: how Kieran had watched her house for weeks, then followed her. But the telling was interrupted by her mobile phone. She answered, expecting it to be the police, to whom she had just given this number. It wasn't.

"Jo? Kieran. Just ringing to check that you're all right."

"You're kidding! After what you just did?"

"I don't know what you're talking about."

"Is that him?" Martin asked. Her boyfriend's voice became high pitched when he was angry.

"Yes, but…"

Martin snatched the phone from her and yelled into it. "Listen to me, you creep. If you come near Jo or me again, you're dead! Got that? I know where you live!"

In the distance, Jo heard a siren. Martin handed back the phone.

"He hung up."

"I'm not sure that threatening him was a good idea," Jo said.

"He tried to kill us."

"He wanted to scare me, probably. Kieran's not violent, just … warped."

"Whether he meant to or not, he could have killed both of us," Martin said. "We're going to tell the police that. We're going to have him arrested!"

Clare and Jan were on patrol when they picked up a call about the attack on Jo McCord and her new boyfriend. They got to Kieran Manders' Wilford house ten minutes later. There was no car outside, no sign of life inside. They rang the doorbell several times, and were about to leave when an annoyed voice made them turn around. Kieran was on the street behind them.

"My mum's in bed and she can't get herself into the stair lift on her own. You'll be upsetting her. What do you want?"

"Kieran Manders?" Jan said.

I've seen him before, Clare thought. *Where?*

"Yes. So what?"

"Could we come inside?" Jan asked. "It's about Jo McCord."

"*Again?*" Kieran said. His irritation was convincing. "When's she going to get it through her head that it's over?"

Kieran took them inside. He put the kettle on while he went upstairs to check on his mum. He made tea the proper way, in a pot. Kieran looked older than he was supposed to be, Clare thought – twenty-six rather than the twenty-one he claimed. He wasn't bad-looking, though too scrawny and baby-faced for Clare's taste. There was something anxious about his face, except when he was speaking. Then, he sounded confident, plausible. His mum would vouch for the fact that he'd come straight home from work, he said. He'd just popped to the chemist's for her.

"And you ran into Jo McCord," Jan suggested.

"Jo? No. I did ring her up though, while I was waiting. Thing is, I feel guilty about finishing with her. I mean, I tried to let her down lightly. She's a nice kid, but that's all she is, a kid. When I met her, I thought she was sixteen, seventeen. We'd been out a couple of times when I found out how old she really was. Some blokes might not mind being with a girl that young, but I do. Her parents were suspicious of me, and I don't blame them. I decided that it'd be pretty heartless of me to dump her before Christmas, so I left it until then. But I blew it, I guess. When I suggested that we just be friends, Jo went mental on me. Started saying she'd get back at me if I didn't go out with her."

He was talking far too much, Clare thought. Sure sign of guilt.

"Jo says that you were watching her house," Jan pointed out, "as you well know, Mr Manders. We had you in the station over it."

"I sorted all of that out with your boss," Kieran claimed. "It was a misunderstanding. If anything, she's the one who's been watching me. You wouldn't believe the number of times I've looked through the window and, suddenly, there she was. Scares me sometimes, she does."

"Let's talk about your car," Clare said.

"What car?" Kieran protested. "I can't drive."

"If I didn't know Jo," Clare told Jan as they were leaving, "I'd find him quite convincing. He's more intelligent than most of the sickos we get."

"Maybe," Jan said. "He seemed a bit smug to me. We've got nothing on him and he knows it. Jo's identification isn't very persuasive unless we can find the car he used and link it to him."

Clare radioed in. There was no car registered to Kieran on the DVLC computer.

"But he's got a car somewhere," Clare said. "Suppose he tries to do it again?"

"I don't know," Jan replied. "Bear in mind, it may be a coincidence. Jo nearly gets run over by a joy rider. A minute later, Kieran calls. Jo persuades herself that she saw him behind the wheel of the car, even though it came on her so quickly that she didn't have time to see what make or colour it was."

Back at the station, Clare wrote the incident up. Jan wrote a circular urging all shifts to keep a careful eye out for a man of Kieran Manders' description hanging about near the McCord home. When she'd finished, Clare remembered the thing that had been bugging her.

"Where've I seen Kieran Manders before? His face was familiar."

"At his place of work. That was where we found Neil's car, burnt out."

"That's it. Of course." Mention of Neil made Clare feel guilty. She hadn't called him since getting back from Ruth's. Neil had saved her life, proving his concern for her. Whereas Clare hadn't told him that she was carrying his baby, which was a kind of betrayal. Clare didn't know where it left them. Nor did she feel up to dealing with the situation. Friendship had to flow naturally. You could never force it. She ought to call Neil. But tonight she was seeing Charlene.

After seeing the police, Martin walked Jo home and they discussed what had happened. Martin was full of macho bluster at first, wanting to take friends round to break Kieran's legs, smash up his car, that kind of thing.

"And what would happen then?" Jo asked. "You and your friends would get into trouble and people would feel sorry for Kieran. He's not worth getting angry over, Martin. He's sick."

"He tried to kill us!"

"Did he? Or was he just trying to get our

attention? Look, we're happy together. Don't let him spoil things."

Martin held her and it was all all right again. They agreed that Jo ought to tell her parents about Kieran trying to run them over. If the police came round, Jo didn't want the story to come as a shock. Martin saw her to the door but didn't come in. Because of the police, he would be late home himself.

"That's it!" Mum said, when Jo finished the story a few minutes later. "If the police don't lock him away, we're going to do something about Kieran Manders."

"Like what?" Jo asked.

"There are laws against what Kieran's been doing. Your dad's got a friend at the Rotary Club, Ian Jagger. He's meant to be a top solicitor. Mr Jagger told your father that we could get an injunction, forcing Kieran to keep his distance. I'm going to ring him now."

Charlene was getting ready to go out and meet Clare for a drink. She dressed in the spacious bedroom which she shared with Ian. It was a very male room, cluttered with antique furniture in dark, polished wood. It had heavy velvet curtains and a thick-pile carpet, both of which would have to go after they were married. Ian was giving her *carte blanche* to make whatever changes she wanted.

Charlene was running late. There was no time to walk across the city, so Ian would have to run her into town. She was looking forward to seeing Clare. They had so much to catch up on – Clare's convalescence, of course, but also the end of the sorry Jed Sutcliffe saga. Ben's conspiracy theories about Ian and Jed Sutcliffe had proved to be rubbish. Sutcliffe, it turned out, was nothing but a blackmailer.

Ian had been magnanimous in victory. He'd told Charlene that the business with Jed Sutcliffe was unfortunate, that the young lad had been duped by a member of the loony left.

"I'd defend him if I wasn't involved in the case. I think that man Shaw was exploiting Jed. I doubt whether the lad seriously meant to blackmail me."

"Why have the anti-racist groups got it in for you so?"

"I defended a bunch of Nazis in those riots a year ago," Ian explained. "But what am I supposed to do? If we turned down clients because we didn't like them or agree with them, we wouldn't have any clients left."

This was true, but Ian was being disingenuous. Solicitors tended to attract the kind of clients they wanted to attract. Barristers were the ones who had to work to the cab-rank principle, taking whichever client came along. Even then, they could usually exercise some choice.

"In future," Charlene had proposed, "I'd like to see us sending people like that elsewhere. I want us to build a black clientele. We won't do that if we represent racist thugs."

"All right," Ian had replied. "If that's what you want. Do I take it that you've been thinking about my offer?"

"Yes," Charlene said. She'd been thinking about the matter long enough. "If it still stands."

"It does."

"OK. After we're married, I want to become a partner. I want a full, equal partnership."

"We can change the firm's name to Jagger and Jagger," Ian had announced, delighted. "You've made me the happiest man on earth."

Now Ian sat on the Chesterfield sofa, doing the *Telegraph* crossword. He was a solid, strong man at the peak of his career. Any woman would envy Charlene being married to him. But there was a question which she kept putting to the back of her mind. What about when Charlene was his age, at the height of her career, while Ian would be over seventy? How would they cope with that?

"Could you give me a lift?" she asked him. "I was meant to be at Via Fosse two minutes ago."

"Sure. Who are you seeing tonight?" he asked as she put on her coat.

"Clare."

"Give her my best," Ian said, following her outside. "She's had a tough time."

"Clare's a survivor," Charlene told him. "She'll get over this."

"Are you sure?"

"You can never be sure about anything," Charlene said. "But – and I wouldn't say this to her, obviously – I think she's better off without a baby. Clare's too young. It's no picnic, bringing up a child on your own. It limits your choices."

"Sure," Ian said, "but with Paul gone, the baby was all she had to show for him. Losing a child as well…"

His words trailed off and he went almost misty eyed. Talk of children got him that way. Partnership or no partnership, Ian would want Charlene to have a baby as soon as possible. He didn't just want Jagger and Jagger, he wanted Jagger and Son. Charlene didn't intend to come off the pill for a year at least, more likely two. But she wasn't going to tell Ian this, any more than she was going to tell her fiancé that Paul Grace hadn't been responsible for Clare's pregnancy. He wasn't the only one who could have secrets.

Clare was already waiting in an upstairs bar when Charlene got to Via Fosse. Her hair was cut unfashionably short and she'd lost a lot of weight. Her skin was pasty and spotty. There were two drinks in front of her.

"I got you a vodka and tonic," Clare said, and launched into a story about a little boy who'd been killed by accident in some old building. His death made Clare angry, so Charlene tried to be sympathetic, apportion blame. But accidents happened. Finally, Clare finished the story.

"It's good to see you," Charlene said. "You look…"

"I look like shit," Clare said, "but I'm getting over it. Let's talk about something other than work. People there treat me like I'm a fragile flower. And they keep making these subtle hints. They seem to think that because Neil saved my life I'm bound to fall back into his arms and marry him."

"He *saved your life*?"

"Didn't I tell you on the phone?" Clare, despite what she'd just said, launched into a detailed description of what had happened six and a half weeks before. Charlene was taken aback. She'd sent flowers, but not visited Clare when she was at her mother's. She hadn't realized how serious the situation had been.

"If this were a movie, you'd have to marry him," Charlene said.

"Yes, and you'd be marrying Ben after he saved you from the evil Bluebeard." Charlene laughed and Clare continued, "Only Ben got egg on his face when Jed Sutcliffe was arrested."

"Ben was there?" Charlene asked, surprised that Ian hadn't mentioned this. "I didn't hear that. What happened?"

"Ben's pretty cagey about it," Clare said. "He went along, thinking that Jed was going to expose Ja … Ian, only it worked out the other way round. You know the rest."

"Yes. Jed got arrested for blackmail," Charlene filled in.

"The charges against Jed were never formally made," Clare added.

Charlene hadn't known about that. She'd thought that Jed was out on bail, awaiting trial. She was confused. "Do you know why that was?" she asked.

"I think because a trial would have been bad publicity for your fiancé and his pal, Roger Wellington. Jed laid all the blame on this Simon Shaw guy, who wrote the book with Jed. Shaw was meant to be at The Trip with him that night, but mysteriously failed to turn up. He hasn't been seen since."

Charlene thought hard about this. She couldn't work out why the police had let Jed go. A trial, Charlene reflected, would have allowed Jed to make his accusations about Ian. She ought to be relieved. She'd meant what she'd told Ian about wanting to attract black clients to Jagger and Jagger. Publicity about taking money from racists, even if disproved, would have destroyed that. Yet she felt uneasy. Ian enjoyed bending the rules, maybe even broke a few. The law was a game to him. No, it was more than that. Life was a game which he had to win. But Ian had never done anything which might backfire on him. At least, not until now.

"Something about this doesn't feel right," she told Clare.

"They can always charge him later, of course," Clare said. "Maybe after Shaw turns up, or if Jed tries to publish his allegations."

Charlene nodded. "Keep your ears to the ground, would you? Let me know if there's any more to the story."

"Like what?" Clare asked. "I mean, you must have discussed this with Ian."

"I have," Charlene said, "but … he's evasive sometimes. It's hard to describe what he's like, Clare. Part of him's mischievous, child-like. He enjoys playing games, especially when he gets together with Roger Wellington. I still don't think he's telling me the whole truth about what went on with Jed Sutcliffe."

Clare was dismissive. "You don't really think that Ian might be part of some international racist conspiracy?"

"God, no! He's no more a racist than I'm a Roman Catholic. I'm probably being paranoid," Charlene said. "In a month's time, I'll be married to him. There'll be no secrets then, we've agreed."

"Wouldn't it be a good idea to get the secrets out of the way before you're married?" Clare suggested, summoning the waiter to order another drink. "Just in case there are things he's done that you can't tolerate?"

"I suppose so," Charlene said, convincing neither Clare nor herself.

20

It was a biting cold day. Grey clouds threatened rain. On the other side of the road, Mr Thomas was coming out of the post office. He waved as Kieran wheeled his mother along. Kieran waved back, hoping that the old man wouldn't come over and try to spark up a conversation.

Mum didn't know that Kieran kept a car in Mr Thomas's garage. The old man felt sorry for Kieran, mainly because of his mother, who he'd known since she was a child. No longer well enough to run a car himself, he was happy to lend the garage to Kieran at no cost and for Kieran to register the car in his name. What Mr Thomas didn't know was that Kieran had applied for a replacement driving licence in the old man's name (Kieran not having taken a test). Kieran's car also had a stolen tax disc. There was no MOT or insurance.

Kieran could take Mum to the library in the car, but if she knew he had it, she'd probably have a third stroke. She certainly wouldn't let him drive without passing his test. The second stroke, three years before, had disabled Mum down the right side, hence the stair-lift, the wheelchair, the home help and the meals-on-wheels. Even so, Mum couldn't get by without someone there at night. If Kieran left, she'd have to go into some kind of a home. Kieran couldn't have that on his conscience.

As Kieran wheeled Mum up the ramp into the library, he almost bumped into Jo. His ex-girlfriend was on her own and in school uniform. Her hair was pushed back and she looked very young. No, she looked her age, which wasn't quite fifteen. Kieran stopped and stared, unsure what to do. Jo stopped too. This was, Kieran realized, the first time he'd come upon her by accident since that very first time, when he saw her in town. His heart leapt. It was a kind of magic.

Mum broke the spell. "Hello, Joanne," she said. "How are you? We haven't seen you for a while, have we?"

"No," Jo said, in her best, polite voice. "I've been busy. School."

"I wish Kieran had worked harder at school,"

Mum said. "He'd have a better job now." Kieran felt like kicking her.

"He's got a pretty good job all the same," Jo commented, still avoiding Kieran's gaze. At least the police hadn't told her that he was only a glorified receptionist.

"Jo," he said, as she edged away from them. "Could I have a quick word in private after I've taken Mum in?"

She hesitated, unable to think of a way to say "No" in front of his mother. Her heart was good. That was what he loved most about her.

"I suppose," she said.

Inside the library, they all knew Mum. One of the assistants came to look after her. Kieran hurried back outside. He half-expected Jo to have done a runner, but she was still there, shivering slightly in the cold breeze. In just a few minutes, the weather had changed. It was now a clear blue day, beautiful to look at but less thrilling to be outside in.

"We could go for a coffee," Kieran said, pushing his luck. "There's a place down the road."

Jo shook her head. "I have to get home."

"I got a letter," Kieran said, "from some solicitors, threatening an injunction."

"You were lucky we didn't take out a private prosecution," Jo told him, "for trying to run us over."

"That wasn't me!" Kieran protested, though of course it had been. It was only his second time out in the car. He'd parked up near the school gates, meaning just to watch. But then he'd seen Jo, hand in hand with that *jerk* and seen red. Had he meant only to scare them, or something worse? Kieran hardly remembered. He was so inexperienced at driving that anything could have happened. But, somehow, he had got away with it. The police had no evidence against him. Nobody knew where the car was.

"I saw your face," Jo said. "You could have killed us!"

"I'm sorry you were scared," Kieran said. He'd had a fantasy in which he had killed her boyfriend and not been caught, then comforted Jo, won her back. But this was not a fantasy. This was the real Jo, standing in front of him.

"What do you want?" she asked.

"I want you."

"That's not going to happen," she said, kindly but firmly. "Look, Kieran, I'm glad you've stayed away from me since the solicitor's letter. That means that when we do bump into each other accidentally, like today, we can be friendly. Right?"

"Right," Kieran said.

She shook his hand and he wanted to pull her towards him. Perhaps a passionate kiss would persuade her that he was still the one. But he didn't dare.

"Goodbye, Kieran."

"Bye Jo. Take care."

He stood outside in the cold, watching her walk away. Despite the school bag draped over her right shoulder, she moved elegantly. He wished he had his video camera with him to record this poignant departure.

Kieran watched until she turned the corner. Sadly, his recent tapes of Jo were nowhere near as good as those he'd shot last year. That was because he had to conceal himself in the car. He kept suit hangers draped over both back passenger-windows and hid behind them when watching or filming. So far, it had worked. Jo didn't suspect. But Kieran wasn't satisfied. Luckily he still had his Jo highlights tape, the one he kept concealed in the *Rear Window* box. In that way, he still owned her.

Back in the library, Mum had selected her Georgette Heyers and Catherine Cooksons, plus a tape of Dirk Bogarde reading one of his autobiographies. In the reference section, Kieran found a legal almanac with a section on the 1997 Protection From Harassment Act, the one which those solicitors, Jagger and Co, had cited in the nasty letter they'd sent him. He photocopied the relevant pages. At the issue desk the librarian was all smiles.

"Your mother must be very proud, the way you look after her. Not many sons would be so good. How long has it been now, since the first stroke?"

"Five years, nearly."

"It's thanks to you that she's still alive, I'm sure."

Kieran didn't comment. No point going into what might have been.

"Time for me to get her home," he said. "See you same time next week."

Getting Mum home took twenty-odd minutes, all of which Mum spent talking about Jo, what a nice girl she was. Kieran had told Mum that the two of them had split up because she'd lied to him about her age. Now, having seen Jo in school uniform, Mum believed him. Such a pity, she said, that Jo was too young for him.

"But stay friendly, pet. In a few years, the difference won't seem so big. Then, maybe…" She smiled beatifically as a romantic fantasy swept over her. Kieran pushed the wheelchair a little faster, anxious to get home and view his video of Jo, while the real girl was still fresh in his mind.

The transfer deadline was three days away and Forest's season was effectively over. They had eleven games left. Only if they won nine of them did they have a chance of staying in the Premier League. But that was an impossibility, Gary knew. For months now he had been reconciled to Umberto leaving Nottingham. Yet they avoided the topic of conversation as much as possible. The *Nottingham Evening Post* kept doing *Whither Umberto?* stories on the back page, alternately asking why the striker wasn't scoring more goals (how could he, when he had got so little service from the other players?) or which club was going to buy him and for how much.

The local paper seemed much more interested in Umberto than they were in who was responsible for the death of Tom Johnson at Wordsworth Hall. The police had spent days trying to find out who owned the hall. First they'd found a London holding company, followed by a bank in Switzerland who represented a partnership of unknown nationality. Finally, they had a name: Tennyson Associates. No other information was available.

Wordsworth and Tennyson: the city was littered with streets and houses named after both poets. Somebody, Gary thought, was taking the piss. The evening paper, despite making a fuss after Tom Johnson's death, hadn't bothered following the ownership story. They were too busy talking about Umberto.

Even if the Italian moved to another English team, Gary wasn't free to follow him, not until his probationary period was over. That was in a year's time. Anyway, most of the clubs who'd shown an interest had been foreign. Inter Milan were the best bet. Umberto would like to return to Italy. But he had to play things close to his chest. If he asked to be transfer-listed, he would forfeit his percentage of the transfer fee. So far, the only teams formally to approach Forest for him had been Celtic and Benfica. Neither had offered anywhere near enough money.

Gary was in Umberto's riverside house when the front doorbell rang. Umberto was in the bath and called down for Gary to answer it. Gary opened the door to see a familiar face. It was the famous manager who had been brought in to save Forest from the drop.

"Who are you? The butler?"

"I'm security," Gary said. This was the cover story which he and Umberto sometimes used.

"Oh aye, since the burglary. You know, I got done by the same lot."

"So I heard."

"Is he in?"

"Having a bath. I'll give him a shout."

"If you wouldn't mind."

Umberto came down in his bathrobe. Gary thought it best to stay out of the living room. The damp made his boyfriend's curly hair look longer. He resembled a rock star more than a footballer. Gary felt that constant tug of surprise in which he wondered how an ex-butcher from Worksop came to find himself with such an Adonis. His boyfriend left the door open so that Gary could hear the conversation.

"Is it Inter?" Umberto wanted to know.

"Yeah. Not quite as much as we wanted. Still, beggars can't be choosers."

"How much?"

"Thirteen."

Gary couldn't help himself. He whistled. Umberto, because he hadn't asked to be transferred, would be on five percent of that fee. Over half a million. That was more than Gary would earn in a lifetime.

"They want you to fly out tomorrow, discuss personal terms."

"Fine."

"Planning to take your *bodyguard* with you?"

Standing in the hall, Gary blushed. Was it that obvious? He didn't hear Umberto reply. A minute later, the manager was gone. Gary saw him out, then returned to the living room, where he and Umberto embraced.

"Come with me tomorrow," Umberto said. "You'll love *Milano*. It's a fantastic city."

"I'm sure it is," Gary said, "but I'm working."

"Resign," Umberto said. "Come to Italy with me."

"And do what?"

Umberto shrugged. "Do whatever you want. Live a life of leisure, if you like. I've got enough for both of us."

"I couldn't do that. I have to be independent."

"Then be my bodyguard. I'm sure I could get you put on the club payroll, so that you aren't directly dependent on me, if that's what's bothering you."

"That'd be worse," Gary said. He had already given this idea a lot of thought. "I'd only be in a job because of my connection with you. I hardly speak any Italian. It wouldn't be long before people worked out what our real connection was."

Umberto conceded that this was true. "All right, but please think about coming over. You can pick up the language in no time. And there's bound to be something you want to do."

"You're being sweet," Gary said, "but I can't see it working."

"I came to your city," Umberto pointed out. "I made a go of it. Why can't you do the same? We're only talking about another part of Europe, a short flight away. What's the problem?"

"You're a famous footballer," Gary reminded him. "You'd have to keep me quiet. Your team-mates wouldn't like playing with an *homosexualle*."

"So?" his lover protested. "You're a copper. You can't tell me that the police force is less homophobic than the football world. Yet you've managed so far. It's not the dark ages over there. Italy's my home. At least say you'll think about it."

"I'll think about it," Gary promised, and the two men kissed.

In bed, a few minutes later, as they made love, Gary found himself hiding tears. He could think about it all he wanted, but soon their relationship would be over. The best thing which had ever happened to him would be gone.

* * *

"You look fantastic," Clare told Charlene as she stood in front of the mirror and inspected the fit of her Versace wedding dress.

"It's terrific," Charlene said, "but you don't think it's a little tight … here?"

"Does it hurt?" Clare asked.

"Not at all."

"Then the tighter the better."

The assistant, who had kept a discreet silence so far, now began to inspect Charlene's apparel carefully for defects or potential improvements, all the time murmuring superlatives. After five minutes she declared the dress perfect and helped Charlene to take it off. Once the dress was whisked away, as the bride-to-be was standing in her underwear, Clare began talking about the ownership of some derelict building where a child had died. Charlene didn't listen to her, concentrating instead on the radio news which was playing in the background.

The Home Office has announced that police forces across the country have carried out a series of early morning raids on supporters of the racist organisation, Combat 18. Twenty-five people have been arrested for possession of racist literature and other offences. They include at least three soldiers in the Parachute Regiment who have had racist material confiscated from their barracks. The police say that further charges are likely to arise from information gathered as a result of these raids, which were the climax of a year-long investigation.

As Charlene dressed, the assistant interrupted Clare and began talking to her about what she would wear at Charlene's wedding. The police-woman couldn't have heard the item. Charlene tried to blank it out. Why did this racist stuff keep coming back to haunt them? Why did she still feel like Ian was involved?

"Plans for the weekend?" Charlene asked as they walked along Lower Parliament Street.

"I'm having dinner with Neil on Saturday night."

"Oh." Charlene found it hard to understand why Clare kept seeing Neil. Once a relationship was over, it was over. Male-female friendship was a myth, as far as she was concerned. "Do you think he's getting interested again?" she asked.

Clare shrugged. "I haven't given him any encouragement. I can't believe that he's still carrying a torch for me."

"But if he is?"

"Then I'll have to let him down gently," Clare said.

"Are you ready to start dating again?" Charlene asked.

It was only five months since her boyfriend's murder.

"I can't get my head around that," Clare said. "I was celibate for two years before I met Paul. I don't mind if I go that long again before meeting some-body. It has to feel right. I have to feel right. There are other things in life than romance."

"Like a career?" Charlene asked. "Your probation's nearly over, isn't it? Are you still thinking about applying for CID?"

Clare, deep in thought, didn't reply. Charlene had been trying to nudge Clare towards the Law. Clare was clever, would easily get into one of the two local universities to do a Law degree. Perhaps Jagger and Co could sponsor her, Charlene had suggested. She would mention it to Ian when the time seemed right. Clare had been non-committal. All the new building work in the city kept reminding her of her first real ambition, to be an architect. While staying at Ruth's, she had rung her old tutor. Manchester University would have her back, he'd said. Clare could, if she wanted, resume her Architecture degree in October.

The two women parted at Chapel Bar. Clare went into Arcade Records to buy some new music for the weekend. Charlene crossed the subway beneath Maid Marion Way and returned to her office. There was a police car outside the office. That was not unusual. The door opened and two uniformed officers led her husband out. That was. They put Ian into the back seat of their car. Charlene hurried over.

"What's going on?"

"Nothing to worry about," Ian assured her. "I've told the office to cancel my appointments for the afternoon. Here," he said, getting out a key, "you'll need this to get into the house."

Charlene nearly protested. She'd had her own

key for months. But Ian's expression stopped her. She knew what it was as soon as he handed it to her. The key to the safe in his office. "Better let Roger know what's going on," Ian added.

"I will," Charlene promised. Then she lowered her voice. "That is, if they haven't taken him in too. The radio said that they'd arrested twenty-five Combat 18 supporters."

Charlene expected Ian to laugh at the idea of a former Home Secretary being arrested, but he didn't. Instead, a shadow crossed her fiancé's face and he looked every one of his forty-eight years.

21

Curt was going out on a double date. It sounded like something from some tacky teen drama but it was real enough. He was going bowling with Natalie, Jo McCord and Jo's boyfriend, Martin something.

"You, bowling?" his sister teased as she fed Tammy. "I'd like to see that!"

"Yeah, well..." Curt mumbled. So what if it wasn't his kind of thing? Natalie didn't have things easy. Her dad had scarpered, disappearing as completely as Curt's mum. Her mum was an alcoholic who had a different bloke every week, or so it seemed. Natalie wanted to do normal-type things with a normal boyfriend, and Curt wanted to please her. Sometimes it felt like they were playing at it, that this was a game of pretend: Julie said everybody felt that way some of the time.

"Where's Ben?" he asked his sister.

"Out."

Julie's boyfriend seemed to be out a lot these days. Studying, that was the story he gave Julie: holed up in the library on Angel Row or at one of the universities. His exams were before Curt's, it was true. But nobody could study that much. If Ben was at home more, he would have noticed something.

"When are you going to tell him?" Curt asked his sister.

"Tell him what?" Julie looked away, evasive, and began to change Tammy's nappy.

"You *know* what," Curt said. "Ben might not know what you're like when you're pregnant, but I do. You've been making banana milkshakes again. And you're starting to show."

His sister burst into tears. Awkwardly, Curt put an arm around her shoulder.

"Don't tell him," Julie begged. "I want to choose the right time."

"What do you think I am?" Curt asked, as the doorbell rang. Natalie's mum was driving them all out to Megabowl on Redfield Road.

"Do you think he'll be pleased?" Julie asked as she wiped her eyes with kitchen towel.

"Shouldn't you have asked him that first?"

Curt had to go but felt guilty, leaving his sister

upset in the kitchen. Getting pregnant was probably a good idea, Curt reckoned. It would seal them together as a family. Ben might even marry her. Then he would be Curt's brother-in-law. Having a black brother-in-law would be cool. Pity he was a copper.

They picked up Martin first. The lad sat in the back with Curt. He seemed all right. A bit brainy, perhaps. He was in a top stream, you could tell without asking. Good looking, Nat reckoned, but Jo was a looker herself. She could take her pick.

When they got to Jo's, Martin went in to get her. Curt looked around. He was sure he'd seen that dark car across the street before. It had been outside the school when he went to meet Nat after skiving off the other day. The reason he'd noticed it was the owner had a suit hanger on each of the back passenger windows. Not only that, but the back window was hard to see through because of all the clutter: a coat, a shoe box and several plastic bags.

Curt, used to looking out for such things, was wondering whether the car was a new kind of police surveillance vehicle. If so, it would be a good idea. The vans they generally used were easy to spot. Maybe the Drug Squad were trying to track down the dealer who was flooding the school with cheap E's.

Jo got into the car. She squashed in the middle of the back seat between him and Martin, which felt pretty good, actually – so good that Curt almost forgot to mention the car until they were past it.

"Stop a mo'," he told Nat's mum. "That car right behind us," he said to Jo.

"The black Fiesta. What about it?"

"Do you know who it belongs to?"

"No."

"Seen it around before?"

"I think so. But it is pretty nondescript."

"Thing is," Curt said, "it was outside your school the other day." He explained about the suit hangers. "I reckon somebody's hiding in the back."

Jo and Martin looked at each other. "Kieran!" they said, in chorus.

Charlene didn't begin to go through the contents of the safe until everybody else had left for the evening. She had spoken to Roger Wellington earlier. He'd assured her that there was nothing to worry about.

"Ian will be clear of all that business soon," were his exact words.

Her wedding was two weeks away. *Soon* was not good enough. Ian had assured her that there were no secrets. Now she would put him to the test.

The safe was an old one. It had survived the fire which devastated the building a year ago. Ian kept the firm's financial records there. His personal records, or so she thought, were all at home. However, the first thing she came across was a copy of his marriage certificate. Ian rarely talked about his first wife, Pamela. Charlene put the certificate into a bag and began to remove other documents which looked like they might be personal. Why had he given her the key? There must be something he wanted her to remove before the police came back with a search warrant.

There was the manuscript of a book, for instance, already typeset. Why was it hidden? Someone's saucy memoirs perhaps. Or a leaked copy of something which Ian was meant to check for libel? Charlene flicked through a few pages. This appeared to be a book by Jed Sutcliffe and the missing journalist, Simon Shaw. Why had they gone to the trouble of writing a whole book if they meant to blackmail Ian? Had they really meant to publish their allegations? And how come Ian had a copy? Charlene put it in her bag with the other papers.

She nearly missed the red folder. It had no writing on the outside. Once she'd opened the expensive fabric folder, it took her a few seconds to work out what it contained: statements from a bank. A Swiss bank, Charlene suspected, but couldn't be sure. You would expect Ian to have an account on which he didn't pay tax. Most rich men paid less tax than the middle classes. However, as a solicitor, Ian had to be more careful than most about what avoidance schemes he used. Charlene put the folder into the bag, next to the book, and added a set of property deeds. There was nothing else. She relocked the safe.

Instead of going back to Ian's, Charlene walked to her own flat. If the police got a search warrant, they were as likely to get one for Ian's apartment as his office. She would hide the papers here. Was she doing anything illegal? Charlene doubted it. Anyway, she was marrying the man. He had to be worth taking some risks for. Charlene picked up her post and put the bag on the table. She didn't take her coat off because it was cold and she didn't intend to stay.

Despite the coat, Charlene shivered. It was tempting to look through the papers she'd brought, see what secrets they contained. Better, maybe, to wait and let Ian tell her. But before she made up her mind what to do, the doorbell rang.

The police? No, she was being paranoid. Even so, Charlene shoved the bag full of papers behind the sofa before going to the door.

In a sense, it was the police.

"Hi," said the man who she'd gone out with for over five years. Ben added, in a slightly embarrassed tone, "I find you in at last."

"I spend most of the time at Ian's," Charlene answered, coldly. "The flat's nearly sold and we get married in a fortnight, in case you'd forgotten."

"I hadn't forgotten," Ben said. "Can I come in? It's important."

"Then I suppose you'd better," Charlene said.

*　　*　　*

At Jo's request, Natalie's mum drove round the block and back to Montague Street from the other direction. Kieran's car was gone. Jo suddenly realized that she hadn't looked at the Ford Fiesta's registration number.

"Did anyone see the licence plate?" she asked. No one had.

"Let's try and find him!" Curt suggested.

"What do you think this is, a police car?" Mrs Loscoe objected.

"I can drive," Curt offered.

"Like hell you can!"

"If we follow him, we might find out where he keeps the car," Jo suggested. "Could you head towards Wilford, please? We might catch up with him."

"If that's what you want," Mrs Loscoe said, "but you're missing good bowling time."

Nobody but her minded about the bowling, so Mrs Loscoe accelerated on to Melton Road. A hundred yards on, they turned on to Wilford Lane. The car still wasn't in sight, so Jo gave directions to Kieran's home. He'd have to be parking his car somewhere near there. If they could tell the police where, maybe they'd find it and do him for attempting to run her and Martin over.

"Turn left here!" she said when they got to Compton Acres. Suddenly, there the car was, a rusty old black Fiesta a hundred and fifty yards in front of them. Mrs Loscoe began to speed up. This time, Jo got the registration number.

"Don't get too close!" Curt ordered, "or he'll realize we're on to him and clear off."

"And what do *you* know about car chases?" Mrs Loscoe asked.

Curt, tactfully, didn't reply.

Kieran turned left on to Rugby Road, past the shopping centre and past his own street. Then they lost him. Mrs Loscoe went up and down several roads. She had to turn awkwardly in a couple of cul-de-sacs. No Kieran. They returned to Rugby Road and were about to head for Clifton Boulevard when Jo spotted him, on foot.

"There he is!"

Kieran had his head down, hands in pockets. By the looks of it, he was walking home.

"Let's get out," Curt suggested. "Sort him!"

"I'm with you," Martin said.

"I'm not having violence," Natalie's mum told them. "Jo, what do you want to do?"

Jo thought about it for a moment. "Don't let him know we've seen him," she said. "We'll give the police his registration number. Then, next time he parks outside, we'll call them. Maybe that'll finally get him out of my hair."

"It's about your ... fiancé," Ben said. "I know that your marriage is none of my business, but I can't help myself. If I don't say something before you marry him, I won't be able to live with myself."

"If you want to rake up the Jed Sutcliffe business again, you're wasting your time," Charlene snapped. "I know it all already."

"All?" he said, pointedly. Charlene felt a sudden weariness. Before they began to talk, she turned the central heating on. Then she dug out a bottle of wine which had remained here only because it didn't have a classy enough label to take to Ian's. Finally, to insult Ben, she rolled herself a small joint. He began to speak.

"There's a book which Jed was planning to publish. Maybe still is, for all I know. Jed was certain that your ... *boss* was taking money from European racist organizations, spending some of it on racist groups in this country, but using most of it to line his own pocket."

"And you believe that, do you?" Charlene asked, licking the cigarette paper.

"I think that Jagger and Roger Wellington are, or at least were, working together," Ben asserted. "If the Europeans were sending as much money as Jed claimed, then Ian must have had a political heavy-weight behind him."

"And where did this money go?" Charlene asked, putting the spliff in her mouth and lighting it. "Ian lives well, but not that well. Do you think he's given all this money to racist thugs?"

As Ben stumbled to answer that, Charlene realized that she already had the answer herself. It was in the large plastic bag which she'd stuffed behind the sofa.

"I used to think that, but now I don't," Ben said. "Jagger's not a racist in the conventional sense. I'll give you that. Maybe his only motive is money. Yet I can't believe you're marrying a man like that, Charly."

"Don't call me *Charly*," Charlene snapped.

"I'm sorry, *Charly*'s how I think of you. I can't help it. You can't wipe out the past."

"That's true." Without thinking, Charlene passed Ben the joint. He began to smoke it, although, as far as she knew, he hadn't smoked anything since they were both students. He sucked deeply on the slim cigarette.

"Oh, that feels good," he said. "My head's been wound so tight…"

He smiled and, for a moment, it was like they were students again, sitting in her tiny room at the hall of residence in Reading.

"What is it you want from me?" Charlene asked, softly. "Why did you come round?"

"I want you back," Ben said, softly, returning the joint to her. "This last year without you, I've been miserable. I made a big mistake and I want to rectify it."

"I can't believe I'm hearing this!" Charlene said.

She attempted a sarcastic laugh, failed. "You've worked your way through two girlfriends since me. You wait until I'm about to get married before you come back to mess with my head…"

"I'm not here to mess with your head," Ben interrupted. "Listen. I made a mistake … more than one mistake. By sleeping with Jagger, you paid me back. As for marrying him … you couldn't think of a better way to humiliate me."

"You think this is all about you!" Charlene said, almost shouted. "Can't you see that I'm past you? I'm marrying Ian because he's what I need."

"Maybe," Ben said, measuring the words which followed carefully. "I'm sure that's why you think you're doing it. But at some level, Charly, I think you're doing it to hurt me. Whatever your motive, it worked. I'm hurt. And maybe you'll never have me back. I was a fool. I had the best thing in the world but I was too young to realize what I had. I threw it away.

"You don't have to throw it all away too. Don't get married to spite me. Don't marry Jagger unless you're a hundred per cent sure that you love him and that he's not got any nasty secrets waiting to come out and stab you in the back. Are you sure of those things?"

"The police took Ian in for questioning today," Charlene told him. "Is that what gave you the nerve to come round here?"

Ben looked surprised. "That's the first I've heard of it. What did they want with him?"

"I assumed it was connected with the raids on Combat 18 members," Charlene said, then regretted being so open with Ben.

"That'd be it," Ben said. "They'll have found Jagger's name in a list of lawyers who're prepared to defend racists."

"You don't think it's more than that?" Charlene tried hard not to show how worried she was.

"How should I know?" Ben said. "But Jagger's not the sort of man who leaves many hostages to fortune. I doubt you have anything to worry about."

Charlene hated the way he referred to Ian by his surname. She wanted to protest, but couldn't think of the right words. She shouldn't have smoked so much of the joint. Her mind was beginning to cloud. "So let me get this straight," she said, offering the spliff to Ben, who shook his head. "You no longer think that Ian's a racist?"

"That depends how you define racist," Ben said. "But if he was prejudiced against blacks, I guess you would have spotted it by now."

"And you're also saying that you want me back."

"Yes," Ben said, then softened his voice. "Will you have me?"

Charlene stubbed the spliff out. "I don't know. I'll have to think."

"Will you at least meet me again, discuss all this?"

"I guess," Charlene said. She needed time. Also, any meeting between them needed to be kept quiet. Vaguely, she remembered that Ian planned to play golf on Sunday.

"There's an exhibition at the Castle that I'd like to see before it finishes," she told Ben, trying to keep her voice calm, professional. "Meet me in the Art Gallery at eleven on Sunday."

"OK," Ben said, looking forlorn.

Charlene could still read Ben's mind. He'd have been building up to this meeting for weeks. Now that it was over he didn't know what to do. Charlene showed him to the door. She watched as he considered kissing her cheek, then decided not to push his luck. They said good night.

As soon as he was gone, Charlene put on some coffee. There was no milk, but that was all right. She splashed her face with cold water until she felt fresh. As hot water gurgled through the filter, she took the plastic bag full of papers out from behind the sofa and emptied it on to the table. She spread the papers out on the floor, then began to read.

22

In an internet café on Charing Cross Road, Jed Sutcliffe finished reading the stories about the previous day's arrests. He'd found tons of coverage, including the names of those arrested. Ian Jagger's, of course, wasn't among them. Nevertheless, the people Jed most feared were in prison. He was surprised by how efficient the police operation had been: their intelligence, this time, was shit hot. For the first time in over a year, it was probably safe for Jed to go home.

Jed had been living in London since January, when the police let him go. The charges against him had been left on the record – allowed to "lie on the file" was the technical term – which meant that the police could still arrest him at any time. It could still go to court. Jed had been silenced. All of his papers had been taken away. He had no proof against Ian Jagger and Roger Wellington any more. Should he discover any, and try to publish it, Jed would find himself in prison, sued for libel, or both. That was the way this country worked. The establishment looked after its own, no matter what they did.

Jed had screwed up badly by putting his faith in Simon Shaw. Shaw had taken Jagger's money, Jed was pretty certain about that. Simon had known that Jed would be arrested that night. He had probably already left the country by the time that Jed was taken into custody. How much cash had he settled for?

The journalist wouldn't be able to return. Jed had made certain that Shaw's former colleagues in both the Socialist Workers' Party and *Searchlight* knew what a traitor he was. But that gave Jed little satisfaction. Now he had to decide what to do next. Stay in London, he decided. There was no need for him to leave the country. London was anonymous enough. And he would not give up. Despite yesterday's arrests, there was still plenty of anti-fascist work to be done, always would be.

While he was on the computer, Jed decided to write a letter. He owed Ben Shipman an explanation of what had happened. Ben hadn't let him down. Jed needed Ben to know that he appreciated what he'd done. Ben had put his career on the line for him, for the cause. Not many other coppers would have done that. The police or security services might still be monitoring Ben's mail or phone calls, but Jed, like Ben, was from Mansfield. He knew where Ben Shipman's parents lived, and would send the letter there.

Ben got to the station at nine. He said "Hello" to Ted, the middle-aged sergeant behind the desk.

"Get anywhere with tracing the owners of that hall where the lad was killed?" Ted asked.

"'Fraid not. The boss handed that one over to CID. What's the word on Ian Jagger?"

"Still being questioned."

"Who's holding him?"

"It's a National Task Force," Ted said. "Nothing to do with us."

"I didn't know there was a National Task Force," Ben said.

"Me neither," the sergeant said. "You're not the first person to ask after Mr Jagger, by the way. He has some powerful friends."

"Roger Wellington," Ben guessed.

"And a senior skirt from Major Crimes."

"Sue Petit?"

"That's the one."

"Did either of them get to see him?" Ben asked.

"Nope. And here's the funny thing."

"What?"

Ted folded his arms and smiled. "Mr Jagger hasn't asked for a solicitor."

"Perhaps that's because he doesn't need one," a new voice said.

Ben turned around. Ian Jagger was standing behind him. His suit was ruffled, his shirt sweat-stained and his face more lined than usual.

"Come to gloat?" he asked Ben.

"No. I came to find out what was going on."

"My name was mentioned in relation to some racists arrested this morning. The Task Force thought I could help them. I answered their questions satisfactorily and now I'm going home. Sorry to disappoint you."

"If you did it," Ben told the solicitor, "they'll get you sometime."

"You're still very naive, Officer," Jagger said. "In my job you soon learn that stupidity, not culpability, is what gets people caught."

"Does Charlene know you think like that?" Ben asked, then regretted bringing her name into it.

"Charlene thinks that way herself," Jagger said. "She's changed a lot in the last year, Benjamin."

Benjamin. Nobody ever called him that. Except… As Ben began to think of DSI Petit, the woman herself walked into reception.

"They let you go at last," she said. "Poor Ian, you must be exhausted."

"Nothing that a deep bath and a stiff drink won't sort out," he said.

The Detective Superintendent nodded, acknowledging Ben's presence but not quite sure what he was doing there. "I'll drive you home," she told the solicitor.

"Cosy relationship," commented the custody officer when they were gone.

"Is there a history there?" Ben asked.

"You don't know?" asked the custody officer, with a smug smile. He'd been on the force at least twenty years, knew what was what.

"I wouldn't be asking otherwise."

"Sue Petit was the youngest sergeant in the history of the force. Twenty-eight when she got her stripes. Very pally with Jagger's missus, too. What was her name? Pamela. After Mrs Jagger snuffed it in a car crash, our Sue took on the role of comforter. Broke up her marriage, it did. Practically lived with him for a while. Marriage was assumed, but never happened, probably because Mr Jagger prefers – no offence meant here – dark meat."

Before Ben could ask more about Sue Petit, a familiar-looking woman came in. "We want to report a stalker," she said.

There were two lads and two girls with her.

"What are you doing here?" Curt asked.

Ben groaned. "Are you in trouble again?"

"No, not at all… But what are you doing here?

You're meant to be at home. Julie never knows where you are these days."

"My sergeant's exams are next week."

"You ought to get back to her," Curt said, sounding like his mother. "Don't you know that she's…"

"She's what?" Ben asked.

"…missing you a lot. You'd better not be playing away, mate."

Ben frowned. "I don't expect that sort of talk from you."

"Get used to it," Curt said. Since he got that reward money, he had become arrogant again.

"I'll see you at home," Ben said.

He left the station quickly. If Ben had had a car he could have followed DSI Petit to see if she went home with Jagger. Was that the way to split Charlene from him? But perhaps Charly knew about Jagger's relationship with the DSI? Ben must be careful not to dive in feet first. He would do some digging around. Maybe he would have a clearer picture of things by the time he met Charlene, on Sunday.

The phone rang just before nine, while Charlene was still going through the papers. She let the machine take it.

"I'm home," Ian's voice said. "Storm in a tea cup but they took their time. Are you there? No? OK. I'm taking a bath. We ought to talk. If you get this, call me. Better still, come over."

The message finished. Charlene ought to go back to Ian's, but her fiancé might ask for the key to the office safe. She thought for a moment. Ian would not be going back to the office, that was for sure. So she would go back there herself.

It was well after ten when Charlene left Jagger and Co. She returned to her flat, where she hid the pile of papers (which she'd photocopied) in the safest place she could think of: her laundry basket. Then she rang Ian, calling his mobile with hers in case his phone was being tapped.

"Is everything all right?" she asked.

"Fine," he promised. "I've just got out of the bath. Will you come over?"

"It's late," she said, "and I've got this feeling that we have to have a conversation which, if we start it tonight, won't see either of us getting much sleep."

"You're right," Ian told her. "Maybe we should leave it until tomorrow."

"That's what I thought."

"As long as you don't doubt me."

"Why should I doubt you?" Charlene said as she turned the pages of Jed Sutcliffe's book, *I was a Teenage Racist*.

"Did you take anything out of the safe?"

"I took what I thought you'd want me to take," Charlene said. "Shall I bring it back to the office tomorrow?"

"A red file?"

"Yes, together with a set of deeds and a manu-script."

"Good," Ian said in his softest voice. "Do me a favour. Bring the deeds back into work. Put the rest beneath your floorboards, if such a thing is possible."

"I'll do that," Charlene said. "G'night."

The photocopying had been unnecessary. She was to hold on to the crucial papers. There was an area in her small hall where the carpet was loose. Charlene lifted it and prised apart two floorboards. They had been cut when she'd had an alarm system installed. She felt beneath them. It was dry, not too dirty. She put the manuscript and the file into a plastic bag, sealed it, then slid it beneath the boards.

Jo slept badly that night. She'd thought it was over and it wasn't. Kieran had been watching her for weeks, despite the solicitor's letter. He'd probably been at it when she bumped into him at the library, laughing behind that sympathetic, smug face. What more was he capable of? He'd already tried to run her and Martin over. Next time, he might succeed.

Mum took the morning off work and Jo stayed away from school. The sympathetic sergeant from before was on duty.

"Call me Jan," she said, seeing how worried Jo was. "We'll get this sorted, don't worry."

Jo told her story, giving the names and addresses of her witnesses. Jan raised an eyebrow slightly when she mentioned Curt Wilder. Then Jo gave her the car registration number.

"Now we're getting somewhere," the sergeant said. "Why don't you wait here while I go and check it out?"

She returned ten minutes later. "The car exists all right. Its owner lives very near Kieran Manders. He's sixty-nine. Are you sure that this was the car you saw Kieran driving?"

"Yes," Jo said.

"Are you certain that you didn't see it near Kieran's house and, because it was the same number and make, assume it was the same one which had been watching you?"

A shadow of doubt crossed Jo's mind, but she was almost sure.

"I don't … think so."

"We'll check it out," Jan said. "Tell me, have you got a solicitor?"

"We have," Mum told her.

"In truth," Jan said, "there isn't enough here to arrest Kieran. Unless he commits an actual offence, the most we can do is give him another warning. But you have witnesses now. A good solicitor would probably have enough to get an injunction keeping Kieran away from Jo. Then, if he broke the injunction, we'd be able to arrest him."

"Thanks," Mum said. "We'll go there now. You've been very helpful."

The two of them were outside Jagger and Co ten minutes before it opened.

"Do you think he'll see us?" Jo asked.

"If he can't himself, I'm sure that somebody there will be able to," Mum said.

They were in luck. Just then, Ian Jagger himself walked by the car and began to unlock the office. When Mum called out to him he jumped backwards, almost as though he'd been shot. But then he collected himself

"Oh, yes, Mrs…"

"McCord. I know how busy you are, but I wondered whether we could have a few minutes of your time. This stalker business has come back again and it's got us all so worried…"

"Of course, of course," the kindly solicitor said. "Come in."

Their story only took a few minutes to tell. This time, Jo told Jagger how Kieran had secretly videotaped her, before they'd even met.

"You threw the tapes away? That's a pity," the solicitor commented, making a note. When they'd finished, Jagger nodded. He seemed tired, Jo thought. Rather than explain the situation, he got out a box file from which he withdrew a copy of the Protection From Harassment Act 1997.

"Let me refer to this. For it to be a crime, what

Kieran is doing has to be something which amounts to harassment of another, or which he knows or ought to know amounts to harassment of another."

Jagger paused. "The following you, the watching the house – both count as harassment. His watching you from the car is slightly less convincing, mainly because he attempted to conceal the watching. I can see why the police don't feel able to act formally. But his actions can still be the subject of a claim in civil proceedings. Listen. 'On such a claim, damages may be awarded for (among other things) any anxiety caused by the harassment and any financial loss resulting from the harassment.'

"That seems to apply to you," Jagger said, "especially with the following part: 'where in such proceedings the High Court or a county court grants an injunction for the purpose of restraining the defendant from pursuing any conduct which amounts to harassment, and the plaintiff considers that the defendant has done anything which he is prohibited from doing by the injunction, the plaintiff may apply for the issue of a warrant for the arrest of the defendant.' That's the injunction which we threatened him with earlier," Jagger finished.

"But first we have to get the injunction and then he has to break it," Mum said. "That could take months."

"Yes," Jagger told them, "and private prosecutions are fraught with difficulty. For the police to act, they would need more evidence of harassment, and probably a more serious level of harassment."

"Are you saying that Kieran has to hurt me or Martin before they'll arrest him?" Jo asked.

"Not necessarily *hurt*," the solicitor said, "but you should *fear* being hurt. Listen. This is a section called 'fear of violence': 'A person whose course of conduct causes another to fear, on at least two occasions, that violence will be used against him is guilty of an offence if he knows or ought to know that his course of conduct will cause the other so to fear on each of those occasions.'

"The next part says that there must be witnesses," Jagger went on. "Then the situation becomes much more clear cut. You've already had one threatening occasion, when Kieran tried to run you over. If there's a second, with at least one witness, the police will be forced to act. Whether Kieran goes to prison or not, you'll get your injunction. Then, if he does it again, he faces up to five years inside as against a maximum of six months and a fine."

"If he threatens violence…" Mum murmured.

"Exactly."

"But Kieran isn't like that," Jo said. "Apart from that one time when he drove at us, but, even then, I think he was only trying to scare Martin. He didn't mean to hurt us."

"But he could have killed you," Jagger pointed out. "Listen, Jo. You want to get rid of this man.

Sometimes in life, it's necessary to exaggerate, to *gild the lily* as the police often say. That's why I read out the law to you, so you know exactly what has to be done. If you want rid of this man, those are the conditions which have to be met. And that is the only advice that I have to give at the moment. You may start a civil action against Manders with what you've got already, but I don't advise it. Next time he turns up, if you call the police and say you're afraid that he's about to become violent, they will respond more strongly."

"Are you saying that I should…" Jo began, but Mum stopped her finishing her sentence.

"Thank you so much, Mr Jagger. You've been extremely helpful."

"That's what I'm here for."

There was a knock on the door. "Mr Jagger, your first appointment is … oh, sorry, I didn't know that you had anyone with you."

"We're just going," Mum said. She thanked the solicitor again and led Jo out of the office.

"I can't lie," Jo said. "I don't think Kieran really means to hurt me."

"It's not lying," Mum said. "Mr Jagger explained."

Had he? Jo wondered, as Mum drove her to school. If so, his logic had been so slippery that it had already escaped her.

23

"Sir, can I have a word?" Clare asked.

"What is it?" Inspector Winter looked up from his paperwork, irritated.

"Wordsworth Hall. Where are we on that?"

The inspector frowned. "*We* are nowhere. The matter was passed on to CID. If any crime took place, it's their responsibility."

"What do you mean *if*?" Clare said.

"I talked to DSI Petit, who has ultimate control of the case. She told me that it's a civil matter, not a criminal one. Now, if you don't mind…" He returned to his paperwork.

Clare left the office, frustrated. A boy had died. Somebody ought to be responsible. Who? The mother, who thought that Tom was at school? The school, from which he was an unauthorized absentee? Or the owner (whoever that was) of a derelict building which he shouldn't have been able to get into? Clare wanted to discuss this with Jan, but the sarge seemed preoccupied this Friday morning.

There was something different about Jan. She'd stopped slagging off Kevin, her husband, for a start. Maybe the bitterest part of the break-up was over. Or was Jan seeing someone...? No, she would have mentioned it. Anyway, who did Jan meet? Only police officers. And, at work, Jan still wore her wedding ring. Only Clare and Inspector Winter knew that she was separated. That was the way Jan wanted to keep it.

"Fancy a drink tonight?" Clare asked.

"Can't," Jan said. "Sorry."

"Oh, babysitters, I forgot," Clare apologized. "But I could come to yours. Wine. A video. I thought maybe you could use some..."

"I've got company tonight," Jan interrupted. "An old friend. But thanks. Another time? Tomorrow, maybe?"

"Can't," Clare said. "Neil's coming to dinner. Finally."

Jan smiled. "That's good. Ready to go on this call?"

"OK."

As they walked down to the car, they discussed Wordsworth Hall. Jan, as it turned out, knew less than she did.

"What did you say this was about?" Clare asked as they drove to Wilford.

"A car – probably the wrong car, but we've got to check it out. It belongs to a Peter Thomas, but Jo McCord reckons Kieran Manders was driving it last night."

They got to the address where the car was registered, a small semi with a dilapidated garage on the side. Both buildings were in bad need of fresh paint. Daffodils were blooming in a small garden at the front. An old man wearing a bush hat was weeding around the flowers and rose bushes.

"Mr Thomas?" Jan introduced herself. "We're checking the details of your car."

"Car?" The old man said, without looking up. "I don't own a car."

"According to our records, you do. A black Fiesta, fifteen years old?"

The man smiled and stood, slowly unbending his body. "That's not mine. It belongs to the son of a neighbour of mine."

"But it's registered to…" Jan began to say. Clare interrupted her.

"The son's name?"

"Kieran Manders. A good lad. His mother's been housebound for five years. Kieran dropped out of college – came home to look after her, took a job near by. I like to help him."

"Can we have a look at the car?"

"I think I have a spare garage key somewhere. Wait here, would you?" Mr Thomas went into his house.

"Where does this leave us?" Clare asked.

"I doubt that we've got enough to do Kieran Manders for stalking," Jan said, "but we can probably get him for falsifying the records on the car. Also, what's the betting that he hasn't got tax or insurance?"

The car's tax disc, when they came to examine it, had six months left to run. Clare took a closer look.

"This tax disc is for an Escort," she said. "It must be stolen."

"I don't know anything about that," Mr Thomas said.

"There may be a simple explanation," Jan said, to avoid alarming him. "Thank you for your help, sir."

They drove to the business park where Kieran Manders worked. They found him in the glass booth where he did his door-man duties.

"Why've you come to see me here?" he asked. "It's embarrassing."

"Tell me, Kieran," Jan said. "Do you have a driving licence?"

"A provisional one."

"Yet you were seen last night, driving a car, on your own."

"Must be a mistake," Kieran said, but he looked nervous.

"No mistake. We've just been examining the car in the garage of a neighbour of yours, Peter Thomas. It has a couple of suit hangers in the back. Any of that ring a bell?"

"I know the car you mean, yes."

"Care to explain why the suit hangers were there, Kieran?"

Kieran seemed to suppress a smile. He had already worked out his story, Clare realized.

"You'd have to ask Mr Thomas about the suit hangers. But I know how this has come up. I've been out in Mr Thomas's car a couple of times, having lessons. He's even talked about giving me his car. But he gets a bit confused sometimes."

"When did you last go out with Mr Thomas?" Jan asked.

"Before Christmas."

"That's funny," Jan said, "because that car was bought at auction in January of this year. I think you'd better accompany us to the station, Kieran."

"But … my job! I can't leave reception unattended. They'll sack me."

"You should have thought about that before you started telling us a pack of lies," Clare said, as the smug smile faded from Kieran Manders' face.

Charlene finally got Ian to herself at lunchtime.

"Want to grab a bite?"

He shook his head. "Not hungry."

"Me neither. And I daren't put on any weight or I'll never fit into my dress in eight days."

Ian tackled the issue head on. "You're still going to marry me, even though I'm a suspected member of Combat 18 and the British National Party?"

Charlene didn't answer. She slid the bolt across on his office door.

"I've seen how much money is in your Swiss bank account," she said.

"I have to warn you that most of the money is spoken for, invested."

"In property?" Charlene asked, handing him the deeds to Wordsworth Hall, which she'd found amongst the personal papers in his safe.

"Precisely."

Charlene sat down, crossed her legs and composed the question which made all the difference. "Where does the money come from?"

"Europe," Ian said. "A lot of it was, I'm pretty sure, siphoned off from EC grants, backhanders, overpayments, call them what you will. The money's clean, but the people who gave it to Roger and me aren't."

"They are…?"

Ian's eyes narrowed. "You already know the answer to that: far right organizations – or racist groups, if you prefer that term. There's a loose alliance across Europe who support each other. Over the years, they've been very disappointed by how little support their policies receive in the UK."

"So they came to you," Charlene said.

"No, they went to Roger, just after he stopped being Home Secretary. They thought that Roger had been sacked for being too right wing. The racists asked whether Roger needed funding to promote policies they might hold in common: immigration controls, repatriation – that kind of thing. Roger being Roger, he asked how much was on offer. The answer came back, *How much do you need?*"

Charlene was momentarily taken aback. "So Roger Wellington, the former Home Secretary, funds half the far-right groups in the country."

Ian managed a laugh. "Hardly. Roger's no more a racist than I am. But he talked to MI6. They said they'd be very interested if he could maintain contact with the people who'd approached him. So Roger drafted me in. He said, 'There's all this money floating about. If I don't take it, they'll only give it to some idiot who'll do real damage. Whereas, if you and I take it, MI6 aren't interested in the money, they just want to know the names.'"

"So the two of you made money while MI6 got top grade information about the far right?"

"Precisely." Ian permitted himself a slight smirk. "I travelled to France for the first time eight years ago. The people I met were very impressed. We invented big plans for financing educational and political campaigns."

"And did you do any of it?" Charlene wanted to know.

"Not unless you count funding the odd fracas here and there – just to show faith to our paymasters."

"Like the people Jed Sutcliffe was involved with last year?"

"Exactly. We were getting pressure for results. I thought that Jed was brighter than most of the morons I'd had to deal with. More fool me, I didn't work out why. He caused us some embarrassment. That was when I decided to get out."

This was what Charlene had hoped to hear. "You've finished with it?"

"Both of us have. We decided to cash in. There's never been a better time to invest in property in Nottingham. We set up a company, Tennyson Associates, which has already bought one piece of prime real estate, as you know."

"Do MI6 know that you're out?" Charlene asked.

"Indeed they do. After the Labour government was elected, we were hardly flavour of the month. They were glad to be shot of us."

"And how did your European paymasters take it?" Charlene asked.

"They understood that we couldn't risk exposure. And they're preoccupied. The *Front National* in France is badly split, as is our own National Front. On the whole, I suspect, they were glad to get rid of us. Let's face it, Roger and I weren't very good value for money. The biggest event we managed was a riot in which most of the racists were arrested."

"But you still caused real damage," Charlene pointed out, surprised by how little shocked she was. "A mosque was attacked. People were hurt."

"You have to look at the big picture," Ian suggested. "People get hurt all the time. It would have been a lot worse if a real racist had taken the money – he would have bought weapons, bombs…"

"You must have broken the law, taking all that money?"

"Technically," Ian admitted, "I might be guilty of income tax evasion, nothing more. The records which Simon Shaw and Jed Sutcliffe obtained would have proved that. So yesterday, when the police took me in for questioning, I thought the Inland Revenue might be behind it."

"And were they?"

"No. MI6 were. The police only took me in to protect my cover, to make sure that the BNP and Combat 18 didn't get the idea that I'd given the Task Force any information."

"You gave them information?" Charlene said, finally working out what Ian had been up to.

"My parting gift," Ian said. "I made sure that most of the most dangerous racists in the country were put away. So, you see, I balanced what little harm I did with a greater good. The Home Secretary rang this morning. He wanted to thank me personally."

Charlene was staggered. She'd thought that she was marrying a villain, but perhaps Ian was – if what he was saying was true – some kind of hero.

"So you're completely in the clear?"

"Yes. I have all the papers. Shaw's been paid off. Jed Sutcliffe daren't speak. Even so, the Inland Revenue might yet get wind of what happened. That was why I wanted all the documentation well hidden."

There was one matter which Ian hadn't dealt with, Charlene realized.

"What about the bank fraud which Ben accused you of?"

Ian laughed. "Oh yes, the cash cards which I handed out to the racists. They looked fake, but were actually linked to a genuine account which Roger and I funded. We couldn't let ourselves be directly connected with money going to racists. But there was no bank fraud involved."

Charlene was shaken. Had he told her everything? It had the ring of truth about it. She wanted to believe him, to trust him completely, but she had to be sure what she was letting herself in for.

"I don't know how to react to this," she said. "You say you don't subscribe to racist politics, yet you take their money. You encourage them, pretend to share their philosophy. What does that make you?"

"An opportunist," Ian said. "Racism will always

be with us, Charlene. Look at all the ethnic conflicts around the world. I'm not a racist. I'm a realist."

"You ought to be an anti-racist," Charlene said.

"I'm too old to play the politically correct game," Ian said, resignedly. "You think that every person in the race relations industry believes in what they do? They do it because it's a job, a well paying one which allows them to be cleaner than clean, to utter sanctimonious twaddle. But they're no better than you or me."

Before she could respond to that, there was a knock on the door.

"Your next client is here, Mr Jagger."

"I'll be five minutes," he called out, then seemed to calm down. "We'd better continue this discussion tonight."

"No," Charlene said. "I'll be staying at the flat tonight. I have to think all this through."

Ian spoke anxiously. "I haven't lied to you, Charlene. I've protected you from a few facts, that's all."

"But they're funny facts," she said. "You've been playing a confidence trick on a bunch of racists. Am I meant to be proud of that?"

Ian shrugged. "They deserved to lose their money. I haven't committed any crimes – at least, none that can be proven."

Charlene thought about the boy who had died in Wordsworth Hall. But that was an accident. She decided not to complicate things by mentioning him. "What about Jed Sutcliffe?" she asked. "Did he deserve what happened to him?"

"Nothing serious happened to him," Ian said. "The police didn't charge him. I would have paid him off, just like I paid off the journalist who co-wrote the book with him. But Jed couldn't be bought, so he had to be discredited."

Charlene almost believed him. "I'm taking the afternoon off," she said, finally. "I have to think this through. I can't concentrate on work."

"Very well. Will I see you tomorrow, then? We're supposed to be having…"

"I know." They were meant to be dining out with Roger Wellington and his latest girlfriend. "I'll let you know."

"I love you, Charlene. Never doubt that for a moment."

His gaze was firm, sincere.

"I don't doubt it," she said.

She unlocked the door and let herself out, keeping her head down so that the other staff couldn't see her troubled face as she left.

By the time the police let him go it was hardly worth Kieran returning to work. The damage had been done. He headed for Jo's school instead, arriving just in time to catch her as she was coming out. The boyfriend wasn't with her, though her chum Natalie was. Kieran charged towards Jo.

"Have you any idea what kind of trouble you've got me into? I could lose my job!"

Jo glanced at Natalie, then began to shout. "Don't hit me!"

"What?"

Natalie was looking around, calling out to the teacher on bus duty. "Sir! Sir!"

"What's this about?" Kieran said, unclenching his fist as Natalie ran to the teacher.

Jo shouted. "Leave me alone!"

"I haven't done anything to justify you bringing in the police," Kieran said, more quietly. "Calm down."

"Get away from me! I'm afraid of you."

"Stop shouting, for God's sake. All I'm guilty of is wanting you back."

"Forget it," Jo said, sarcastically. "I've got a proper boyfriend now, one who can do what you couldn't manage on Christmas Day."

"No!" Kieran moaned. "Don't…" He was reaching out to her. He wanted to shake her. The next moment, the teacher was pulling him away. "Leave here now or I'm calling the police. D'y'hear?"

Kieran backed off.

"Sir, will you call the police anyway?" he heard Jo ask. "My solicitor says…"

Kieran began to walk rapidly away, reminding himself that he hadn't touched her, although she had tried to get him worked up, almost as if she wanted him to hit her. What had she said? *Afraid*? He had done nothing to make her afraid of him. He had only loved her, put her on a pedestal. And, yes, he had found it hard to take her off that pedestal, to make love to her. She had wanted it too much, that was what had upset him.

He walked faster, a sweat building up even though he was only wearing his work suit. It was over now. Jo had given herself to that Martin creep, even though she could only have been seeing him for a few weeks. She was a common slut. The first thing he would do, when he got home, would be to throw out the video he'd kept, the highlights of his hours of taping in the unoccupied house on Montague Street. She looked so innocent in those tapes, but now the innocence was gone. Jo had soiled her body and called the police on him. She wasn't worthy of him.

"Kieran, is that you?" his mum called from the living room. "Help me to the loo, would you?"

"Just a minute, Mum," he said.

She hadn't touched the hot dinner which meals-on-wheels had brought round earlier.

"Hurry, please," she called.

"Why are you downstairs?"

She had a bedpan in her bedroom. Normally she would be up there by now.

"The home help was off sick. I said I could get by, but…"

"All right, I'm coming."

He took her to the loo. Kieran was used to it now, having this intimate, unpleasant contact with his own mother, but it still embarrassed her. When she was finished, he helped her out into the hall and on to the stair lift. Soon he had her settled in bed.

"You're a good lad," she said, as he went down to make them both a brew.

He put the kettle on, then found the *Rear Window* box on the shelf, removed the tape from it. He pushed back the flap and pulled several metres of tape out, then snapped and twisted the tape so that nobody could retrieve the video from the dump, watch it. While the tea was mashing, he took the tangled tape outside to the wheely-bin.

"Kieran Manders?" Standing in the back alley was a uniformed police officer, one he'd not seen before. Kieran panicked. Tape still in hand, he ran back through the house, into the hall and out through the front door, where two more uniformed officers were waiting. They arrested him. Then, even though he told them about his mum, they took him away.

"Are you ready to eat?"

"No hurry."

"Come here then."

Neil dropped his towel and took Jan into his arms. She was an inch taller than him. The way her body pressed against his was fantastic. He had never imagined that two bodies could fit together like this. Everything else fitted too. Neil didn't have to try and impress Jan, as he had Clare and Melanie. He and Jan got on because of, rather than despite, knowing each other's weaknesses.

Jan had taken Henry round to Kevin and Carol's before Neil arrived. Neil had come straight from work to Jan's. He had showered, then gone to bed, then showered again. Now they were no longer in a hurry and kissed tenderly, exploratively.

"Why didn't we do this years ago?" Jan asked.

"Because you were my boss."

"No one kicks up a fuss when a bloke sleeps with a probationer."

"And you were married."

"I wish I'd known you before I married Kevin."

Neil grinned. "I would have been – what? – fifteen when you tied the knot."

"I'll bet you were a gorgeous fifteen-year-old."

They kissed again, and went back to bed.

An hour later, as Jan was cooking pasta, she asked Neil what he was up to the following night.

"I'm having dinner with Clare."

"Oh yes," Jan said, slightly awkwardly. "I think she mentioned it."

"There's nothing to worry about."

"I didn't think there was," Jan said. "I mean, I used to … obviously. But since we… I guess what I do worry about is – are you going to tell her?"

"I don't know," Neil said. "I wanted to discuss it with you tonight."

The sauce began to spit and Jan put an apron on over her kimono.

"If she wasn't my partner, I'd want to keep this secret as long as possible. I don't want anyone else in the shift to know. Not for now."

"You think we might not last?"

"You might get bored with me."

He went over to her and slipped his hand inside the silk. "Never."

The doorbell rang. "Would you mind getting it?" Jan said. "It's probably somebody collecting for charity. I left an envelope in the porch."

Neil went, slightly embarrassed because he was wearing an old dressing gown of Jan's which was way too short and showed his knobbly knees. He should have got dressed. He opened the door and reached for the charity envelope at the same time. Because of this, he didn't see who was waiting outside.

"Hello… Neil?"

"Kevin. Hi."

Jan's husband looked him up and down. Neil got over his embarrassment.

"What can I do for you?"

"Henry forgot to bring his cuddly today and he's throwing a fit. I wondered if…"

"You'd better come in for a minute."

When Neil turned round, Jan was in the hall.

"I think it's down the side of his cot. Would you get it, love?"

"Eh, sure." It only took Neil a split second to realize that the *love* she was referring to was him. When he returned Kevin was still in the hall, frozen in position, but Jan had returned to the kitchen.

"There you go," Neil said, handing over the tatty blanket. "See you."

Kevin left without another word. Neil joined Jan in the kitchen. She was grinning from ear to ear. "Did you see the look on his face?" she said, triumphant. "That couldn't have gone better if I'd planned it for months."

They hugged. "I put a bottle of sparkling wine in the fridge," Neil said. "I think this calls for a celebration."

By the time they got round to the pasta, it was burnt dry.

24

The duty solicitor told Kieran that he didn't have too much to worry about.

"Harassment's a hard thing to prove, particularly as both sides admit that you had a relationship with the girl. Now, let's look at the particulars. They say you tried to run her over, then to hit her."

"It wasn't me in the car," Kieran said. "I was with my mum when it's supposed to have happened." He'd admitted that it was him to Jo, but she had no witnesses to his confession. "And I didn't hit her," he added.

"We'll have to see what the witnesses say on that one, I'm afraid. The police have several."

"I ran up to her," Kieran protested. "I only wanted to let her know that she'd got me in trouble about the car. Suddenly, Jo started shouting, 'Don't hit me'. She acted like she was afraid, but she wasn't. It was an act."

"It sounds like she was trying to ensure that you gave her grounds for an injunction against you, Kieran. Did she take legal advice before this happened?"

"Yeah, I even heard her mention her solicitor. Jagger, he's called."

"Ah, yes, Ian Jagger. A very tough customer. I'm afraid that Joanne may have enough to succeed."

"But it's her who's been stalking me," Kieran protested. "Following me, begging me to go out with her again…"

The solicitor gave him a suspicious look. "We can, of course, make a counter-claim if you have any evidence to back that up. In the meantime, though, we have various driving offences to consider. You don't deny buying this car at auction?"

Kieran didn't reply. He needed to talk to Mr Thomas, find out how much the old man was willing to lie for him. Why did things get so complicated?

"I need to see my mum," he said. "She's been on her own for hours. I'm the only one who can look after her at weekends."

"Is there a neighbour who can come in?"

"Nobody I can rely on." There was only Mr Thomas and he was a decade older than Mum.

"Perhaps Social Services…"

"No!" They would put her in a home, and she would never get out.

"I'll talk to the police. Maybe they can get you out tonight."

"She's already been on her own for a day," Kieran pointed out. "Without me to help, she's bed-ridden."

"I understand. Now, we'd better return to the matter of the car…"

Ian came by at two, without calling first. Charlene hadn't slept well. She'd gone over Jed Sutcliffe's manuscript several times, trying to pick holes in what Ian had told her. There were none. It was the truth, as far as she could tell. But Charlene still didn't know what she thought about it, how she felt. Part of her admired Ian's gall. But what about the money? When you got down to it, Ian and Roger were some kind of thieves – thieves with the police and politicians on their side – but thieves nonetheless.

Only a year ago, she'd been proud, principled. Then Ben had left her and she'd begun a descent into Jagger's world. Now Ian stood before her, contrite, asking whether she was still going to marry him.

"I don't know," she said.

"If you want to call it off," he said, "we ought to give people notice."

"I know." The wedding was exactly a week away.

"Then there's the honeymoon."

"I haven't said that I want to call it off," Charlene

told him. "I'm *conflicted*, Ian. You behaved so cynically, yet I can't hate you for it. It's the way you are. Then there's the law. What if you're charged, put away? Where does that leave me?"

"You've done nothing illegal," Ian pointed out. "Assume the worst: the police manage to find something to charge me on, get a conviction. There's no way they'll get their hands on any of my assets. Therefore, as my wife, you'll be running a law firm for however long I'm gone. Does that sound like a bad thing?"

"No," Charlene said.

"Talking of assets, I'd better take those papers you were good enough to hide. I think we'll let Roger have the responsibility of looking after them."

"Good idea," Charlene said. So he didn't trust her completely. He was right not to. She still had the photocopies, which she hadn't told him about, tucked away in the laundry basket. They got the plastic bag out from beneath the floorboards.

"Will you be joining us for dinner tonight?" Ian asked.

"I don't think so," Charlene said. "Roger Wellington's the last person I want to see at the moment." But he would be best man at her wedding, unless she pulled out. "I'll let you know what I decide tomorrow," she told him.

He whispered. "Please don't let me down." Then they hugged.

She watched him drive away. Tomorrow morning, she was seeing Ben, who wanted her back. Part of her still wanted Ben, the first love of her life. A larger part was in love with Ian – not just the man, but everything he represented: culture, power, money, sophistication. Had he broken any laws? Maybe. Maybe not. Maybe, when you balanced things out, he had done far more good than harm. But there were many people who would see it a different way. Charlene had the evidence which would bring both Ian and a former Home Secretary down. The publicity would destroy both their careers and their land deal. While Charlene's silence would both save them and make her a rich woman.

The Charlene of a year ago would have known what to do. But now she saw the world partly through Jagger's eyes. It was a crueller, colder place. You had to have the means to buy kindness, to keep yourself warm at night. People were blamed for being poor, not rich. Charlene needed someone to talk this over with. But who could she trust? Not Ben. He was too compromised – both in his feelings for her and in his feelings about Ian. She knew what her parents would say. *Leave him. Come home.* They didn't know Ian, hated her marrying a rich Tory twice her age. They hadn't even answered her wedding invitation.

Which only left Clare. Charlene respected Clare. She'd made some duff decisions in her life, but always for good reasons. She had a sharp brain, and a good heart. But could Charlene trust Clare to keep quiet if she decided to accept Ian's behaviour, marry him despite it all? Was that a risk which she was willing to take?

Neil arrived promptly at eight. He was wearing a new collarless shirt with dark moleskin jeans. He smelt nice. CK1. That was new too. The first thing he commented on was the "For Sale" sign outside.

"Are you about to become homeless?" he asked.

"I don't think it's imminent," Clare told him. "Sam's had no luck renting out Ruth's room. Plus Steve wants the two of them to move to London so he can work on his acting career."

"And Sam's prepared to follow him there?"

"She's ready for a change," Clare said. "Also, I guess she loves him."

"And does he feel the same?" Neil asked as Clare opened a bottle of Chianti.

"They've been together a fair while," Clare pointed out. "True, she's a few years older than him, which is always worrying…"

"Is it?' Neil queried, his voice a little petulant. Clare couldn't quite work out what mood he was in. Neil didn't like Steve much, which made Clare want to defend her landlady's lover.

"Only in that it puts pressure on the woman to have kids quickly."

"Yes," Neil said, more thoughtfully. "I guess that's true."

Clare got a little worked up, more for the sake of conversation than because she felt strongly about Steve. "I hate that it's all right when a man dates somebody several years younger but when a woman does it, people treat her like a tramp. That's one of those sexist double standards."

"I'm with you there," Neil said, and, suddenly, his face cracked into a smile. Clare stopped pouring the wine. "You've got something to tell me, haven't you?"

"I'm seeing someone," Neil said. "It's serious."

"You're wha…?" Clare found herself cracking into a smile too. She felt happiness for Neil, relief for herself. This evening was already turning out much better than she'd feared. "Come on, then," she said. "Tell me everything."

"She's thirty-one. She's got a kid, a toddler. She's separated."

"How long have you known her?" Clare asked.

"I've known her for a long time but things started to change at Christmas. We took it very gently at first but recently it's been…"

Clare had never seen Neil this happy, not even when she'd agreed to go out with him, all that time ago.

"I'm moving in with her," he said. "Next weekend. I'm going to tell my mum tomorrow. I wanted to tell you first."

Clare hugged him. "Your mum'll probably freak out," she warned. "A married woman with a kid."

"No, Mum'll be fine with it. She's known her ages, likes her a lot."

"That's good," Clare said, realizing that Neil had mentioned no names and that she, too, might know this person, whoever it was. "Have I met her?" she asked.

Neil nodded. "She said I could tell you as long as you promise not to get mad with her for keeping it a secret."

Clare's mind suddenly made the connection. "You and Jan?" she blurted out.

"It's Jan," he admitted, grinning like a five-year-old.

"I knew that something was different," Clare said, thinking aloud. "These last two weeks, she's looked so radiant, really blooming…" Then she collected herself, hugged him and said, "I couldn't be happier for you both."

Twenty minutes later, they were starting to eat when the telephone rang. Clare had left the machine on but, hearing Charlene's voice, apologized to Neil.

"I'd better answer this." She picked up the phone. "What's wrong?"

"I've found this … stuff," Charlene said. "I need to talk it through with someone. Can I come over?"

"Of course you can," Clare said. "There's food if you haven't eaten."

*　*　*

"I'm not hungry," Charlene said when she arrived, fifteen minutes later. With her was a large plastic bag, but she didn't refer to what was in it until Neil started to make his excuses. "Mind if I call Jan?" he said.

"Only if I can talk to her too," Clare told him.

They went into the hall and had a whispered conversation. "Looks like Charlene needs you alone," Neil commented.

"Do you mind?"

"No. I just wanted to see you, to make sure you heard it first from me," Neil said. "There's one other thing. I told Jan about … you know."

"No secrets," Clare said. "That's the only way."

"She won't tell anybody else."

"I know she won't."

Neil dialled Jan's number. "Something's come up here," he said, in his gentlest voice. "Is it OK for me to come over?" Clare found it weird, hearing Neil talk to his ex-boss, to her sergeant and partner, as a lover. "I've told Clare," he was saying. "Yeah, she'd like a word."

He passed the phone over. "You're a sly one," Clare said. "How long have we known each other? Three years, and I never even knew you fancied him."

"Took me a long time to work that one out myself," Jan said. "You're all right with this are you, Clare? Neither of us want to…"

"I couldn't be happier," Clare said. "I hope everything works out just the way you want it to."

"I know we might seem to be rushing things, but…"

"Live for the day," Clare said, her voice wavering uncontrollably. "You never know when…" She handed the phone back to Neil.

"Clare's a bit choked," he told her. "I'll be over soon. Bye."

Neil made his goodbyes. After he'd gone, Clare expected Charlene to ask what the emotional scene had been about. But Charlene had other things on her mind. She cleared the kitchen table and started to spread papers across it.

"I want you to look at these and tell me what they tell you," she said.

The police finally let Kieran go at nine in the evening. He'd tried to explain that he was no longer interested in Jo, that there was no need for an injunction or any of that crap, but his solicitor said it was too late, that didn't matter.

He'd spoken to Mum earlier in the day and she was coping. The solicitor had sorted out somebody taking her a meal round. Normally she went to bed around this time but tonight, since she'd been in bed all day, she might want to come downstairs. Kieran didn't know how he'd explain what had happened. He could say that it was about the car, but the police wouldn't have kept him in for so long for driving without a licence. Maybe he'd have to tell her the truth, that Jo had got it in for him and was trying to have him put in prison. Though it wasn't likely to come to that, his solicitor had warned. Kieran would probably have to pay a fine and there would be an injunction to keep him away from Jo.

"Mum, I'm home!" Kieran called, letting himself into the house.

No reply. She was probably asleep. Kieran went to put the kettle on. The tea pot was still full from the brew he'd made the afternoon before, which hadn't been drunk. The back door was still unlocked. They were lucky the house hadn't been burgled. Kieran suddenly remembered the videotape the police had taken from him. He hadn't been asked about it and he hadn't mentioned it to his solicitor. Would they assume that he was throwing it out because it was damaged? Or would they check and see what was on it? If they did that, it could cause more trouble. Serious trouble.

He made the tea and put the tea cosy over it. Then he arranged Mum's favourite floral mugs and a plate of milk chocolate digestives. Kieran was nervous as he walked upstairs. It always made him queasy, confessing to his mum. She would want details. He couldn't tell too many lies. Despite his age, Mum would give him a good telling off if she thought that he'd done wrong.

"Mum?" He pushed the door open. The light was out. He had to put the tray down in the dark and fumble for the switch. As he was doing this, he recognized a familiar smell. She hadn't been able to reach the bedpan. He'd have to clean her up. The light came on.

"Mum?"

She appeared to be sleeping peacefully. Maybe he ought to leave her. But then he saw that something was wrong. Mum looked very peaceful, more peaceful than was usual when she slept. Kieran reached over to touch her face. It was cold.

24

Julie had decided. This was the morning that she would tell him. Curt had stayed overnight at Natalie's. Tammy had had an early feed and gone back to sleep. Julie brought Ben breakfast in bed. They would make love, she hoped. Then, in the drowsy afterglow, she would tell him and he would hold her and be happy.

Only it didn't work out that way. As soon as he'd bolted down his breakfast, Ben was in the shower. "Got to go out," he said, as he dressed with his back to her.

"Where to? It's Sunday!"

"The library's open," Ben told her. "And my exam's the week after next."

"Ben, we need to talk."

"There'll be plenty of time for that soon. Got to go."

He went without even taking the plates downstairs. Julie would have had a go at him, only her morning sickness began to kick in. She hurried to the bathroom, where she puked up buckets. Ben, as usual, wasn't there to notice.

"I can't advise you what to do," Clare told Charlene, who had stayed the night in Ruth's old room. "If it were me, I wouldn't be marrying him, I'd be going to his professional body, or something ... but you're not me."

"Why wouldn't you marry him?" Charlene asked, for the third or fourth time.

"He's corrupt."

"He's not a bad man," Charlene pleaded. "In a way, I'm sure, he sees himself as a Robin Hood, taking from the evil rich, though he'd never say that himself."

"Next you're going to tell me that he gives all the money to the poor," Clare said, caustically.

"He does give to charity, but privately," Charlene said. "I don't know how much. He reckons that you shouldn't make a show of giving."

So how come he told you about it? Clare nearly challenged. She hardly knew Jagger, but had been shocked by the figures travelling through the solicitor's secret accounts. Money and power were an aphrodisiac. Clare could understand Charlene's wanting to be with him despite all the dubious things he had done. Maybe he did some good, too, like helping to put a few racists in prison the other week. But that didn't make him a good person.

"The way it looks," Clare said, "they've had well over two million pounds between them. But most of it's gone, earlier this year. What did they spend it on?"

Charlene looked flustered. "I don't know," she said, unconvincingly. "I think they moved it to a different account…"

She was hiding something. Clare knew that people usually did what they wanted to do. You had to let them make up their own minds. But she couldn't stay quiet.

"Don't do it, Charlene," she said. "You know it's wrong. Talk to Ben. Tell him what you've told me. I'm not saying *get back together with him*, but hear him out."

"I ought to be going," Charlene said, getting up. "I'm meant to be meeting Ben at eleven."

"And have you decided what you'll tell him?"

Charlene covered her head with her hands for a moment. Clare didn't know what she would say. Last night, Charlene had confided that she still had feelings for Ben. But he had broken her heart, badly. Charlene wanted to punish him more than she wanted to make up with him.

"Yes," she said now. "I've decided."

Charlene put on a coat and pointed at the plastic bag full of photocopies.

"Destroy those for me, would you?"

"I can do," Clare said. "If that's what you really want."

Charlene kissed her on the cheek then set off for the Castle. Clare, still in a dressing gown, didn't see her to the door. She looked at the Prada bag stuffed with papers. Would Charlene change her mind? Did she really mean for Clare to get rid of the evidence? It could destroy her husband's career, might even put him in prison. Did Clare have the right to destroy it? Did she have the right not to?

The house was empty. Clare took the bag up to the attic, where she'd left a trunk full of her stuff. There would be time to get rid of it after the wedding, if Charlene went through with it. Clare didn't want to betray her friend's trust, but she had no compulsion to protect Jagger, who was a crook, as far as she could see, and much too cynical for his own, or anybody else's good.

As she was getting out of the attic, Clare realized that somebody was in the room below.

"Clare! What are you doing up there?" It was Gary, packing a suitcase.

"Not much," she said. "Where are you off to tonight?" They began an afternoon shift the following day. It must be a short trip.

"Milan," he replied.

"Seeing Umberto off?"

"No," he said. "I'm not coming back."

"You've resigned?"

"The letter's in the post."

Clare was confused. "I thought you'd turned Umberto down?"

Gary grinned. "I did. I love my job. But, like I've heard you say, you only live once. I love Umberto more than any job. I can't spend the rest of my life wondering what might have been."

"What are you going to do over there?"

"Umberto's found me a job as a security consultant. The club need a fluent English speaker to deal with international clients. If that doesn't work out, I'll find something else. The important thing is, I'll be with him."

"Living in Italy, though," Clare mused. "That's a big step. You don't speak the language."

"I've been taking lessons," Gary said, and rattled off an extremely obscene suggestion in fluent Italian. "Hey, you will come and see us, won't you?"

"Try and stop me!"

"Good. Now, do you fancy helping me to pack? Umberto's picking me up to go to Birmingham airport in half an hour."

Ben wandered around the Castle Art Gallery feeling like a lemon. He ought to be revising, like he'd told Julie. Jagger was untouchable. Jed had said as much in

333

a letter. It was Mothering Sunday, Ben realized. To mark the occasion, two city councillors were handing out disposable cameras to young children. The kids were taking photos of their mums for a community art exhibition. Ben realized that he hadn't sent his own mother a card. He must ring her. Maybe he could take the bus to Mansfield after he had seen Charlene, surprise her. But if he went, Mum would start nagging him about when he was going to take Julie round.

Ben had decided not to introduce Julie to his family. For, even if Charlene wouldn't have him back (and she hadn't said definitely that she wouldn't), Ben planned to leave Julie. Maybe he would do it this very week, once the sergeant's exams were over – no point in creating any aggro before that. Maybe he'd leave it a little longer.

It wasn't because of Charlene. It wasn't the age gap. What was a few years? If anything, it was the education gap. At first, Ben was always explaining things to Julie – anything from who Miles Davis was to how the legal system worked. He'd enjoyed it, though he was surprised how little she knew. Lately, however, he'd stopped explaining. And the sex had worn off, like it had with Ruth, after the same amount of time. All that left was affection, friendship. That wasn't enough to keep Ben looking after a seventeen-year-old girl and her fourteen-year-old brother in one of the grottiest parts of the city.

Nearly half-eleven. He'd give Charlene another five minutes, then call it quits. He'd walk into the centre, get the bus to Mansfield. Maybe he'd even stay there tonight, give himself some space. Ben had managed to get tomorrow off work to prepare for his exam. Gary could manage on his own.

She still wasn't there. Ben walked through the Long Gallery, down the winding staircase lined with black and white photographs, past the café and out of the building. Wind blew round the castle. His eyes scanned the scattered tourists as intermittent sunlight dappled the city. There was no sign of Charly. She had stood him up, which meant that she must have made her decision. That was that, then. Jagger was welcome to her.

The phone call came while Mum and Dad were at church.

"You killed my mother!"

"Who is this?" Jo asked. "Kieran?"

"You got me arrested because you said I'd hit you. It killed my mum."

"I don't understand," Jo said, upset. "How? What happened?"

"The police kept me in for twenty-eight hours. Mum was left alone all that time. When I got in, she'd had another stroke. She was dead. If I'd been there, it wouldn't have happened. Or if it had, I might have been able to save her."

"Oh Kieran, I'm so sorry. I never meant…"

"What did you mean? Saying that I meant to hit you, that you were afraid of me? I never meant you any harm. That time I drove at you, I didn't come really near. I was angry and I wanted to scare you. That was all."

"I know, I know," Jo admitted. "I'm sorry."

"So why did you do it?" Kieran asked, angrily.

"The solicitor, Mr Jagger, said that it was the only way to get an injunction, to keep you away. I'm so sorry, Kieran. I know how much you love your mum."

Should that have been *loved*, past tense, she wondered, but Kieran was blubbing now. Jo almost offered to go over, to comfort him. But she didn't feel *that* sympathetic. Mr Jagger had rung up the day before and told Jo what the police had found on that video-tape they'd taken from him.

He was still crying. Quietly, she hung up the phone.

The two lovers recited dialogue from a favourite film.

"We're going to be rich!"

"We're going to be very, very, very rich!"

Ian Jagger licked champagne from his fiancée's naked body. He had cancelled his golf game this morning, preoccupied with what would happen if Charlene backed out of the wedding or, worse, decided to expose him. Instead she had turned up at eleven o'clock.

"I didn't think you'd be here," she'd said. "I was going to get into bed, catch up on some sleep, surprise you when you got back."

"We can go back to bed anyway," he'd told her.

Now he went to the bathroom and, when he returned, Charlene was asleep. She'd been up most of the night, she said, making her decision. What would he have done if it had been the wrong one? He didn't have to think about that now.

"You're a rascal, not a racist," she'd said this morning. "My rascal."

She looked so beautiful, stretched across the cotton sheets, a dead ringer for his first wife, Pamela. That was what had struck him when she first came for interview. That was why Ian had hired her – not because she was black, and certainly not because she was Ben Shipman's ex and he wanted to get back at him. But because of Pamela.

There was one difference between Ian's first wife and the woman who was about to be his second. When Pam found out where Ian's new flood of money was coming from, she hadn't argued, she hadn't been *conflicted*, she had left him.

The suspicion had stained their marriage for weeks. That was why she'd begun an affair with that black boxer. Pamela was going to see Dexter George that night when she lost control of the car. In a way, Ian had blamed Dexter George for his first wife's death. He'd worried, too, about how much Pamela had told her new boyfriend. Still, a few words in the right ears and the boxer had been fitted up for fraud, forced to flee the country. He'd paid for his fun.

When he was sure that Charlene was sleeping soundly, Ian rang Roger.

"Changed your mind about the golf, old man?"

"No, but Charlene's made up her mind about me."

"And…?"

"And I hope you're still willing to be my best man next Saturday."

"That's wonderful news. I couldn't be more delighted for you."

"It's an immense relief, I must say."

"Did she tell anyone what she'd found out?"

"Not a soul, she says. The ex-boyfriend was still sniffing around, but she's stood him up."

"Ben Shipman?"

"That's right. Sue Petit says not to worry about him. Shipman's too interested in pursuing promotion to make waves. And he keeps very dodgy company. If he tries anything in future, there's plenty of dirt to throw at him."

"Good, good. And I have some more news. Our application comes up at the May meeting of the planning committee. It should be nodded through."

That was quicker than Ian had been led to expect. He and Roger exchanged a few more pleasantries, looking forward to the wedding. When he went back to the bedroom, Charlene was fast out. He pulled a sheet over her and went back to his *Sunday Times*.

Where had Charlene spent last night? he wondered. He had called at her flat on his way back from dinner, but there had been no one home. He wouldn't have blamed her for having a final fling with Ben Shipman, but they would have had to use her place. Ben had a girlfriend with a baby at home. So it couldn't be that.

Suppose she had been to see Clare Coppola? It would be natural for Charlene to talk over the issues with Clare. That was worrying. Clare, if she knew, would be a problem. But if Charlene had told everything to Clare – good, Catholic Clare – she wouldn't have come back to him, would she? Her silence confirmed what Ian had long since decided: Charlene was a private person, like himself – good at keeping secrets. They made a good team. Even Sue Petit said so.

Ian leafed through the paper until he found the article about the raids on Combat 18 members, which was buried deep inside. Some of the other papers might have featured the story more prominently, but if any had mentioned his name, Ian would have heard by now. Nobody took the far right very seriously in Britain. The attitude to racism was this: ignore them and they might go away – an attitude which referred to both the racists and those they hated.

Although it was barely midday, Ian poured himself a cognac and lit a Montecristo. He had broken his ties with Europe. The press had not connected him with the raids on Combat 18 members. Only the Home Secretary, MI6, Roger and, of course, Charlene knew what he had done. He had bitten the hand that fed him. He had given the Task Force the names and addresses and the crucial evidence against most of those arrested. Some people would call Ian a hero, but he didn't believe in the concept of heroism. He'd taken a calculated risk. If word got out, there would be a price on his head. But racists weren't terrorists, they were morons. They couldn't organize an assasination in a month of Sundays.

At last, Ian was a free man, in every sense. But some freedoms weren't worth having when you got to his age. In six days' time, he would be marrying a sexy, fertile, black woman who was intelligent yet compliant. Nobody would accuse him of being a racist again. And the land deal would go through only a few days after they returned from their honeymoon. Life was sweet.

Ian blew fragile smoke rings which floated in the air like halos. He had what every man wanted in middle age: money, status, and a beautiful young wife. Soon, Charlene would give him a son and heir. Then his life would be complete.

APRIL

26

Julie had put on weight, Ben noticed as she lay beside him, asleep. It had been a warm night and they had slept unclothed. They had also had sex, for the first time in weeks. But they had not *made love*. Ben had been trying to use sex with Julie to stop himself thinking about Charlene's marriage. He had failed, hardly slept at all.

Was Julie putting on weight because he'd been neglecting her? Ben had made up his mind what to do about the future, but wasn't going to rock the boat until his exams were over. He would miss her when he moved out. Julie was a gem. But if he stayed much longer, he would be in too deep.

Charlene was going to marry Jagger, today. Ben was reconciled to that. He'd had some childish daydreams, but that was all they were. He didn't plan to crash the wedding, which was at some posh hall out in the country, make a scene. No, Ben would get them back the best way he knew how. *Success is the best revenge*. Whoever said that was right. And Ben had one big thing on his side: youth.

In sixteen years' time, Jagger would be sixty-five, retirement age. Ben would have just turned forty. He planned to be a superintendent by then. Maybe he'd even have DSI Petit's current job. How would Charlene feel about that, as she went to the post office to collect her husband's pension? Sure, she might have money, but money wasn't everything. How would Charlene feel, seeing Ben in a position of power, probably with a young family, too? She'd be gutted.

Julie wasn't part of this daydream. Ben couldn't see Julie as a superintendent's wife. Pity. He looked at her, thinking about what he was losing. Julie might be ignorant in some areas, but she knew human nature. She had a sharp mind, which he would miss. And she was very beautiful, lying next to him, naked.

There was another possible reason for Julie putting on weight, Ben realized. He took a quick look at the table on her side of the bed. Tissues. A magazine. No contraceptive pills. Quietly, he got out of bed and went round to her side. He looked beneath the table. No pills.

She wouldn't get pregnant without telling him,

would she? They had had that discussion in Spain, but he'd been distracted by Dexter Gordon at the time. Dexter turned out to be a complete red herring, a waste of time. Ben had been out of his mind, going over there. He'd been clutching at straws.

Julie wouldn't con him into it, would she? The force was full of blokes who'd been caught that way. Babies were one of the dangers of the single life, a life which Ben planned to enjoy soon. He looked at the bump in his girlfriend's stomach. She'd been wearing loose clothes lately. Julie – who was always so thin, almost as thin as one of those waif-like super models – Julie would never let her body go like that. She must be – what? – three, four months gone. Since Christmas, in fact. God.

The alarm clicked, which it always did a second before it went off. 5.15. Ben pressed *off*, so that it wouldn't wake his pregnant lover. *Pregnant*. Shit. *Shit*. He was on an early today and couldn't talk to Julie until mid–afternoon at the earliest. While Charlene was getting married, Ben would be getting trapped. What the hell was he supposed to do?

He got up, dressed in a daze, then couldn't face eating breakfast. At six, when he got in to work, Jan immediately took him aside.

"I thought it was time to sort you out a new partner," she said.

"I'd like another probationer, if possible," Ben said, his ambition making him articulate. Being a probationer's mentor was good for his career prospects.

"I don't think so," Jan said. "If you pass your sergeant's exams, you'll be leaving us soon."

"Even if I pass, I might have to wait months for a move," Ben pointed out.

"In your case," Jan said, "I doubt it." She meant *with your colour*. "Sorry," Jan went on. "It wouldn't be fair to the probationer."

"OK," Ben said. "So, who?"

"I'm letting you have my partner," Jan said. "I've been giving Clare an easy ride for a while. It's time for her to pull her weight again. But she needs someone reliable. That's why I'm pairing her with you. All right?"

"Fine," Ben said. "As long as Clare's happy."

"She's fine with it," Jan said.

"Great." Clare must have forgiven Ben for dumping her best friend, Ruth. Ben wondered what it would be like to have a female partner again. Weird, probably. One of his weaknesses was that he couldn't be with a woman without wondering what it would be like to have sex with her. Even when there wasn't the slightest chance, even when he hardly fancied her. Jan Hunt, for instance, had crossed his mind, many times. Clare too.

At first he'd thought she wasn't his type. That was probably because she'd been with Neil, who was his friend. Whereas, now, Clare was free, as he was about to be. Clare was classy, had been to university, like him. And she'd lost a lot of weight lately, was beginning to look quite tasty again.

"Hey, Ben," Clare said, barely looking at him. "How's Julie?"

The question brought him back down to earth with a crash. They were alone in the parade room. Ben mumbled something about Julie being OK. Then, this being the last day of their shift, he asked Clare what she was up to over the weekend.

"I'm meant to be going to a wedding after work," she said.

"Anyone I know?" Ben asked.

Clare gave him a funny look.

"Someone you used to know," she replied, then said no more.

Christ! Did Clare know Charlene, too? And they were friendly enough for Clare to be invited to the wedding? What was Ben's world coming to?

Their patrol was a disaster. Ben, preoccupied with Julie's bump and Charlene's wedding, found little to say. Clare, too, seemed to have things on her mind. It was a warm spring day and there was no crime, which made the shift seem longer than usual. By twelve, they were back at the station with two hours to kill.

Clare had just got out some paperwork when Jan interrupted her.

"There's a phone call for you. Dan Rossiter from the *Evening Post*. Will you take it?"

"Sure." Clare picked up the phone.

"PC Coppola? I hope you don't mind me calling you. It's just that the motorway-team trial is due to finish this week. I wondered if I could get a few quotes from you – material we can add to the story once the verdict's announced."

"I don't know," Clare said. She'd been trying to keep the trial out of her mind. "I'll have to think about it."

"I could come over," Rossiter said. "We could have a drink when your shift's over, discuss the matter."

Was he after information, or a date? Clare wondered. "I'll tell you what," she said, "why don't I come to you? I'd like another look round your new offices."

"Not that new any more," Rossiter said, "but be my guest. I'll see you in a few minutes."

In the Ladies, Clare did her face. Not yet twenty-two, she could pass for thirty at the end of a shift. She toyed briefly with giving the Jagger story to Rossiter, who was the *Post*'s crime correspondent. But no, if anyone was going to get the proof, it had to be Jed Sutcliffe. He'd earned it.

She walked along the canal, crossed at the magistrate's court, then walked around the shiny green *Post* building, which sparkled in the spring sunshine. Two men in their twenties were washing the cobbles outside. They didn't appear to find the job demeaning, but it depressed Clare. *Welcome to the twenty-first century,* she thought. *Just like the nineteenth century.*

The *Post*'s headquarters reminded her of the new university swimming pool, one of her favourite buildings. Its form was simple and functional. The outside was in cool, relaxing, light green glass. Sometimes, places like this fuelled her old desire to be an architect.

The *Post* building had a flashy atrium on Castle Boulevard, but the doors at the front, Clare soon found, were false. Signs directed visitors to the back of the building, where Dan Rossiter met her. As they walked through the building, Clare saw that the building was like many other modern ones. Forget form and function going together. This one was all front, no function. It wasn't just the fake entrance. There were several attractive balconies, but the doors which led on to them were kept locked. Reporters were herded together while the big spaces went to men in suits. Rossiter showed Clare the empty editor's office, which had a great view of the canal and the new city archives centre. Then he took her to his desk, which overlooked the Castle Boulevard job centre.

"Like to keep you in your place, do they?" Clare asked.

Rossiter laughed. "It's a useful reminder when the job gets me down."

"How's the trial going?"

"Pretty smoothly. They're all pleading guilty, after all."

Although Clare had been involved in the motorway-team case, she wasn't being called as a witness. The men were being done for several robberies, but had not been charged with the murder of Paul Grace, for the simple reason that they'd all been in prison when it happened. They would each get about fifteen years, serving ten at most.

"I don't see why you want a comment from me," Clare said. "I'm a beat copper, a plonk."

"I think you're more than that," Dan said.

"My boyfriend was murdered, that's what makes me interesting. But I don't want to be part of some tabloid sob-story."

"Once the three are sentenced, we'll be able to publish the full details of Paul's death."

Sub judice laws had restricted the coverage of the murder investigation because aspects of it over-lapped with the trial of the motorway team.

"Fine," Clare said. "But it won't bring Eddie Broom back from South America, or wherever he is. Sorry, Dan. I don't want to give an interview about it. I want to get on with my life. Want to do some real journalism?"

"Of course," Dan said.

"Then find out who Tennyson Associates are. They own the building where a boy was killed last month. They ought to be held to account."

"They are being held to account," Dan said. "I believe an out-of-court settlement is being made."

"How much?" Clare asked.

"A few thousand. Dead children aren't worth more, not legally. If he'd been badly injured, needed nursing care, it would have been a great deal more."

"So the company pay off the mother for peanuts and keep their anonymity?"

"Oh, I know who they are," Dan said. "I spent two days in Company House, following the paper trail. I wrote the story a fortnight ago."

"What?" Clare said, shocked. "I didn't see any story."

"That's because my editor spiked it. The people behind Tennyson are too important to upset. The editor plays golf with one of them."

"Who?"

"More than my job's worth," Dan said.

"I need to know," Clare said. "Look, you can have your sob-story interview, if that's what it takes. Now, tell me. Who?"

He told her.

Clare came back into the station just as the shift was ending.

"Shouldn't you be rushing off to Charlene's wedding?" Ben asked her.

"I've decided not to go."

Clare hung around until they were alone in the parade room. Maybe she *was* interested in him, Ben thought. Most women were. And he was interested in her. But it would be a bad idea to make a move while they were partners, and while he was still with Julie. Best wait until he got to be a sergeant.

"Have you got a few minutes?" Clare said.

"Sure."

"Somewhere private."

This was getting interesting, Ben thought: Clare skipping Charly's wedding to have a private meet with him. They agreed on a seedy pub a stone's throw from the station, the sort of place that nobody they knew would visit. Clare bought him a coke. She had apple juice.

"Are you still in touch with Jed Sutcliffe?" Clare asked.

"Not really. Why?"

"I need to talk to him."

"You'll need to give me more than that," Ben said.

"So you do know how to find him?"

"I've got a mobile number."

"Do you have it with you?"

Ben nodded. He had memorized the number, then torn up the letter, knowing Jed Sutcliffe was no longer likely to be helpful to his career.

"Do you trust me?" Clare asked.

"Yes," Ben said. Clare had her faults, but she was straight as a die.

"I'm going to help Jed nail Jagger."

Ben trusted Clare, yet he didn't believe her. He had come to believe that the lawyer was invulnerable. But that was one of Clare's faults, a naive optimism which had seen her through some horrible times.

"You've got proof, solid proof?" he asked.

"Yes," Clare said. "I've got everything Jed needs."

"Why can't we do it, then?" Ben asked, sceptically. "Why Jed?"

Clare gave him a condescending look. "You're compromised. The whole Notts force is compromised, for that matter. Jed had the right instinct – find a journalist, publish a book. He chose the wrong journalist, that's all."

"Tell me more," Ben said.

"No," Clare told him. "Steer well clear, you've got your career to think about."

"And you haven't?"

Clare didn't reply directly. "The number?" she said.

"I'd better call him," Ben said. "Introduce you. Then I'll leave you to it."

"OK," Clare said. "There's a box down the street. We'll use that."

He followed her out of the pub, their drinks left unfinished. Ben hoped that Clare wasn't going to be this bossy as his partner, but knew that she probably would be, if he let her. Their bodies pressed closely together in the the phone box, but there was no sexual tension, only the other, scary kind. Clare handed Ben some coins and he fed a couple in. Once Jed's phone began to ring, he put in more.

"Who is it?" a terse, familiar voice asked at the other end.

"Jed. It's Ben Shipman. Are you all right? Can you talk?"

"I'm fine. What do you want?"

"I've got somebody with me who wants to give you some information, about Jagger."

Long pause. "Someone you trust?" Jed asked, finally.

"Completely," Ben said, then added, "it's Clare Coppola. Know who she is?"

"I know," Jed said. Another pause. "OK. Put her on."

Ben handed the phone to Clare, who nodded, then waved him away. As soon as Ben closed the door of the phone box, she began talking, intensely.

Ben didn't know what to do, or think. Jed getting Jagger was too much to hope for. He couldn't face going home to Julie, so walked instead to the university library, where he would continue to revise for his final exam.

27

Kieran had lost the love of his life. Not Jo, he was over her. His mother. Nobody could replace your mum. No one would ever love you the same way again, unconditionally, no matter what you did. Kieran had devoted years to looking after Mum. He would happily have done it for the rest of his life.

Mr Thomas said maybe it was a merciful release. But what did he know? Kieran was alone now. He had nothing to live for. He was due in court in fifteen minutes. He ought to be there by now, waiting for the inevitable sentence. It would probably be in the papers, how Kieran had secretly taken dirty videos of a fourteen-year-old girl. Jo's name wouldn't appear. Oh no. She was under age. But Kieran's would. He would get a fine. He would have to move house. He might even get sacked. People would always talk about him behind his back.

Who was to blame? Kieran had been a fool. There'd been a love-shaped hole in his life and he'd believed that Jo could fill it. Wrong. He blamed Jo. She had over-reacted to his following her, videoing her. Everything would have been all right, maybe, if Kieran had been sexually experienced, had known how to make love to her. It would definitely have been all right if Jo hadn't gone to that lawyer, Jagger. It was Jagger who'd told Jo to lie about Kieran hitting her.

Kieran was driving to court. His car was illegal, with no insurance, tax or MOT, but he didn't care. Mr Thomas still let Kieran keep it in his garage. The old man hadn't asked any questions when he took it out this morning. All Kieran had to do was drive into the Broadmarsh car park, then walk over to County Court. He should be just in time, though he was cutting it fine.

But Kieran didn't want to go in. He drove by the back of the car park. There was building work going on. There was always building work going on in the city at the moment. Kieran crossed a lane of traffic and pulled up between two red and white plastic bollards. He put his emergency lights on and turned off the engine. Buses drove past, ignoring him. Now he had the time to get to court. It was only two minutes' walk away, if he chose to go. The car would be towed off if Kieran left it here, but so what? He wasn't meant to drive it anyway.

The four lanes of traffic between him and the other side of the road cleared, then filled again. The lights changed. The road cleared, then filled again. This repetition was relaxing to watch. It gave Kieran an idea.

Mr Jagger was wearing a wedding ring, Jo noticed.

"Are congratulations in order?" she asked him.

"Yes, I've just returned from my honeymoon."

"Go somewhere nice?"

"Jamaica. My wife's family come from there."

"Sounds brilliant," Jo said, as the judge entered and they were asked for silence. Was that bastard Ben Shipman from Jamaica? Jo couldn't recall. Ben had finished with Curt's sister two weeks before. Even when Julie told Ben that she was pregnant, it didn't change his mind. He'd urged Julie to have an abortion, go back to college, get herself an education. Julie, poor fool, was heartbroken.

Jo, by contrast, was in heaven. Martin had been revising a lot in the Easter holidays, but he'd still found plenty of time to see her. And Kieran had kept out of her way. Jo would have liked to go to his mum's funeral, but Mr Jagger had advised against it. Jo felt sorry for Kieran, sorry that she'd had any part in his mum dying. It must have hit him hard. She felt bad about trying to get this injunction against him today, but Mr Jagger said that it was too late to back out. Jo wasn't looking forward to standing in the witness box, pretending that she was afraid of Kieran. Really, she pitied him. She wasn't sure she could go through with it.

Jo needn't have worried. Kieran didn't show up.

"My client has reported regularly to the police station," his solicitor said, grovelling to the court. "His absence today is a mystery. The defendant has been greatly disturbed by the death of his mother, and is on medication."

The session only lasted a few minutes. Jo, it seemed, had a strong case. She discovered that Kieran had lied to her about his age, deducting three years. He'd lied about his job, too. In fact, he'd lied about everything, from the very start. Even his love was a kind of lie, she decided.

The judge granted the injunction in Kieran's absence.

"Thank God that's over," Jo said, as she walked along Canal Street with her mother, father and Mr Jagger. The lights were red and the four traffic lanes between them and the Broadmarsh car park were empty. "He'll have to stay away from me now."

"Let's hope so," Mr Jagger said. "And if he doesn't, we'll have him arrested."

Somewhere, Jo heard a car being started. "I hope it doesn't come to that," she said. "If he can only put what happened behind…"

"Look out!" The solicitor shouted. He'd seen the car, which had come from near the bus station and was speeding across the empty highway towards them. Kieran's car.

As the car mounted the pavement, Mr Jagger pushed Jo aside, then tried to get out of the way himself, but failed. Kieran drove over Jagger, narrowly missing Jo and her parents, then smashed into the red brick wall of the law courts.

Jo got up off the ground and hurried over to help the man who had saved her life, but he was already dead.

THE FOLLOWING YEAR

EPILOGUE

N ew building had begun near the forest, Clare
saw. Not on the Wordsworth Hall site. That
stood empty, unwanted, the building left to rot after
the City Council withdrew its offer for the land at the
last minute. At one time, there'd been talk of calling
the new leisure complex *The Roger Wellington Leisure
Centre* in honour of the former Home Secretary
who'd died of a heart attack in the summer. Then
Private Eye magazine broke the story of how
Wellington had taken money from racist organizations in Europe. The *Eye* also asked whether Welly
had used this money to buy Wordsworth Hall and
land around it.

That was only the beginning. Shortly after
Wellington's death, a book had revealed the full

extent of his and Ian Jagger's corruption. Both men were dead, so they could not sue its author, Jed Sutcliffe, for libel. They would have had trouble anyway, for, as far as Clare could see, every word in Jed's book was true. She ought to know: she had given Jed back his manuscript, together with documentary proof of Jagger's financial dealings.

Clare got off a bus at the Victoria Centre. She had been away from Nottingham for nearly a year. Now she wondered whether she would ever live here permanently. She had returned to her studies in Manchester, although she could just as easily have taken up her new course at one of her home city's two universities. Nottingham was home, but it held too many ghosts for her.

Clare needed to buy a wedding present. She'd left it late to get anything off the list, so would have to rely on inspiration. She walked through House of Fraser, heading for the top floor, where they kept the kitchenware and fancy household stuff. As she stepped on to the escalator, another woman almost bumped into her.

"Oh," Charlene said. "It's you."

"Hi," Clare replied.

They were going up the escalator. It was impossible for either to walk away. There were lines beneath Charlene's eyes, Clare noticed, and her suit was more austere, more formal than she used to wear. That was probably because she was the boss now.

"I didn't think the university term was over yet," Charlene said.

"Jan and Neil are getting married tomorrow," Clare explained.

"I didn't know," Charlene said.

"Gary and Umberto are coming over, Ruth too. Should be a great do."

Clare, having failed to attend Charlene's wedding, didn't mention that she was the maid of honour. Nor did she refer to Ben, who was a sergeant now, the youngest in the city. He had taken Jan's old job shortly after she was promoted to Inspector. Ben and Charlene didn't speak any more, not since Ben realized that Charlene knew all about Ian Jagger's corrupt dealings, yet married him anyway.

"Have you got time for a coffee?" Charlene asked. "I think we have some unfinished business."

"I haven't got long," Clare said. It was true. But she couldn't deny Charlene this confrontation. They had once been friends – close friends, nearly. As they went down to the store's small restaurant, Charlene asked Clare about her course.

"What's it like, studying Architecture again?" she wanted to know.

"I decided not to," Clare said.

"Why?"

Clare tried to explain. "All those long years of study, and what's it for? I love great buildings, but even the best architects are often fifty before they get to design one which actually gets built. Also, I'm not sure I have enough talent. So what does that leave? Car parks? Shopping centres? Forget it. I went into architecture partly because I wanted to impress my dad, design places that he would build. But Dad went bust and, anyway, I have to live for myself. I wanted to do something which makes a difference."

"So what did you choose?" Charlene asked. "Social work? Medicine?"

"Don't laugh," Clare said. "But I chose the Law. That's where the real power is, not in the police force."

"You're right," Charlene said, thoughtfully. "Hey, maybe you can come and work for ... I mean, *with* ... me when you graduate."

Clare didn't reply to this. She didn't know what kind of lawyer Charlene was, but suspected that it wasn't the kind she wanted to be. The two women ordered a snack and a drink.

"There's something uncomfortable I've got to ask you," Charlene said, as the waiter poured wine. They had each opted for alcohol over coffee. Clare knew what was coming.

"It's about Jed Sutcliffe's book," Charlene said. "He had some financial figures in there which I was surprised to see. As far as I knew, only four people in this country had seen copies of those papers. And two of those people are dead. I expect that Jed got fresh copies the way he got the first lot, but I need to ask…"

Clare interrupted. "I gave them to him," she said.

"You *what?*"

Clare had been waiting for over a year to justify herself. Now the words tumbled out. "You showed me the papers, Charlene. You left them with me."

"I told you to destroy them!"

"If I'd done that, I'd have been doing wrong. They were evidence of a crime."

"You betrayed me," Charlene said, bitterly.

Clare took a sip of wine to steady herself. "Maybe I should have told you what I was going to do, but you already knew what was in those papers. You chose to do nothing. What I knew was on my conscience. Then, when I found out that Ian and Roger owned Wordsworth Hall, that they were responsible for that little boy's death and had washed their hands of it … then I couldn't take it any more."

Charlene looked at the ceiling, furious.

"Did you know about Wordsworth Hall?" Clare asked.

"The firm paid the appropriate compensation to the boy's mother," Charlene said, not answering directly, which meant she knew.

Clare continued. "Instead of going to your wedding, I got in touch with Jed Sutcliffe, gave him the photocopies. After all, the originals of most of those papers were Jed's anyway. The other stuff only confirmed what he'd already found out."

Charlene's eyes narrowed. "Do you know what you've done? My husband died a hero. He was a hero. You destroyed his reputation. I was starting to get black clients for the firm. Now they won't come near me. Most of Ian's money is tied up in a frozen bank account, while Inland Revenue investigators see if they've got grounds to confiscate it, which could take years."

"You've still got the firm," Clare pointed out.

"Yes, but I've lost my three best members of staff and I can't get decent applicants to replace them."

"I'm sorry."

Charlene gave her a hard stare. "No, you're not. You think that the truth is sacrosanct. Now your precious conscience is clear. That's all you care about."

"Is it?" Clare said, draining her glass and lowering her voice. "Shall I tell you something? I haven't been to church since I lost my baby. I don't believe in God any more. I don't know what I believe in. All I know is this – *you are your actions* – nothing more, nothing less. And I can live with myself."

"Whereas I can't," Charlene snapped, eyes blazing. "Is that what you're saying?"

"Maybe I'd better go," Clare said, standing up and removing her coat from the chair.

"Yes, maybe you had." Charlene stared ahead, poker-faced, as Clare left the store. Beneath the table, Clare saw, one of her hands was shaking.

It wasn't yet two. Clare walked through the city, wedding present forgotten. A shift was coming to an end. On impulse, Clare called in at the station. There was a recruitment poster on the wall showing Sue Petit, Notts' new Assistant Chief Constable. She was surrounded by black police officers, Ben Shipman among them.

Clare was about to go upstairs when Julie Wilder came into reception, a crying baby in her arms. Hesitantly, they greeted each other. A stranger seeing them together would have said that Julie was the older of the two women. Clare admired the little boy.

"His father's having him for the weekend," Julie said.

Clare took the baby, held it carefully, imagining the child that she might have had herself and the child she might still have, sometime, when she was older, if she met the right man.

"I hope he doesn't cry at Jan's wedding," Julie added, as the door to reception opened and an attractive young policewoman came out.

"Can't Ben get his mum to babysit?" Clare asked Julie.

"I don't think he's dared tell her that she's a grandmother yet."

"The sarge'll be down in a minute," Hannah Knight told Julie. "Oh, Clare, hi. How're things?"

"Fine," Clare said, realizing that she shouldn't have come, that she didn't belong here any more. "I wanted to wish you luck in your new job."

"That's brilliant of you," Hannah said, entirely at home in her smart new uniform. "I know you told me I should go to university first, but when they lowered the recruitment age to eighteen and a half, I couldn't wait. This is all I've ever wanted to do."

"I understand," Clare said, returning the baby to its mother before backing away. "I wish you all the luck in the world."

"If I can be half as good as..." Hannah started to say, but Clare didn't let her finish.

"It's time for me to be off."

"Thanks for everything," Hannah called out, as Clare left the station, not looking back. "Mind how you go."

Have you read the other titles in THE BEAT series...?

Avenging Angel

Introducing Clare Coppola, Neil Foster and Jan Hunt...

When Angelo Coppola is tragically killed in a hit-and-run accident, the police are unable to track down the culprit.

But Angelo's sister, Clare, cannot rest till she has discovered the truth. Who was driving the car that killed him? And what is the significance of "blaze" – the last word that Angelo uttered?

Clare is soon convinced that she has found the killer. But can she prove it? And is she putting her own life in danger?

Missing Person

Introducing Ben Shipman, Ruth Clarke, Sam Holt and Steve Garrett...

Fifteen-year-old Hannah Brown is missing – just another teenage runaway. Or is she?

Only PC Clare Coppola, working on her first police case, thinks otherwise. But how can she prove that Hannah is in danger? And what connection can a missing teenager have with a spate of local burglaries?

Black and Blue

Introducing Jed Sutcliffe and Ian Jagger...

Violence is brewing on Ben's beat – deliberate, organized violence. But who is behind it, and what are they trying to achieve?

Ben is determined to find out. And he's got more than just a professional interest – because some of the violence is directed against *him*. Being a black police officer could be harder than he thought...

Smokescreen

Introducing Chris Dylan and Charlene Harris...

There's a serial arsonist at large, going by the name of *Phoenix*. First Clare's school is burnt down, then the local library. What will be the next target?

Now Neil has been transferred to CID, Clare is determined to prove her worth and find Phoenix. But how can she track down an arsonist who's as elusive as a puff of smoke?

Asking For It

Introducing Paul Grace and Melanie Byatt…

A thirteen-year-old girl has been raped, and Neil is assigned to the case. Then there's a second rape. This time a student. And the man wore a mask.

Could the two crimes be linked? Or is it just coincidence?

Neil is determined to find out. But if the rapist isn't caught soon, he could attack again…

Dead White Male

Introducing Gary Monk…

When nineteen-year-old Scott Travis is found battered to death, the police are baffled. What motive could there be for such chilling violence?

But as Clare delves deeper into the victim's past, small clues begin to come to light. Clues linking a student, an ex-prostitute and a police officer in a web of lies and deceit. Could one of them have killed to keep their secret hidden…?

Losers

The first of three novels featuring the gang known as the Motorway Team, and introducing the Wilder family and Eddie Brown...

Life on the Maynard Estate is hard, and Julie Wilder wants out. A winning scratchcard could be her ticket to a new life...

A life such as Gordon Loscoe's. He won the Lottery and lives in the lap of luxury. That is, until his house is burgled and his wife is violently abducted...

Called in to investigate, Paul and Clare uncover a network of crime based on greed and betrayal. But proving it could be quite a gamble...

Sudden Death

When Dean Sutherland gets picked to play for Nottingham Forest, he's over the moon. It means a whole new start. Of course, he's always been into team games, just not always *legitimate* ones...

Deans old friends are not so happy, though. They think he owes them something, and there's only one way he can pay. But now he's sharing a house with a police officer, he has to be careful. Neil Foster's no fool...

As the motorway team move in for another big-time burglary, Dean has to decide which side he's on. Whichever he chooses, there'll be a penalty to pay.

Night Shift

The motorway team are still at large, but a key witness is behind bars. The police are just waiting for him to sing like a bird...

But Joe isn't stupid. He knows what happens to people who cross the team. They end up dead. As least no one can touch him while he's inside.

Back at the station, the night shift is beginning. That means eight long hours on duty for Clare – her first shift after the funeral. Eight hours during which anything can happen. Like a prison break-out...

Victims

Events from Ruth's past come back to haunt her final appearance in the series...

Alan Wallace has just got off scot-free. The locals are outraged. But the police are duty bound to protect everyone. Even perverts...

Then a two-year-old boy goes missing. According to the police, Wallace is not a suspect. But the community's not so sure...

When justice fails, do you turn the other cheek? Or take the law into your own hands? Because shouldn't the punishment always fit the crime...?

Suspects

Introducing Jo McCord…

Mark Murray's soap-opera smile made him an icon.
But with his face caved in, he's not so pretty.

Jealous husband, the police reckon. Mark could never
resist a married woman. His co-stars reveal a catalogue
of one-night stands.

The national press can sense a scandal, so CID must
work fast. With so many suspects, there has to be a lead.
But in the theatre everyone's playing a part…